POOLE

LIGHTHOUSE SECURITY INVESTIGATION WEST COAST

MARYANN JORDAN

Poole (Lighthouse Security Investigation West Coast) Copyright 2023

Cover by: Graphics by Stacy

ISBN ebook: 978-1-956588-46-0

ISBN print: 978-1-956588-47-7

❦ Created with Vellum

1

You've won a five-day, fun-in-the-sun Las Vegas vacation. Five-star hotel accommodations. Award-winning restaurants. Famous bars mixing signature cocktails. The best in entertainment, including adult shows. And, of course, the famous casinos. All for you!

Frederick Poole scrubbed his hand over his face at the plans for his vacation, secretly wishing he was more enthusiastic about the proposal of a *free* Vegas holiday. Free except for the small print at the bottom of the gift certificate—taxes, gratuities, premium shows, certain gambling rooms, alcohol, and travel.

What he really wanted to do was drive to a small B&B somewhere off the path of tourists and chill. Read. Relax. Swim. Hike. Maybe hit a few small breweries. Now, that kind of trip sounded like the perfect vacation.

"Got your days off sorted out?"

Poole blinked, startled out of his musing, and turned from his computer screen to find his co-workers all grinning at him. Dolby chuckled. "Man, you had an expression that looked like you were already at a Vegas hotel gaming room with a blonde hanging onto your side, cheering you on."

Maintaining the facade of looking forward to Vegas, he wiggled his brows and quipped, "Don't gotta be a blonde, Dolby. I like 'em in all shapes, sizes, and hair colors." That much was true. He didn't have a traditional *type*. He wasn't opposed to an occasional one-nighter, but to be interested in a woman, he wanted someone who cared about themselves without being high maintenance. Conversation, wit, intelligence... now those were traits that sparked something inside.

At the moment, he was surrounded by fellow Keepers, the name given to the employees of Lighthouse Security. Their boss, Carson Dyer, would be arriving soon for an end-of-week meeting, having been home today taking his little boy to the doctor for a checkup. Carson had always fostered a sense of family among his employees. Since marrying Jeannie, a woman he'd met on a mission, and then becoming a parent, Carson was even more dedicated to taking care of his employees' needs.

A satisfied smile spread across Poole's face as he watched his fellow Keepers combine work with a fun, casual atmosphere. Each member, a seasoned military Special Operations background veteran, would not hesitate to give 110 percent during a mission unwaveringly. Now, though, he was grateful they were working on more straightforward security tasks.

Looking back at the computer screen in front of him, he typed his electronic signature on the system he'd just designed for a house and sent the file to Rachel, their invaluable, intrepid business manager. Without her, LSIWC would not be able to run with such efficiency.

Relishing a moment of respite, he reclined in his chair and stretched his hands over his head, hearing the familiar snap and crackles from jumping out of an airplane too many times as a former SEAL. With the completion of his final assignment, he was ready to finish the Friday workday and start his weeklong vacation, even if the destination wasn't his first choice.

"I'm glad you can use the Vegas vacation instead of me," Bennett said.

He glanced to the side at one of his close friends, a former Army Ranger sniper, and snorted. "Just because you had to go to Vegas on a mission and had a shitty time doesn't mean I won't enjoy spending some time in Sin City."

"Well, it didn't turn out so bad for me after all, did it?"

Still grinning, Poole shook his head as his thoughts drifted to the events involving Bennett's recent assignment. Fate had surprised his friend when he'd been assigned to escort a scientist to a conference in Vegas. Bennett dreaded the assignment, but once Diana, the beautiful chemist, captured Bennett's heart and then was abducted, he and the other Keepers rushed to her rescue. Falling in love had changed Bennett's perspective on life, and he was now more protective of his beautiful girlfriend than ever.

And when Bennett won a five-day Vegas vacation

that neither he nor Diana wanted to accept, it had been given as a gift to Poole.

Poole sure as fuck wasn't looking for love, but since receiving the gift, he felt obligated to immerse himself in the delights Las Vegas had to offer—at least the free hotel room and food.

Natalie sauntered over, placed her hands on his shoulders, then leaned down to whisper, "I have a feeling when you come back, I'll be singing 'Another One Bites the Dust.'"

He would have flipped her off if he didn't consider her to be a good friend. Instead, he tossed out a smirk and winked. "Don't think I'm gonna find the right woman for me in Vegas." *Especially not at the gambling tables or a show.*

Natalie rolled her eyes and laughed as she returned to her husband, Leo, another Keeper. They'd met as Deltas, and now both worked for Carson.

Carson walked through the door just then, and Poole was glad for the diversion away from the talk about his vacation. Looking up at his boss, he asked, "How's your boy?"

Their iconic leader displayed a broad smile lit by a light inside that he'd had since his little boy had been born. Poole had never experienced that kind of light but wasn't opposed to marriage and fatherhood with the right woman and at the right time.

"Growing like a weed," Carson said. "Ninety-fifth percentile for height and ninetieth percentile for weight. Hitting all the right growth markers."

Everyone greeted the news with congratulations, then Abbie asked, "Did he have to get any vaccinations?"

She was a Keeper in her own right, as a former Army and CIA special operator, now married to another Keeper, Rick. And though her past endeavors and missions exemplified she was just as badass as Natalie, she had a softer side that manifested when it came to her co-workers.

Glancing over at Carson's pinched face, Poole knew the answer before it was given.

"Yeah, he screamed, and my heart dropped. Jeannie just rolled her eyes at me. But they gave him a cute bandage, and he got a popsicle to suck on, so he was fine."

"Did you get a popsicle," Leo asked, laughing.

Carson scowled, then chuckled. "No, but they should have ones just for dads who can't stand seeing their kids hurt."

As much as Poole enjoyed hearing the banter about his co-workers' lives, he was anxious to get home and finish packing. The sooner he left work, the sooner his vacation week started, and while the destination wasn't his first choice, a chance for days off was exactly what he needed. So when Carson called them all to the table for their end-of-week review, he was the first to be seated, giving his attention to their boss.

"Since our last major mission, we've been able to have a few weeks of just focusing on security systems," Carson began before going around the room, checking the various aspects of where they were on each of their client's cases.

LSIWC only designed security systems for individuals with specific needs and usually deep pockets. Not a run-of-the-mill security company, they focused on cases from the FBI, CIA, and clients with unusual security requirements. They did not install the system but contracted out to various electrical businesses vetted and trusted to handle the advanced and intricate work.

When Carson turned to Poole, he reported, "I just signed off on the Hamilton estate system and sent it to Rachel. I reviewed some of my past work and discovered the Pence Realty estate was never completed, or at least I didn't get a final notice. When I checked with Rachel, she said that Carolyn Pence, the real estate agent we dealt with for the design, said her clients had moved more slowly on the build than she'd expected. But she also said that the house was almost move-in ready." He held Carson's gaze. "If that's so, I should have gotten the final notice from the electrician. I'd like to request that we look at the electrical businesses we use to do the wiring."

That statement gathered looks from around the room, which he expected. "Is there a problem?" Carson asked. "Or are you just being preemptively cautious?"

"The last one I designed wasn't up to their usual standards. Now, the house is ready for occupancy, and the company never sent the final notice. It's not something that I expect from the electricians we use."

"Agreed." Carson nodded and turned to Jeb. "Can you look at all of the companies we contract with? It's been a while since we've vetted them."

"No problem. I can probably have that done by the time Poole returns from his vacation."

Carson looked over and grinned. "Are you still going to Vegas for your week off?"

Poole didn't even have a chance to answer before the others tossed wadded pieces of paper like confetti. He threw his hands up to bat them away, but several popped him right in the head. Laughing, he said, "You all are just envious!"

"Don't need a showgirl when I have Marcia at home." Dolby grinned, wiggling his eyebrows.

Poole had no doubt his friend meant what he claimed. Most of his fellow Keepers had met their significant others on missions. The women were smart, beautiful, and had a tenacious personality that made them the perfect blend to be with a Keeper. He hoped that one day he'd find the same, but sure as fuck didn't figure he'd even come close to finding that on vacation in Vegas.

Just before Carson dismissed the meeting, Poole tapped his fingers on the table, gaining his boss's attention. "I was looking at my route the other day since I'm driving. I'll stop at the estate we were just discussing—the one Pence Realty handles. Since she says it's close to being occupied, I'd like to look at the system to see if we need to bring in a new electrical company while Rachel chases down the paperwork from them."

Carson nodded but added, "I have no problem with that. But it's your vacation time, and I hate to see you spend part of it checking on something work-related."

Poole shrugged and shook his head. "It's on the way.

I talked to the real estate agent's assistant. They said the property would be open tomorrow. It might be an hour detour since it's stuck way the fuck out in the desert, but I can check on the current situation, then let you know what the status is. It's no big deal."

With a sense of purpose, Poole joined the group as they said goodbye with handshakes, hugs, and back-slaps. On the way home, he stopped at a gas station to ensure he had a full tank, grabbed a few snacks for the trip, and then drove straight home, wanting to spend the evening getting ready.

Years of military training had taught him to pack efficiently. Thinking of his plans, he chose a few clothing options in case he decided on an upscale dinner or show. By the time he finished, he'd primarily packed casual clothes, nice dress pants and shirts, and running shoes. Last, he tossed in the basics and toiletries before setting his duffel bag by the front door. He was prepared to leave at dawn... old habits are hard to break.

Pausing, he glanced into the kitchen of his spacious rental apartment. The desire to purchase a home had lingered in his mind, but he hadn't decided what appealed to him more—a house with a view of the mountains or the water. Turnkey was a must since he had no desire to spend his precious downtime with a fixer-upper. When he moved to the area to begin his employment with LSIWC, he'd opted to rent but wasn't about to move into a tiny-ass apartment. So now, his home was a roomy two-bedroom, two-and-a-half-bathroom apartment that gave him ample space to relax and unwind.

Then he heard the familiar sounds of the couple next door arguing. A-fuckin'-gain. *Okay, time to move house hunting up on my list of shit to get done.*

His phone rang, and he looked down with a smile before hitting the video call button. His parents' faces popped onto the screen, big smiles greeting him.

"Hey, Mom. Hey, Dad. What's up?"

"Your mom and I wanted to call to wish you a safe trip and to have fun."

"I don't know if I want you to have too much fun in Las Vegas," his mother said, a little pretend glare on her face while her eyes twinkled with mirth.

"Life's too short not to be lived, Son," his dad interjected.

At one time, his dad would have never said those words, but Poole understood the emotions behind them.

He held his dad's gaze and offered a chin lift, then smiled at his mom. "I promise I'll be good." He settled his hand over his heart. Hearing his mother laugh out loud, he grinned. "How is everything else at home?"

"The grandkids are coming this weekend, and you know your dad... He's trying to get the yard ready for the summer but nearly threw his back out mulching."

"Brenda, you know you're exaggerating," his father grumbled, then turned to the screen. "I just strained a muscle. Nothing I haven't done before."

Poole's father would never admit to overdoing

anything. He'd played professional football years before and had back injuries to show for it. Not that Frederick Poole Sr. would ever complain. To hear him tell it, he'd loved every minute of his career. And for years, Poole and his dad had butted heads over him turning down football scholarships to join the Navy. It took years before his dad finally came to terms with Poole's choice of career.

His mom rolled her eyes and turned back to the screen as well. "When are you leaving, sweetheart?"

"I'd like to get there early, so I'll leave soon after I wake up. I'll be on the road by dawn." Ringing off with promises to stay safe and love, he hit disconnect. Heading off to bed, he breathed a sigh of relief. *Tomorrow, I'll be in a luxury hotel with a steak dinner in my gut and sleeping on a thick, king-sized mattress.* Somehow, though, he wasn't as excited about the trip as he'd hoped.

2

Poole drove six hours and was almost to the property he wanted to evaluate. He had completed the home's security design based on blueprints given by the real estate agent. That last step occurred after the electrician signed off on the completion of the project, and one of the Keepers verified the system had been installed according to the plan.

He looked around as he drove, eagerly taking in the magnificent panorama. Poole enjoyed long drives, finding the solitude a time to listen to music or audiobooks while scanning the ever-changing scenery.

The vast desert sprawled in every direction, broken up by rolling hills and mountains in the background. The terrain grew increasingly rugged as he continued his journey toward the property. Large boulders dotted alongside the two-lane asphalt road. Having studied the blueprints when he designed the security system, he knew the house would be modern, blending in with the untamed environment. Since he's spent time in opulent and grandiose estates in his work in security, his curiosity intensified as he drove closer.

The road curved around colossal boulders as it ascended the hillside. Suddenly, an open gate was just in front of him, the rock fence traveling from either side. The gate concealed the entrance so artfully that it was almost indiscernible. It would be hard to find unless someone knew where it was. Following the lane, he continued upward and around the boulders, seeing a few outbuildings equally as camouflaged until the main residence appeared. Studying blueprints did not prepare him for the architectural masterpiece that seemed to rise from the earth while being part of it. He was awestruck at its complexity disguised as simplicity.

Since the house was ready for occupancy, his gaze roamed the area as he drove past the front of the house. *House?* More like a palatial compound. He'd only designed security needs for the house. He wondered about the rest of the estate.

The front of the main house was the same tan color with a slight pinkish hue that he imagined would capture the evening sunset light. The front of the house was two stories tall, with a flat roof. A wide veranda was on the first level, and various balconies were on the second level. Still not seeing vehicles or people in the area, he continued to follow around to the back. He spied multiple outbuildings as well as a connected four-car garage.

Finally, near a back door, he discovered a lone pickup truck with a magnetic vinyl sign attached to the side doors, declaring Roche Electrical Company.

"I can't believe they're still fucking working on this house!" he grumbled aloud. "Someone is ready to move in, and the security system isn't finished." Determined to speak to the electrician inside, he parked next to the truck. Climbing from his SUV, he glanced inside the truck, surprised to see it spotless. No food wrappers. No soda or beer cans. No tools lying about. Stepping back, he looked inside the truck bed and found it equally neat.

Turning, he walked toward the closest door and grasped the handle, pulling it open with ease. Stepping inside, he walked into a large room with hooks on the wall, cabinets, sinks, and counters. He continued into the house, not hearing any noise besides music playing in the distance. He moved into a tiled hallway and spied more closets lining the hall and what appeared to be the kitchen at the end. A set of stairs was on the left, obviously built for the staff to gain access to the second floor, whereas the owners would have a much more elaborate staircase near the front.

Ascending to the second floor, he followed the sound of the music as it became a little louder. At the top of the stairs, he looked toward the end of a long hall and spied a tall stepladder under an open ceiling trapdoor. Discovering the source of the music, he stared at the top of the ladder. There perched two booted feet and, leading upward, the bottom part of denim-covered legs.

Initially struck by the small size of the boots, he acknowledged the advantage of having an electrician of smaller stature. With their diminutive frame, they

13

would have the agility to maneuver within tighter spaces, a feat that would be considerably more challenging for someone of his larger build.

Approaching with caution, he called out, but the electrician didn't appear to hear him. He stopped close to the ladder and glanced up, unable to discern anything above the knee with the electrician's top half in the attic.

He hated to frighten the man, especially if he was actively working on the electricity, and he sure as hell didn't want them to fall off the ladder. But he came all this way and had questions about why the system wasn't ready. Poole didn't plan to leave until he had answers.

"Hey! Buddy!" he shouted.

Suddenly, the legs stiffened just before the music stopped. One booted foot kicked out, barely missing Poole's head. He grabbed the boot and shouted, "Chill out! I'm from the security company. I'm here to check on the system you're installing."

The electrician dropped to a squat, still balancing on the top step of the ladder. Their torso lowered, a head popped down through the trapdoor hole, and their eyes landed on him. Poole jerked slightly, stunned to see a woman's face staring back at him, her dark brown eyes wide.

"Who are you?" she asked.

He threw his hands up, palms out instinctively, both in an effort to catch her if she happened to tumble off the ladder and to show that he wasn't armed or a threat. "Sorry to scare you, ma'am. I'm from the security company that designed the system. Frederick Poole."

She turned deftly on the top of the ladder, came down two steps, then plopped her ass on the top where her boots had been, staying at a height that caused him to lean his head back to see her face— not a position a tall man was used to.

"Seriously?" she asked, her gaze still locked onto his face.

"Yes, ma'am, seriously."

"Why haven't I ever seen you before?"

"Why would you?"

"Because I've been working on this project for a while, and no one has come around."

His hands planted on his hips as he tried to figure out if she was stalling or giving him a truthful answer. And if it was an honest answer, that still didn't explain why the project took so long. But the more he stared, the more interested he became. Initially, he hadn't noticed her appearance other than she was a woman. But on closer inspection, he was intrigued that she captured his attention.

Her soft brown hair was thick and wavy, and while unremarkable at first glance, now he spied natural highlights that looked touched by the sun, not an expensive salon treatment. It was pulled away from her face into a neat ponytail, with a few wispy waves curling around her forehead. It appeared she didn't have a trace of makeup on, yet her complexion was smooth and clear, with a hint of blush on her cheeks that also looked sun-kissed. And her lips were full, with only a slight sheen, no doubt from a swipe of lip balm over them. Her hands were unadorned, but she wore three tiny silver hoop earrings in each ear. Her brown eyes were dark with light amber flecks around the edges of her pupils.

Her blue jeans were not painted on in the way he'd seen on many women. They also weren't overly baggy but fit loose and comfortably. A long-sleeved Henley shirt, also worn loosely, completed her outfit. A leather electrician's belt hung around her waist, with various small tools tucked inside for easy reach.

"Are you just going to keep staring? If you don't believe who I am, I have my company ID here in my pocket."

Jerking slightly, he was startled that he'd been caught staring at her appearance. "Yes, I would like to see some ID," he snapped, then immediately hated that his voice was so harsh.

"Fine, I'd like to see some ID, also."

Huffing, he reached into his back pocket with one hand, grabbed his wallet, and slid out his LSIWC employee ID. Stepping close, he handed it to her. The ladder was so tall that she had to reach down to take it in her fingers. She carefully reviewed it and looked between him and the picture several times. "Okay, Frederick Poole. I guess you are who you say you are."

She lifted her ass off the top step and reached behind to pull out a small wallet. Leaning down, she handed it to him. Like her, he carefully perused the photograph, surprised at how photogenic she was even with a crappy employee identification picture. The company logo matched the magnetic sign on the side of her truck.

"Patricia Burrows."

"Tricia."

He looked up, his brow lifted.

"My friends call me Tricia."

He lifted his hand with her ID clutched between his fingers and noticed she accepted it without touching his hand.

She tilted her head to the side and held his gaze. "Can I ask why you're here, Mr. Poole?"

"Poole."

She blinked. "I said Mr. Poole."

"No, it's just Poole."

She blinked again, but he explained, "My friends just call me Poole."

Her lips twitched, but she simply nodded. "Okay. Poole… why are you here?"

"I could ask you the same thing. It's early on a Saturday morning. There are no other employees or workers around here of any kind. You're out here all by yourself."

"I get the feeling you don't trust me," she said, her lips quirking upward.

Much to his surprise, he really wanted to see a broad smile on her face. So far, one side of her mouth lifted higher than the other, turning what might have been an ordinary grin into an interesting and beautiful one.

"I hardly think I would be standing on top of a ladder with my head stuck up in the attic on a Saturday morning if I didn't have a job to do."

A chuckle left his lips, and he nodded. "I admit, it would be an unusual pastime. I talked to the realty company, who told me someone would be here, so I assume you're here at your employer's behest."

Something flashed across her face that caught his notice but was undefinable.

"My employer doesn't have the same standards I do. Hence, my reason for being here on a Saturday morning so early." She cocked her head to the side again and added, "I've been working for a while and have never met anyone who designed the system. I'm usually long gone before they come in. I have to admit, this is an imposing system you designed."

Poole was confident in his abilities, never needing false praise, but pride coursed through him that she was impressed with his work. Instead of showing his pleasure, though, he jerked his chin upward toward the door in the ceiling and said, "What are you working on? How far is this from being finished? I thought this project would've been completed a long time ago."

If his line of questioning offended her, she didn't show it. Instead, she crinkled her nose and said, "To be honest, I'm not sure. I wasn't initially put on this project. I was installing a system in a large building that took a couple of months to complete. Then I overheard my boss talking about this estate. He was dealing with the real estate agent, to begin with. I'm not sure he ever met with the actual owners. Then I think the project stalled for a little while due to building difficulties." She shrugged. "At least, that's what I heard. My boss put me on this job two months ago after he'd fucked up some of the work. When I came out here, I was stunned. The house was nearly finished, but only basic wiring was completed for the system. As you can imagine, I had a conversation with him that didn't go well."

"So he told you to make it right."

"Absolutely. I'm the best."

A snort slipped out, and he was hit with her glare just as quickly.

"What's wrong, big guy? You can't imagine that a woman can do this job?"

"Didn't you just objectify me?"

Her lips pinched together. "Touché. I apologize."

He really didn't want her apology and, in truth, felt stupid for bringing it up, but there was just something about sparring with her that he enjoyed.

"So," she began again. "You can't imagine me in this job?"

"No, Tricia. That's not what I think at all." He held her gaze. "I guess I enjoy meeting someone confident in their abilities."

She peered at him, and he battled the urge to squirm, finding her intense perusal unusual. Many women looked at his size, muscles, hair, eyes... anything to convey they liked his looks. But her eyes held a sense of discernment that was more curiosity than blatant interest.

"Would you like to see what I have?"

His head jerked up, and the unprofessional reply of *hell yeah, I'd love to see what you've got* flew through his mind. Instead, he simply tilted his head to the side, flexed his fingers that rested on his hips, and waited.

3

Tricia's gaze locked onto the imposing figure standing below her, his presence commanding her attention. She'd remained perched on the top of the ladder, savoring the height advantage it granted her over him. At five feet, six inches, she knew she'd have to tilt her neck backward to meet his eyes, but he had to stare up at her right now. It was a subtle power play she didn't usually engage in, but she couldn't deny the satisfaction she derived from this tiny advantage, especially since he was a stranger.

Her frustration with her boss repeatedly making empty promises to clients had reached its limit. This wasn't the first Saturday she had driven to the estate to rectify his subpar work. His misguided attempts to install the intricate system had quickly spiraled beyond his capabilities, so he'd called her in. She had painstakingly checked his work, re-done much of it, and completed the system. Today, she was finishing the last of the work, determined to ensure everything was working, and planned on spending the day enjoying the mansion and breathtaking scenery.

Feeling safe in the deserted estate, she was relieved that all the work had been completed, and according to her boss, the owners would move in soon. Lost in her thoughts, Tricia was caught off guard when a man's voice called out. Startled, she scrambled to see who was there. At first, she thought the owners or real estate agent had caught her still working.

Instead, once she dropped her ass to the top of the ladder and was able to peruse the man standing below, she was gobsmacked. *Damn.* He was tall, his broad shoulders exuding strength. A thick mane of tousled brown hair gave him an effortlessly rugged charm as if he'd stepped out of a shower and casually ran his hands through the length. A well-groomed beard adorned his face, adding a touch of sexiness despite her usual preference for the clean-shaven look.

An air of danger emanated from him, although it wasn't aimed in her direction. Remaining cautious and unwilling to trust him implicitly, she requested to see identification. *Double damn.* His ID photo looked as delicious as he did in person.

By the time they finished with introductions and established their identities, a surge of excitement coursed through her. Meeting the person who had designed such intricate security systems was a thrill she couldn't deny. As a licensed electrician, she understood how to install the systems and often entertained thoughts of designing her own. But in this case, his design was superior.

She offered to let him examine her work, then caught a glimpse of the little smirk on his face and realized the double entendre she had suggested. Refusing to look away, she held his gaze even though she felt her cheeks pinken with the heat of a blush.

Thank God he was a gentleman and didn't take her up on an offer she hadn't meant. "I'd love to see your work," he agreed.

Smiling again, she nodded. "Great, come on up." She turned and stepped back on the top of the ladder, then hoisted up through the trap doorway leading to the attic. As she moved out of the way, she heard him clamber up the ladder's steps. As tall as he was, he didn't have to stand precariously on the top, which was never advisable but necessary for her. He could easily pull himself upward and into the attic, but once there, he had to duck low to keep from hitting his head.

"If you came by the front of the property, I'm sure you saw that the house has two stories, but it forms a U-shape toward the back, where the courtyard, pool, and gardens are. The front is a massive two-story entryway with fucking amazing views. Each side of the U is actually two floors, and the wiring had been done in the whole house. The side we're on right now also controls the garages attached to the house."

She pointed out where the security's electrical lines were as they crawled along the most extended space.

"Impressive," he said, and she wanted to beam under his praise.

Confident in her abilities and training, she had grown used to her boss's miserly withholding of any praise. For that matter, he was miserly with everything.

Continuing, she walked him through the work she had completed in following Poole's system. She hoped she had erased any skepticism about her competence as a master electrician. When they finished in the attic, she stood to the side to let him go down the ladder first. Casting her gaze around the attic for the last time, satisfaction filled her chest. She stowed her few tools back into her utility belt, then dropped her feet to the top of the ladder. Navigating her way down the ladder with practiced ease, she reached up to pull the trapdoor closed above her. Easily scrambling the rest of the way down, she found Poole standing near the bottom. He was close enough that he would have caught her if she fell, but maintained enough distance to avoid intruding on her personal space.

Unused to displays of male gallantry and not needing it in the workplace, she was surprised. But she was also intrigued to discover that she wasn't upset.

"Are you all done here?"

"Yeah, I'm finished in this area. In fact, this was the last of my checking the system."

She reached for the ladder, but he had snapped it closed and hefted it into his hands. She stared up at him, neither pleased nor displeased that he was taking it upon himself to carry the ladder, but wanted to make sure he understood it wasn't expected.

"You don't have to do that, you know. I got it up here

alone, and I can take it back myself." She tried not to stare at his broad shoulders flexing as he hefted the ladder upon his shoulder.

"I have no doubt of your ladder-carrying abilities any more than I have no doubts about your electrical skills. But I also know that my mama would skin me alive if I walked with a woman, even one as capable as yourself, and let her carry a ladder while I didn't."

Pressing her lips together, she finally nodded. Her dad would've done the same, so she nodded, turned, and headed down the hall. Stopping outside a closet door, she turned suddenly. "Set the ladder down, and I'll show you the safe room."

He laid the ladder gently on the floor and turned his attention toward her.

"I know this was part of your design, and I must tell you it was really cool to work on." She opened the closet door to expose a linen closet, then reached inside, her finger skimming until she found the button she was searching for. Pressing it, the back of the linen closet swung open. She stepped forward and glanced over her shoulder with a smile. "Come on."

She led him into a room and flipped the light switch, illuminating the interior. A sleeper sofa sat in the back corner, and a desk in front of a bank of computer screens was in the other. A sliding door revealed a toilet, sink, and small shower. To the side were bunkbeds, each already supplied with a mattress.

She turned toward him and said, "It's not as luxurious as I would've imagined in a house like this, but it's

25

functional. Certainly, a family of four could safely hide out with a sofa bed and bunks until help came. The computer screens show the security cameras around the compound. On the side was a counter with a sink, mini-refrigerator, and microwave.

"We designed another one downstairs," he said.

"Yes. From the office. We'll look at that when we get down there." Her lips curved upward before a smile graced her face. "I have to admit, I loved the use of Smokecloak. I'd heard of their products but had never seen them installed. Brilliant!"

He smiled for the first time, and her heart performed a strange flip-flop inside her chest.

"They're a great product. Once the family is in the safe room, it can create a smoke fog that makes it hard for the intruders to find the safe room or make them think the house is on fire, and they leave."

"The company sent someone to install it, but I was here. I'd like to learn more about it. Add that to my repertoire of services offered."

His gaze jumped to hers, and she thought about the words she'd just uttered. Heat seared her face. *God, could I be more of a doofus?* Turning hastily to keep her red cheeks from his intense perusal, she walked back into the hall. She closed the safe room door as he picked up the ladder from the floor. "We can head down now."

Once on the first floor, she called over her shoulder, "You can bring it through here."

She led him through a doorway that opened into a garage. Inside were several ladders, painters' equipment, more electrical equipment, and a few odds and ends. "From what I can tell, this would be the secondary garage. On the other side, the garage is pristine, and it leads into a hallway that takes you through the kitchen, dining area, and more of what I consider to be the owners' area of the house."

He nodded, saying nothing. She continued, feeling the need to fill the silence. "Of course, you've seen the house plans. My guess is that their main housekeeper, cook, or higher-level house staff should be able to park in here." She shrugged and laughed. "I'm afraid this setup is a bit above my pay grade."

He stood, towering over her, but she felt no fear. Something about him was almost teddy bearish. He chuckled, and her gaze snagged on his slightly lopsided smile as he laid the ladder on the floor.

"You've got that right. It's above my pay grade, too."

She sucked in a breath and let it out quickly to hide how the deep sound of his chuckle reverberated through the empty oversized garage before it settled inside her.

She had initially planned to check over her boss's other electrical work but wasn't sure if Poole was staying or expected her to leave with him. "I was going to check on more of the work to see if it was ready for the owners." She peered up at him. "Do you have to leave now, or would you like to see it? Since you designed it, you might like to check it out."

He hesitated for only a second before placing his hands on his hips and nodding. "I'd love to see it. This is an impressive estate, and I like to see my designs come to life."

A wide grin spread across her face, and she led him back through the door. Looking over her shoulder, she waved. "Come on, this will be fun."

4

Surprise passed through Poole as he realized he'd accepted Tricia's invitation to stay longer to tour the estate. He'd left his apartment at the crack of dawn, allowing plenty of time to check on the security system at the estate before hitting the road to Vegas. While he wasn't on a rigorous time schedule, he'd hoped it wouldn't take long—get in, see what had been accomplished, and then get back on the road.

But the allure of exploring the labyrinthine network of the security system was a pull. Plus, the enigmatic Tricia stirred a distinct spark of interest. A flash of the other Keepers darted through his mind, and he rolled his eyes, scoffing. Taken aback by his own reaction, he was relieved to be behind her and not in her sight. He found her attractive, with a quick wit, and very smart regarding the electricity and the security system.

Yeah, you're interested.

In her?

Do you see anyone else around?

She's just a professional showing me around.
Seriously?

The argument in his head sent his eyes rolling once again, and another slight scoff slipped out.

"You okay back there? You sound like you keep choking. The cleaners haven't been through before the family moves in yet, so there may be dust."

She started to turn around, and he dropped his gaze, pretending to study the floor.

A questioning expression crossed her face as she looked downward. They stood on the tile, and she scrunched her nose adorably. "I've been in houses with nicer tile than this." She lifted her head to look at him. "Just wait till you see what's in the rest of the house. If you like this, that will really blow you away."

She turned and walked away, leaving him to follow once again. Rolling his eyes at her retreating back, he thought of how he'd just made up a lie about the stupid floor being so fascinating. Not to mention that if he rolled his eyes anymore, they'd end up cross-eyed— at least, that was what his mother had always told him.

She probably thinks I'm an idiot.

Oh well, at least it's good that you don't care what she thinks since you're not interested.

He hastened to catch up to her, needing to shut down his inner voice.

She turned and looked over at him. Her eyes were bright, drawing his attention. "This place is fucking phenomenal," she said. "I've been inside some nice estates, but this one is really cool. It's got the whole desert vibe going on, with some hacienda and Native

American touches. Plus, the way it seems to rise from the rocks and blend into the surrounding environment, it was designed for someone who wants total privacy. You know… someone who doesn't want to be found!"

She continued walking, and Poole's feet halted momentarily as he pondered her words, suspicion mounting. He'd had the same thought when he'd driven up. Deciding to discover who the real estate agent represented, he'd wait to call Jeb until he found out more from Tricia. His long stride had him back at her side quickly before she noticed he'd lagged behind.

She leaned to the side, her smile still endearingly crooked. "I wish I could come back and see the estate when the owners move in and see what furniture they place here. It's going to be gorgeous."

He nodded, sure she was right. Anyone who could afford this estate could certainly afford the best furnishings and interior decorating. *And what else?* Still pondering the need for massive, disconnected security, he was startled when she stopped directly in front of him.

"So this," she said, spreading her arms wide as she turned in a circle, "is the front foyer. I thought if we were going to take a tour, you'd like to see the house as though you just walked in through the front door. Of course, the security cameras are mounted on the front veranda, aimed at the front door and out toward the driveway." She shook her head and muttered, "Obviously, you know where the security is since you designed it."

With someone else, he might have been insulted that

they were giving him a tour when he already knew the system in place, but he found her enthusiasm to be infectious and laughed. "I designed it, but the company you work for installed it, so it's fine for you to give me the full tour since I haven't seen it in place here yet."

At that statement, she tugged on the corner of her bottom lip with her teeth, her brows lowering. "I've worked with the company for a number of years and know that someone usually comes out to do the final walk-through. Is this your formal walk-through assessment?"

"Nope," he said, shaking his head. "I wanted to stop by because our records show that your boss never signed off on the system as being completed."

Her lips pinched together, and her gaze dropped down as she sighed. "Probably because it wasn't finished. Or he knew that it hadn't been installed properly." Turning, she waved him to follow. "Come on, let's explore. You'll love seeing this place."

Her enthusiasm was contagious, and he found her interestingly refreshing. They walked through the wide marble-tiled entryway, and he glanced up at the two-story ceiling holding a massive wrought-iron chandelier.

He also knew the locations of the security cameras in the entranceway, and his gaze moved to their placements, satisfied to see they were where he intended them to be installed.

"From here, let's go to the left."

Tricia walked ahead, and it struck him that he was willing to follow her lead, which didn't often happen.

Somehow, letting her play tour guide through the mansion allowed him to see a more relaxed Tricia than the one he'd encountered on the ladder.

"This room is too small for a formal living room, but I think it's called a receiving room on the blueprints. I assume it's for guests who come for business because the next room is the office."

While many mansions had elaborate home offices and libraries, he couldn't imagine a house this remotely located having many visitors who would show up to meet with someone. Rubbing his chin, he wondered again who might have bought this estate.

The office held a private half bathroom and a door that led to one of the back hallways. He knew another safe room was behind the closet door. Tricia opened it, and he stepped inside. Smaller than the one upstairs, it was similarly furnished with a small full bathroom, sink, mini-fridge, desk with computer monitors, and a sofa sleeper. "Looks good," he said, appreciating the chance to see the work.

He walked back into the office and continued to look around. The rooms were painted soft ivory with stained wood trim around the windowsills and doorways that matched the ceiling.

The expansive windows drew his attention. The landscape of the desert hills just outside was stunning, but he quickly recognized the privacy glass used. It would prevent anyone from seeing inside while allowing the residents to have a perfect view out of the window. Narrowing his eyes, he peered closer and recognized that the windows were also bulletproof. Stepping back, he gazed upward and observed roll-up security shutters that could be lowered quickly, effectively locking down the residence.

"Do you know anything about the owners of this place?" he asked.

Tricia shook her head. "Nope. As far as I know, my boss has only talked to the real estate agent. I've talked to her a couple of times when she was here while I was working." She stepped up next to him. "It's impressive, isn't it? Quite a design you came up with."

His head jerked to the side, seeing her smiling up at him. "Did your company install these windows and shutters?"

"No way. Roche Electrical only handles the electrical systems, not windows like this."

It was on the tip of his tongue to admit he'd never added some of these security measures to the design but kept quiet instead. "Hm," he muttered, staring at the windows, no longer seeing the beauty outside but the actual windows.

"What would you put in here?" she asked.

He turned from the window and looked at her, finding her standing in the middle of the room, her gaze moving over the bare walls. "I'm sorry?"

She blushed and scrunched her nose. "Sorry, I guess that sounds kind of dumb. Empty houses are like a blank canvas, and I wonder how I would decorate if this were my place. What would be important for me to have in here?"

He looked around. "I suppose a desk and some chairs. Obviously, some bookcases and a credenza."

Her hands landed on her hips, and he wondered if he'd said something wrong as he stared at the scowl on her face. "You don't think that's what should go in an office?"

"Of course I do. But what kind of desk? What kind of bookcases? What kind of chairs?"

Unsure, he deflected. "You tell me. What would you put in here?"

She smiled widely. "I don't think anything heavy or dark should go in this room. I also don't think anything modern should go in here. I see a lightly stained white oak or ash desk with matching bookcases along the wall. Something that won't take the eye away from the outside view."

Envisioning what she described, he had to agree it sounded perfect. Deciding to play along, he said, "A sofa should be in here, along with two or three chairs. But, like you said, not dark leather. Maybe either pale ivory or tan."

Her eyes brightened, and he found that he liked that look on her. And he liked it when it was directed toward him.

"Come on," she encouraged, reaching out to tug on his sleeve.

He glanced down, not remembering the last time somebody tugged on him to get his attention. His fellow Keepers would be more likely to slap him on the back or just take off without him. Other men, often intimidated by his size, would just ask if he was ready to go. Women often used the well-practiced expression of lowering their chin, glancing up through long eyelashes, and adopting a sultry tone.

Somehow, the fresh-faced, widely grinning, bright-eyed Tricia captured his attention as no one else had. "Where are we going now?"

"This is just the office area. Wait till you see the rest of the family rooms. They are stunning!"

As they returned to the receiving room, he commented, "The same kind of sofa and chairs should be in here, as well. Something comfortable."

She stopped and turned to look at him. "Oh, I agree! I think that sounds perfect. A few Native American prints or artwork would look wonderful. Although"— she shrugged—"I don't exactly know what a receiving room is for. It seems rather unlikely that multiple visitors will come to see the owner and not meet with him immediately. It's an awfully long way to drive to make your guests wait."

She returned to the entry foyer and walked to the other side. There, with the windows facing south, was a massive living room with wall-to-wall windows overlooking the vista. The room opened in the back to what he assumed would be a dining room with equally stunning views.

"I could get my entire apartment just in this living room," Tricia said, laughing while shaking her head. She turned around in a slow circle, then looked back at him. "Now that I think about it, I think this room is bigger than my whole apartment!"

He chuckled, appreciating her unaffected honesty. "It's fucking huge, I'll grant you that." As soon as he walked into the room, he ascertained that the same bulletproof privacy glass had been used, with the security shutters tucked unobtrusively at the top of each window.

She commented on her living and dining room decorating ideas before saying, "You can get to the kitchen and family room if you keep going through the dining room. But I want to go back into the entry foyer so you get the full experience of going into their family room."

A flash of curiosity flickered through Poole's mind as he imagined what *family* might live in this estate—and it didn't jive with the concept of mom, dad, two-point-five kids, and a white picket fence. He was intrigued and suspicious.

Many people with immense wealth bought real estate that they never lived in, or some collected houses and might use it as a second, third, or fourth house. Others liked opulence, having all the bells and whistles of expensive security they could buy. But Poole couldn't shake the uneasy feeling that the future inhabitants wanted to conceal what was going on inside the house and sure as fuck didn't want anyone to be able to get in.

"What are you thinking?"

Having been lost in thought, he stammered, "Oh, uh... nothing." He followed her into the grand entry foyer. This time, instead of observing a smiling Tricia, she stood with arms crossed over her chest and her gaze staring up at him.

"I know we don't know each other very well, Poole, but... uh... walking around probably isn't really your

37

cup of tea. We can just look at the security, and I'm sure you had more important things to do today."

That was his opportunity. His chance. The perfect moment to nod politely, offer an amiable smile and agree that he really did need to get back on the road. In truth, there was nothing else to see here besides an expensive architect's dream house. If she was finished for the day, he could walk her to her truck as they left together, satisfied that he could talk to her boss and give her kudos for a job well done. All he had to do was open his mouth and make his excuses for leaving.

"No, I don't have anywhere I need to be. I'd like to see more of the house with you."

What the fuck? I'm gonna miss all the shows tonight in Vegas!

Who cares about Vegas? I'm having a nice time with a pretty woman who's sweeter than anyone I've met recently.

Vegas. Shows. Gambling. Drinking. Isn't that what I planned?

Poole silenced the inner battle as soon as her smile widened when he said he'd see more of the house with her.

"Great! Because what I'm going to show you will blow your mind!" She turned and headed straight to the back of the house.

He followed, telling himself not to think about what she could show him that would blow his mind.

They made their way through a vast hall with a large powder room on one side and several closets on the other. Through an arched doorway, he followed her, craving her enthusiastic presence more than a chance to get to Vegas early. When he stepped into the family room that faced the west with wall-to-wall, floor-to-ceiling windows, he took in everything the room had to offer. The ceiling was sixteen feet high, covered and stained in weathered wood. The walls were cream, complementing while not distracting from the desert vista outside.

The room would've been excessively hot without the unique windows when the evening sun hit. However, it was designed to expose the residence to all the beauty outside while still maintaining privacy and keeping out the UV rays. It didn't escape his notice that it also allowed for complete observation of anyone approaching the back of the house. Stepping closer, he spied the stone wall he'd seen from the front of the house and confirmed that it circled the entire estate. Nestled at the very back was a lush garden with a large swimming pool surrounded by palm trees.

"I was right, wasn't I? This blows your mind!"

Turning, he looked at Tricia standing in the middle of the space, arms spread wide, as she slowly turned around in a full circle. A smile spread across his face, unsure he could've stopped it if he wanted to. Seeing her smile, he liked that he was sharing the moment with her. And she was right—the view blew his mind.

5

Tricia wondered if she should pinch herself to see if she was truly awake or lost in a surreal dream. When her alarm jolted her this morning, she'd grumbled at the tiresome drive to the desert to finish the work that her lazy and incompetent boss had neglected. Caught between emotions, she both hated and looked forward to the last time she would be out here. The drive was long, and she was tired of cleaning up after her boss's constant mess. But there was a captivating beauty to the estate that brought peace when she was here alone. It was a respite from the frustrations of being overworked and underappreciated. She was the best security electrician working for a company she'd been proud to be employed with. At least, she used to feel that way. Not so much anymore as those sentiments waned.

Now, she wandered around a one-of-a-kind house, architecturally designed to blend seamlessly with the environment. And, while typically preferring to indulge in her house-decorating fantasies alone, she was in the company of the man who had designed the security system she'd helped install. It didn't hurt that he was easy on the eyes, either. She turned to walk back to the entry foyer and stifled a snort. *Easy on the eyes? Hell, more like a drop-dead gorgeous man who'd likely launched a thousand women's fantasies... and not of the home-decorating variety.*

"Are you ready to show me more?"

His deep voice rumbled throughout the empty room, bouncing off the walls and reverberating through her chest. She hadn't been this affected by a man in a long time. Looking up at him, she had to admit she'd never been this affected by just someone's voice.

Nodding in haste, she walked toward the entry foyer and waved him on. "Sure, let's look at the upstairs rooms you didn't see yet."

She slowed her steps on the open staircase.

"Are you okay?"

She blushed and held the railing as she glanced over her shoulder. "Open-back staircases always make me feel a little dizzy."

"You're kidding, right? You work on ladders all the time."

"I know! It sounds weird, but it's true. Somehow, climbing straight up a ladder, where my hands are also holding on, makes me feel more secure. I can only go up open-back staircases if I hold the railing tight. Otherwise... I don't know... it's just visually different."

"I promise I'll catch you if you start to fall."

She stood several stair steps above him, bringing her eye level to his. Staring into his face this closely, with his words ringing in her ears, made her long for a chance to see if he tasted as beautiful as he looked. Embarrassed at her unprofessional thoughts, she jerked around to face forward again, hurrying up the rest of the steps, attributing the feeling of unsteadiness to the stairs and not the man.

"You can see how this walkway faces the front and extends from either side to the back. You saw me working on the south wing, with four bedrooms, each with its own en suite bathroom." She led the way, and they stepped into each room, two on either side of the hall. At the end of the hall was a small sitting area with a deck that overlooked the back of the property. "I suppose these would be guest rooms or children's rooms." Standing in the middle of one, she shook her head.

"What are you thinking?"

"I'm thinking of the small bedroom I had growing up and just imagining what I'd do if I had this much space to put my toys in."

He looked around and nodded. "You're right. I had a decent room growing up, but it sure as hell wasn't anything like this."

"Where did you grow up?" The question slipped out, and she realized how easy it was to talk to him.

"I was born and raised in California. Stockton. What about you?"

"I was born in Nevada, but my parents now live in California. I guess we were what you'd call basic middle class. My parents had a nice house, but it was small and not fancy." She shrugged. "It was home, and I was happy there."

Poole held her gaze momentarily, the intensity shooting straight into her. Finally, the side of his mouth quirked up, and he nodded. "Can't beat a happy home. The size doesn't matter as long as it's a place with people you care about."

Eyes widening, she nodded her head quickly. "Yes! That's exactly how I feel, too." She looked around. "I love seeing beautiful architecture and the houses I work in. I appreciate the quality of craftsmanship, but I'm not envious."

He chuckled. "I often look at these big houses and wonder how much it would cost to fill them with furniture. And then I think about how many rooms don't get used."

"I have the same thought. Especially if this isn't going to be the owner's primary residence. It'll sit out here like a diamond in the desert without many people seeing or appreciating it."

"We might be the first people here who actually appreciate it."

She smiled at the thought. "You're right. That makes us very special."

His gaze continued to stay on her face, and a shiver moved through her body. Swallowing deeply, she cleared her throat. "Well... um... let's go to the north wing." Leading him back to the wide breezeway overlooking the front foyer, they came to the next wing. There were two bedrooms with en suite bathrooms, and the owner's suite filled the rest of the wing.

They walked inside to see the high ceilings finished in the same stained wood as the family room. Floor-to-ceiling windows faced the north and west, complete with the same security glass as on the first floor.

They stepped into the massive his-and-her closets, and she exclaimed, "My clothes could all be hung in a tenth of this space!" Looking around with her hands on her hips, she shook her head. "Maybe even less than that!"

"So I take it you don't have a massive shoe collection?"

A barking laugh erupted as she rolled her eyes and thrust out one booted foot. "I'm afraid my shoe collection doesn't extend to much more than my boots, some sneakers, a decent pair of running shoes, flip-flops, and a pair of heels I haven't worn in forever."

Next, she stepped into the owner's bathroom, which included a shower along the back corner, the wall made of glass overlooking the gardens below. "I certainly hope that's privacy glass, or somebody will give the coyotes an intimate view!"

This time, the full-throated laugh came from him, and she looked over her shoulder and smiled. The rest of the room was opulent, but staring at the soaking tub and entirely glass shower with a gorgeous man beside her made her feel heated from her booted toes to her ponytail. Hustling past him, she walked through the bedroom to a sitting room extending from the back.

"And in here? How do you see this furnished?" she asked.

He appeared to study the space, then turned and

grinned. "This room is enormous. I'd put a California king-size bed against the far wall, facing the windows with the mountains in the distance."

"Oh…" She blinked, swallowing deeply at the idea of him in a king-sized bed. *A California king.*

"What do you envision?"

"I… was thinking… well…"

"Come on, don't be shy now. What do you see when you look at all this space?"

Dragging her gaze from where he'd indicated he'd place a bed, she turned and waved her hand toward the sitting area. "I thought this would be perfect for a comfortable chair with an ottoman to put my feet up, recline, and read while the sun rises."

He stared for a long moment, and she battled the urge to squirm under his perusal. Turning, she spied the private deck that bordered large boulders on one side and a hot tub nestled in the privacy of the natural surroundings.

Feeling the need to escape the thoughts of his king-sized bed and her recliner, she stepped through the sliding glass door and walked out onto the deck, sucking in a deep breath of air. Her mind cleared as the beauty of the landscape surrounded her. How many people would only see rocks, sand, desert, and burning sun? The house was nestled among the boulders, and standing on the deck, she was immersed in the scenery. An irrigation system was already in place, and the grass below was lush and green, and the palm trees gently waved in the breeze. The pool was filled, but she'd always resisted the temptation to sit on the side with her legs dangling in the cool water.

Desert hills surrounded, leading to the purple mountains in the distance. There were no trees, but cacti and scrub brush dotted the desert soil. Caught up in the vista, she almost forgot Poole's presence. *Almost.* The reality was he was not a man easily ignored or forgotten. Especially as he walked closer, she felt him nearby.

His hands landed on the railing next to hers, and she glanced to the side to see his gaze looking out over the scenery. She turned away to look out as well and breathed deeply, remaining silent for a few minutes. Finally, she inhaled deeply. "It's beautiful, isn't it?"

"Absolutely stunning," he agreed.

She gazed to the side and realized he was staring at her. For a few seconds, she pretended he was calling her stunning instead of the view. *Yeah, right.* Inwardly scoffing, she looked down toward the gardens and pool.

"Would you like to stick your feet in the water?"

She jerked her head around again, seeing his beautiful smile as he inclined his head down below toward the swimming pool. Her brows furrowed. "Seriously?"

"Absolutely. I don't see why not. No one is here, and no one will know."

She hesitated, looking down at the sparkling water gently lapping against the sides of the pool.

He continued, "Have you ever used the bathroom in a house you worked in before? The empty houses like this, where no one is around?"

Her cheeks heated, but she smiled as she nodded. "Yes, I've even used one of the bathrooms here before."

"Same principle. You're out in the desert, and you've got to go, so use the bathroom. Be glad the plumbing and electricity work."

"Yes, but that's to take care of an immediate need."

"I don't know about you, but I really *need* to see if that water is as cool as it appears."

Throwing her head back, she laughed. "Okay, let's go. Anyway, I have another room to show you that'll be on the way." She turned and started to lead the way back through the owner's bedroom, but this time, she noticed that he stayed beside her instead of walking behind her. When they came to the staircase, she reached to hold the rail on the right, and he gently placed his hand on her left elbow, providing the calm stability that made it easier to walk down the open staircase.

Rounding the bottom of the stairs, they walked back through the expansive family room toward the kitchen. Grinning, she looked up at him and said, "My mom always said the kitchen was the heart of the home, and for me, this is a great heart!"

His eyes widen slightly. "My mom used to say the same thing." He whistled long and low as he looked around. "Mom would love this. She loves to cook, and damn, she is a good cook."

The kitchen was fitted with every updated appliance, including two stainless refrigerators, three double sinks, a top-of-the-line dishwasher, a microwave, three ovens, and an eight-burner induction stove, the black glass top blending perfectly with the marble countertops.

She leaned against the counter, her fingers trailing lightly over the surface. "Every time I'm here, I imagine my mom cooking a meal in here when my brothers and I were little. She'd be able to move around without all of us getting under her feet like we used to."

"How many brothers did you have?"

"Two. One older and one younger." She hadn't asked him any personal questions, but since he'd broken the seal, she decided to go for it. "And you? Any siblings?"

There was a second hesitation before he replied, "There were three of us. Two sisters."

She wanted to ask more but held back. It was one thing to make polite conversation and quite another to probe for information from someone she'd just met.

He glanced at his watch, and his eyebrows lifted to meet the hair swooping over his forehead. "Jesus! I can't believe it's almost noon!"

She had planned on spending most of the day at the estate, finishing the work early and then walking around to ensure everything was ready for her boss to sign off on the project. She brought lunch but decided to say goodbye to Poole first before eating.

"I'm sorry the tour took so long. But it was nice getting to look at the place with you. We can skip the pool so you can get back on the road."

A line creased his forehead as he turned to look out toward the backyard, followed by a sigh. "It's going to take a while to get back to civilization. I wish I had more than a few travel snacks to share with you."

"Oh, don't worry about me. I brought something to eat."

Seeing his brows lifting again in an unspoken question, she rushed to explain. "The work is finished, but I wanted to check it out, and I brought something to eat. I know you need to get back on the road, going wherever you were headed, but..." She walked over to one of the refrigerators and pulled open the door, exposing a large pizza box and a six-pack of soda. "Just like you described using the facilities... I use the refrigerator and microwave. If you'd like to eat before you leave, there's plenty, but I don't wanna hold you up if you need to head out."

His gaze moved to the refrigerator and then back to her, and once again, she tried not to squirm under his intense gaze. Then his lips curved upward until a wide grin spread across his face, bracketed by the dark beard. For a second, he reminded her of the gorgeous pirate models on the covers of her mom's historical romance novels. The ones she used to drool over when she was a teenager. *But I am nothing like the voluptuous damsels in distress.* Standing perfectly still, afraid that he could see inside her mind, she watched as he nodded, still grinning.

"Pizza? Damn, Tricia! Sounds perfect."

"You'll stay?"

"Absolutely."

Grinning, she fought the urge to dance a jig in the spacious kitchen. Instead, she pulled out the box and grabbed the sodas. She walked into a large pantry, calling, "This is bigger than my whole kitchen, but I'm not the only one who's discovered it. Some of the painters must have left a few supplies." She returned with a roll of paper towels. "Won't be the best, but it'll work." She placed two slices of pizza onto paper towels and heated them in the microwave. Setting them onto the open pizza box lid, she grabbed two more slices and repeated the steps. "Go ahead and dig in! Not fancy, but as my mother used to say, 'It'll fill an empty spot!'"

6

Poole studied Tricia as she navigated her way around the kitchen. He'd only been in her presence for a couple of hours, but he was drawn to her, desiring more of her company. Strolling around the house with her had been more pleasurable than he imagined. Her effortless beauty and ease of conversation made him loathe to say goodbye. Every layer of personality she exposed compelled him to learn more.

When they'd entered the owner's bedroom, he'd looked at the space, and it was easy to imagine how he envisioned it before she asked. A California king-size bed against the far wall, facing the windows with the mountains in the distance. *Oh yeah, definitely a California king-size bed.*

He'd pivoted, fully expecting to find her staring at the space where he thought it would go. Instead, he was met with her back as she stood in the sitting area, her gaze not on the vista outside the windows. Her vision of a sitting area for reading hadn't occurred to him, but he had to admit, he could imagine her ensconced comfortably, reclining, with her nose buried in a book.

When she'd asked what he was thinking about, he wasn't prepared to admit he was thinking of the bedroom furniture—specifically the bed. Instead, he'd simply mumbled his agreement to her idea of a reading area. Her laughter had echoed in the cavernous, empty room, her eyes twinkling as though she knew a reading area would be the last thing he'd think about.

A blush had crept onto his cheeks, a reaction he couldn't recall experiencing in a while. What was it about her that continually caught him off guard?

The rich aroma of pizza sauce, pepperoni, and gooey, melted mozzarella filled the air, and Poole's stomach rumbled. Looking down at the simple fair, he found it hard to believe he'd overstayed his planned brief visit by hours. His intended quick visit had morphed into two hours of enjoying the company of the striking electrician whose appreciation and enthusiasm for the architecture and surrounding area had resonated with him. It was refreshing to be in the company of a woman who wasn't flirting or expecting him to initiate advances. While Tricia was unaware of the full scope of his profession, her understanding and appreciation of the security system were tangible. Which, if he was entirely honest with himself, he found hot as hell.

"You dig in, too."

They each snagged a slice of pizza, folded it over, and took big bites at the same time. The melted cheese strung between the pizza and their mouths, and she slapped her hand over her face as she chewed, covering her laughter.

"You'd think I haven't eaten in days!" She laughed.

"It was smart of you to bring something."

"I got here early because I wanted to finish the last of the work. Then I planned on staying for a while to check everything out before I get my boss to sign off on this damn overextended project." She shrugged. "I've learned to bring some food when I come since we're in the middle of the desert."

"Tell me more about this boss of yours. Why is this project taking him so long?"

She swallowed, wiped her mouth with an extra paper towel, and sighed heavily. "Harold Roche started the business. He's the one who hired me. A good man. A fair boss. A really nice, all-around guy. And a smart businessman. He started as an electrician and got into security systems, then realized that money could be made by learning how to wire more exclusive design systems for estates and businesses."

Poole recognized the name, Harold Roche, considering LSIWC had used his company for several years. "So what's happening now?"

"He had a stroke and retired, so his son, Harry, took over. And believe me, he's not cut from the same cloth as his dad."

Poole stopped chewing, and his brows snapped together. Swallowing first without actually tasting the pizza, he asked, "We didn't know this." Seeing her questioning expression, he continued, "We vet all the companies that work for us to ensure they're up to our standards. We didn't have any notification that there'd been a change of ownership."

Her tongue slid over her bottom lip, catching a dribble of pizza sauce. His gaze focused on her mouth for a few seconds, and he completely forgot about the topic they were discussing. Blinking, he shot his gaze back to her eyes, not her luscious lips.

"If I had to guess, that's probably because his name is also Harold Roche. *Junior.* But he never uses the junior part. He goes by Harry, but the name of the business didn't change. The name that signed the checks didn't change. The name that signed the contracts didn't change."

"Fuck," he cursed under his breath. Carson and the Keepers prided themselves on knowing who they always worked with. He was glad he'd suggested to Carson that they re-look at all their contracted businesses. He wanted to call Jeb immediately to tell him what he'd discovered but preferred not to have that conversation right in front of Tricia. If LSIWC was going to halt its contract with Roche Electrical, he didn't want an employee to tell the new owner before they were ready. *Although, it sounds like she's not impressed with Harry Roche Junior.*

He peered down at the her and was curious about the enigmatic woman. "Tell me how you got into this line of work?" Her eyes lit up, and her smile widened. Seeing her enthusiastic response to his question, he was struck with the knowledge that he wanted to know more about her, not just about her employer.

"My dad. He's an electrician and is the proud owner

of Burrows Electrical Systems. I used to go on job sites with him, and in high school, I took vocational classes for electricians. Then I earned my electrician certification at a technical college, completed my apprenticeship, and became a licensed electrician." She chuckled. "I wanted to learn more, so I kept going. I earned a bachelor's degree in electrical technology and became a licensed contractor electrician. Then—"

"Holy shit, Tricia," he exclaimed, stunned at her education and impressed with her drive. "What was next?"

She threw her head backward in unadulterated joy. He couldn't take his eyes off her as she seemed to smile with her whole body.

Eyes still twinkling, she said, "I got my licensure to become a security system installer." Still chuckling, she shrugged. "That's it, I swear!"

"That's fuckin' amazing," he said, meaning every word. "How old are you?" As soon as the words left his mouth, he could imagine his mother slapping his arm, prompting him of his manners, and his dad popping him on the back of his head, reminding him that wasn't the way to talk to a lady. "Sorry... that was... well, it's not my business..."

Her laughter rang out again. "I'm thirty-one."

"You're kidding me. You don't look a day over twenty-two."

"Good genes, I guess."

He knew her reference was to genetics but couldn't help but drop his gaze to her blue jeans in appreciation. Lifting his gaze, he blushed again at the sight of her staring at him as he stared at her. "Well"—he cleared his throat—"your credentials are impressive."

Her smile hit him in the chest, another first for him. He'd known and worked with intelligent and professionally exceptional women, but something about her resonated deep inside, sparking an interest he hadn't felt before.

"Thanks, Poole. I appreciate that."

"And you don't want to work for your dad?"

"I do! Or rather, I did. And I will."

His head jerked slightly at her confusing response.

"Sorry, that doesn't make any sense. Let me start over. I worked for Dad at first. Then, he suggested when I got my first license that I should work for someone else. And with each subsequent license and degree, he still wanted me to experience different work environments, bosses, and locations. The goal was always for me to go back and continue with Burrows Electrical. In fact, he says that as soon as I rejoin the family business, he wants to rename it Burrows Electrical and Security Systems."

"Did your brothers go into the business?"

Her face softened, and while a pleasant smile remained on her lips, it no longer met her eyes. "My older brother, Trent, is in the Marines. Recon."

Poole hid his surprise, but he was impressed. "And your other brother?"

"Marcus followed in Trent's footsteps and joined the Marines. He also was in Recon but was one of the marines killed in a helicopter accident during a training incident."

His heart skipped a beat before dropping into his gut. "Oh shit, Tricia. I am so fucking sorry." Thoughts and memories bombarded his mind, and he opened his mouth to speak, then snapped it closed. Sharing wasn't his strong suit, especially not with someone he'd met casually. And no matter how attracted he was, this was casual. After today, he'd never see her again. The ache in his chest surprised him, and he lifted his hand to rub it, hoping to ease the pain.

Her lips stayed in a gentle smile, and she shrugged. "It was almost five years ago, but I swear, sometimes it just seems like yesterday. My parents wish Trent would get out of the service, but he seems more determined than ever. And in truth, Marcus would never have wanted Trent to give up his career." A little sigh slipped out, and she dropped her gaze back down to the slice of pizza her fingers fiddled with instead of picking up. She scoffed. "My mother would be embarrassed over my manners. I shouldn't play with my food."

He appreciated her effort to relieve the pall cast over their conversation but wasn't sure what to say.

A moment passed, then she looked up and hefted her shoulders in another shrug. "I'm Dad's last hope for joining the business. He doesn't mind because I was always the one interested in electricity, anyway. But, as I said earlier, he wanted me to get as wide a variety of experience as possible before working with him and one day taking over."

"Your family sounds special, Tricia."

Her smile widened, and it reached her eyes this time.

"They are. The absolute best." She tilted her head to the side. "It sounds like your family is, too."

"They are. We're both lucky."

"I'm determined to be as good an electrician as my dad. And if I follow in my parents' footsteps and have a good marriage and family, I'll consider myself a success." Pride sounded in her voice.

Her words seemed so simple on the surface, yet they struck him to his core. Her eyes sparkled with resolve, not the allure of money, fame, glory, or accolades. She wasn't looking to fill her closet with designer shoes or hoard the latest fashions. She just wanted to be a successful partner with her dad as an electrician and continue the tradition of a happy family. To be honest, it didn't sound a lot different from himself.

As though she could read his mind, she held his gaze. "What about you? I feel like I've done nothing but talk about myself." Her gaze dropped, and a light blush crossed her cheeks, making him grin. Her vulnerability peeked through her confidence. *She wasn't as unaffected as he thought.*

"What do you want to know?"

"Well, you haven't really told me anything about yourself. I couldn't help but notice that when I mentioned my brother was Marine Recon, you looked like you knew exactly what I was talking about."

He chuckled and nodded. "I was in the Navy. A SEAL."

Her eyes widened, and he stiffened. It was a natural reaction from all the years of women immediately having an idea about banging a SEAL. But instead of her gaze morphing into pure, predatory interest, she burst out laughing, throwing her head back. Stunned, he lowered his brows as he waited to see what she found so amusing.

"I'm sorry," she said, her laughter ending with her smile still wide. "My brother used to talk about working with SEALs. It seems like there was a lot of competition among some of the Special Operation Forces. Of course, you can imagine that he thinks Recon is the toughest."

He snorted. "I hate to break it to you, but your brother is wrong."

"Oh yeah? He says he used to eat SEALs for breakfast."

"Well, maybe your brother and I should meet up sometime, and we'll compare stories."

She dipped her chin, her lips pressed together as though to hold back more laughter, and he couldn't help but smile. Talking to Tricia was easy, and the more time he spent in her presence, the more he enjoyed her company.

"I now know you were a former SEAL. Did you always want to be a SEAL?"

"Maybe not a SEAL at first, but I always wanted to go into the Navy." He smiled at the memories cascading through his mind.

"Your smile tells me there's a story there."

He looked over and caught the spark of interest in her eyes. Nodding, he agreed. "Yeah. I was thinking of my grandpa. He was in the Navy. He used to show me pictures and tell me stories. God, I loved listening to him. He was assigned to an aircraft carrier, and I thought he must have had the best job in the world. He was in for about ten years, then got out when his parents needed help. He met my grandmother and said he never regretted leaving when he did, but he was blessed to have served."

"He sounds wonderful and such a good person for you to look up to. What about your dad? Was he in the military, too?"

Poole started to laugh, but it came out as more of a chortle. "No, no. My dad went his own way but had a hard time when I wanted to do the same." He looked over to find her brow crinkled. "My dad was Frederick Poole Sr., a professional linebacker for the Forty-Niners. He was six-foot-two-inches and about two hundred and thirty pounds. He was talented and worked hard. And made sure that I did, too."

A slight intake of breath caught his attention, and he looked toward Tricia again, seeing her gaze move over his torso. She blushed as her hand fluttered toward him. "I can tell. Looks like you got your size from your dad."

He grinned, finding the blush endearing.

"What did he think about you going into the Navy? He must have been proud."

The grin slipped from his face, and a heavy sigh left his lungs. "I'm afraid that was a real problem between my dad and me for several years. I was also a linebacker in high school and had scholarship offers from several colleges. Dad was talking to my coaches, lining up tryouts and interviews. I kept telling him that I didn't want to go to college and play football. Then, when I turned eighteen during my senior year, I signed up to join the Navy after I graduated."

"Oh my…" she whispered, eyes wide. "I assume that didn't go over very well."

A chortle barked out. "You'd be right about that. It made things tense between my dad and me for a couple of years. He was furious. Thought I'd thrown away a promising career. I guess it was also very personal—like I'd thrown his career back at him." He hefted his shoulders, then shook his head. "At one time, I thought I'd just stop visiting my parents when I had leave, but I wanted to see them, as well as my sisters and grandparents. But it was hard to feel his disappointment with each visit."

"I wonder if parents are doomed to want things for their kids and then have to deal with it when the goals are different."

"Are you thinking of your dad and brothers?"

She nodded. "I think my dad always knew Trent had his own path. He craved adventure. Danger. Excitement. And while Dad encouraged me, he thought at one time that perhaps Marcus would follow in his footsteps. But Marcus always idolized Trent. It was obvious that Marcus would join the Marines."

He wondered if she felt like a consolation prize but didn't want to ask in case it was sensitive.

But with her typical openness, she smiled and said, "Dad was thrilled to have me interested in his job and what he did. He never made me feel second best. And he was proud of his sons." Her smile slid from her face as her eyes lowered to stare at her hands on the counter.

"After Marcus was killed, I know that as grief-stricken as Dad was, he was proud that Marcus had followed his own dream, knowing my brother was fulfilling his destiny."

They fell into silence, but Poole's mind raced with things left unsaid. Things he wanted to say. Things he didn't talk about casually. Yet Tricia seemed to easily lay her thoughts out into the open to someone she just met, not keeping them moored deep inside where they became almost forbidden to find the light.

He watched her as she gazed out the window, a soft smile playing about her lips as her appreciation of the breathtaking vista wasn't marred by talking about her brother's death. Her eyes were bright, and the tiny freckle next to her eye that was slightly darker than the others once again captured his attention. Calm radiated from her, and he was gripped with the desire to share in that peace.

Before he could speak, she turned toward him and asked, "How did you and your dad breach the divide?"

"My younger sister died."

Her facial muscles froze for a second, and he wanted to snatch the words back as terror clutched at him. "I…"

Then her expression crumpled as her hands darted to his shoulders, gripping him tightly, as tears welled in her eyes. "Oh, Poole. Oh God, I'm so sorry!"

Before he could react, she pressed tightly to him, her arms snaking around his waist. His arms instinctively wrapped around her back, holding her tight. The feel of her body so close to his at the moment of exposed emotions sent the calm he'd desired to move through every cell.

He was no longer the former SEAL who had to be tougher, badder, and more lethal than anyone else. He was no longer just a Keeper who had to be on point with every mission. He was no longer just a son who'd disappointed his father many years ago. He was no longer just a man who needed to guard his emotions, not wanting to share something so personal with just anyone.

If he had learned one thing, it was that grief had no timeline. As devastated as his family was when his sister, Becky, died, he found his grief came in waves over the years. While she was always in his heart, sometimes the grief receded into the background, and other times, it rushed to the forefront, bringing the familiar ache. And often, when around others, he held it deep inside. Now, with Tricia's arms around him, he felt honest emotion in front of someone else for the first time.

He rested his chin on top of her head and allowed his racing heartbeat to slowly match the steady beat of hers.

7

Poole continued to hold her, knowing he needed to give more of himself, but for several minutes, he simply allowed himself to feel. Tricia didn't speak. Didn't offer platitudes. Didn't offer advice. Didn't probe or prod.

She finally leaned back and held his gaze. For the first time, he noticed her eyes. They were dark brown, but this close, he could discern gold flecks that ringed the iris. Warmth and shine emitted all at the same time.

They were silent, but it wasn't uncomfortable. It was as though they'd shared a moment that needed the silence to process the topic, but it wasn't oppressive. Instead of wishing they'd never traveled down that road, he wanted to know anything she was willing to share. And realized he also wanted to share with her.

"It was discovered close to the time you said Marcus was killed... about five years ago. Becky was only twenty, in college, with her whole life in front of her. She was young and healthy, or so we thought. She rarely went to the doctor. But breast cancer is the second most common cancer in women in adulthood. By the time it was diagnosed, it was too late. She had surgery and chemo but died a year later."

Tricia's arms tightened around him, and her gaze didn't waver. He dropped his chin to stare deeply into her eyes as he marveled at the healing powers of her hug.

"I was able to stay with my family a lot near the end, taking family emergency leave. But when she died, I tried to return to my unit, but it was too soon for the focus needed as a SEAL. I ended up moving to an admin position but hated it. I was thirty years old when Carson Dyer reached out to me about joining his firm. I grabbed on to his vision, glad to become part of his company."

"Change can come to us at just the right time if we let it," she said.

LSIWC had given him a new purpose, one that was true to who he was as a man but also one that let him be near family. Nodding slowly, he held Tricia's gaze as something clicked deep inside his chest. "I think it was the right time."

"Did you and your dad heal the breach?"

"Yeah. At first, just grief held us together as a family. Grandpa had reminded my dad for years that he'd forged his own path when playing football, doing what he loved, and chasing his dream. And Mom was just her steadfast self... you know, always there, cheering in the background. My other sister, Rachel, was right there, also pulling us all together. She was pregnant, and the birth of my nephew solidified the family again. When I came home for his birth, Dad and I talked. Really talked. We've been as tight as I could ever hope since then."

Tricia sucked in a breath and let it out before smiling again. "My dad used to always say that life was to be lived to the fullest."

A smile curved his lips, and it felt real. "That's what my grandpa used to say. Now, everyone in the family agrees."

With a lighter heart, he reluctantly loosened his arms from around her. As she stepped away, he instantly felt the cool air between them and battled the desire to snatch her back into his embrace.

She turned back to the pizza and cleared her throat. "Tell me more about what you do now. What about the company you work for? The one that saved you." She bit back a grin. "The company who may or may not keep doing business with Roche Electrical."

Brows lifted, he snorted, ready to ease into a new conversation. "Let's just say that my company will re-vet all their contractors. The original Harold Roche's contract with us was based on letting us know if there was any change in management."

Her smile immediately dropped. "I understand if your company drops the contract since Harry Junior is not the greatest electrician. But Harold was wonderful, and if it weren't for his stroke, he would still be on top of things."

Poole nodded, then glanced around the kitchen, his mind turning to all of the work Tricia had completed on the house. "It's good that Roche Electrical has you to work here. Whoever the owners are, they'd be incredibly disappointed if this place wasn't as secure as you've made it."

"Well, your company and design made this place secure. When you showed me your ID, it said Lighthouse Security Investigation. Is designing security systems the main thing you do?"

He shook his head, wanting to tell her more but keeping his comments to the standard information anyone could find out. "It's a specialized security company that takes on contracts for systems and personal security. And we're also licensed investigators."

"Then I'd say they're fortunate to have a former SEAL working for them."

A bark of laughter now erupted from deep in his chest, and his eyes caught her surprise as her head jerked back. "Sorry, I didn't mean to startle you. It's just that everyone who is hired at LSI is a former special operator from the military."

"Oh, wow. So it's a whole company made up of people like yourself."

"I can tell you it's a company made up of some of the best people I've ever worked with. So to be in their presence and considered to be one of them is an honor."

Her face gentled. "That's a really nice thing to say." Then she lifted a brow. "And, honestly, it sounds like that's all you can tell me about your job, or you'd have to kill me."

"Nah, nothing that drastic. But most of our cases are secure, so we don't discuss them." He looked around again and added, "We also design specialized security for exclusive clients."

"Oh, I don't think Harry knows who the owners are."

"Actually, we don't. We were contacted by the real estate agent, who initially said she wanted top-of-the-line security to attract buyers with money who might want security since the estate is so far out in the desert. She was willing to pay, and the house hadn't been built yet, so we took it on. Then she gave us the name of an attorney buying it, and he had more specific requirements. The contract installation was awarded to Roche Electrical since we've worked with them before, and I knew their quality work." Inclining his head toward her, he added, "Now that I've met you, I can understand based on your work. As far as I can see, you make Roche Electrical."

She blushed, appreciating his notice of her professionalism. "How did you learn to design the systems?"

His shoulders shook with mirth. "Honestly? By learning how to get past them."

Blinking, she opened her mouth, then shut it quickly. He could see she was confused. "As a SEAL, I had to know all about different security systems and how to get past them. Into them. Around them. Disarm them. You name it, we had to do it. So, from that, I learned what was needed. I don't have the education you do for making them work, but I have the know-how to start with what's needed and create a plan. Then it's up to someone like you to make it happen."

She smiled and blushed, but her eyes held pride. "Does it usually take this long to finish a place?"

"I know a house like this can take a while, but we'd been in contact with the real estate agent almost two years ago. She said that the building had stalled, and nothing was being done. We were paid for the new design, so it didn't really matter to us. But then, it came back up on our list, and when I contacted her, she said yes, that the house had finally been built, and the owner said he was moving in soon. She didn't mention that we are not the only security this house would have. I find it interesting."

Her brows knit together. "If someone wanted to have a super secure place but wanted to ensure that no one person or company knew all their secrets, they could have different components. Your company designed the security and cameras and technology. Another company obviously installed specialized safety glass in all the windows and doors. Another company may have put in security shutters that can be raised and lowered." She nibbled on her bottom lip for a minute, then said, "Damn, it makes me wonder who's moving in here!"

He thought the same thing but didn't tell her that his gut wasn't giving him a good answer. She gave him the perfect out when she said, "If you'll excuse me, I'm going to make a trip to the restroom." She walked out of the kitchen and down the hall next to the pantry, and he heard a door click.

Pulling out his phone, he called the compound, not surprised when Jeb answered, even on a Saturday. "Hey, man. I need to let you know what I've learned and pass this on to Carson and the others."

"I have Carson right here. Go ahead."

"I came to the Pence Realty house in the desert. I found one electrician here who just finished checking the system. She's given me a lot of information."

"She?"

"Don't be sexist, Jeb. Women can be electricians."

"Hell, I was just wondering how charming you were being to get information."

Hearing the water in the sink down the hall running, he knew he didn't have much time. "Listen, I'm still here and have to talk fast. Check out Roche Electrical. The older man who ran it had a stroke, and his son is running it now. Same name, and they didn't notify us. But according to the electrician who works for them, and I trust her, the son is probably not the kind of person we want to do business with. If she doesn't trust him, I don't trust him. Plus, see what you can learn about who's moving into this house. There's more security here than just what we designed. And that makes me wonder who the fuck is moving in."

"Will do. When are you heading to Vegas?"

He heard the door open down the hall and quickly said, "Later today. I'm still checking things out."

Disconnecting, he shoved his phone into his pocket just as she re-entered the room. She smiled but remained quiet, not pestering or begging for information. But he wanted to be honest. Or as honest as he would allow under the circumstances. "I checked in with work and told him about the change in ownership even though the names are the same."

She nodded as she walked to the counter. "That makes sense."

"How long do you plan on working for them?"

She held his gaze for a long moment, and he wasn't surprised. She was intelligent and seemed exceptional at reading between the lines. "How long do *you* think I should continue my employment with Roche Electrical?
"

"Perhaps you might want to start sending your résumé out or consider it time to join your father's business."

Her face remained impassive for a moment, and then her lips curved upward. "Well, it sounds like I'll need to order new business cards."

"I assume you trust your father's business," he joked.

"Absolutely! I can guarantee you that Burrow's Electrical is top-of-the-line." She shrugged and added, "I should let you know that I was actually going to be leaving Roche's by the end of the month anyway. I'm heading back home. My parents are excited, and I feel like it's time to join the family business. I've learned a lot, but now I'd like to use that knowledge and education with my dad."

"Where is he based?"

"Their home is in Fresno, California. That's where the business is based, but he sends electricians all over the country."

"Well, if his company is interested and can satisfy vetting by LSIWC, I would tell him to consider being a contracted security installation company for us." He chuckled and shook his head. "Looks like we're probably going to need another one."

Her top teeth landed on her bottom lip as she held his gaze, seeming to study the veracity of his statement. Slowly, she nodded her head. "Sounds like a good idea, Poole. I'd like to keep working with you."

Her words eased in, and his grin widened. If she wanted to see him again, he was more than ready.

8

Tricia needed to use the restroom but instinctively knew that Poole needed privacy to report to his employer about his findings. She was confident in her work and initially hesitated about sharing her concerns over Harry's business handling. But as she spent more time with Poole, she trusted him and hated to think that Harry's shoddy work would harm Poole's employer's reputation.

Stepping into the kitchen again, she knew it was the right decision to give him a few minutes of privacy. She was thrilled when he suggested that her dad's business could win a lucrative contract with Lighthouse Security. *It's definitely time to go back home and work with Dad!*

Her mind raced with possibilities to continue their conversations, but he'd already spent so much of his day with her. The idea of going home to her tiny, lonely apartment held no appeal after being with him. Sighing, she turned to the counter and began wiping the crumbs with paper towels while he collected the pizza box and water bottles. "Once we gather the trash, I'll carry this out to my truck when I leave." He didn't respond, and she turned to see him staring out the sliding glass door toward the gardens.

"Let's go out there."

Blinking as her chin jerked back, she looked outside and then at him. "Don't you need to get on the road? I hate to hold you up here." Her words were a lie, considering she'd love to continue her time with him. She tried to adopt a casual expression but had a feeling he could see right through her when he stared, and his lips slowly curved up.

"I can check the security out there, also."

"We didn't do the outer wall because that wasn't contracted for us," she hastened to explain.

He nodded, but his smile dropped as he admitted, "We weren't contracted for any parameter security either."

"So what are we looking for?"

"Let's just explore."

"Explore?"

Turning to her, he placed his hands on her shoulders. "Yeah. Explore. Come on, Tricia. You were the one who wanted to check out everything in the house. Let's see what's out there. I might find something I can report back to LSIWC."

She loved the feel of his hands on her shoulders, but his words snagged her attention. "What does the WC stand for?"

"West Coast. There is another LSI based in Maine."

"Are they as good as you?"

His deep laughter rang out, and she was struck by how his gorgeous factor jumped up to the stratosphere level when he let go and really smiled.

"They were the original and, believe me, set the standard." He jerked his head toward the door. "Come on. Forget security. Let's go check out the pool."

At that moment, she would have agreed to go check out the moon if he had asked. "Sounds good." She opened the sliding door and stepped outside in front of him, still hoping to hide her enthusiasm. It had been a long time since she'd been interested in spending more time with a man. Her shoulders hefted with a sigh. *And, of course, it has to be for a man who's so far out of my league and in the middle of a trip.*

They strolled across the patio, meticulously crafted of stamped and stained concrete that gave the appearance of walking across desert stones. She appreciated the artistry and, turning, observed him looking down and seeming to appreciate the patio. As the spring sun beamed down, she was grateful for the shade from the arbor overhead. Keenly aware of how unforgiving the desert heat could be, the inside of the house would stay cool, but an unshaded patio would turn blistering hot. The placement of the palm trees and the overhead arbors made the area beautiful and maintained the shade.

He walked to the pool, bent over to unlace his boots, and pulled them off before shedding his socks. He rolled up the legs of his pants to just below his knees. She stared at his calves, strangely mesmerized by the play of muscles as he moved.

"What are you doing?"

Puzzlement filled his face. "I'm going to put my feet in the water."

Her eyes widened, and she stammered, "I know you said we could, but should we?"

"I don't see why not. The owners haven't even moved in yet. We've been checking out the security. There's no reason we can't check out the pool with our feet, either."

She laughed and nodded. Bending, she repeated his actions, unlacing her boots before pulling them off and ridding her feet of her socks. Rolling her pants legs up, she sat beside him on the pool's edge and dipped her toes into the water. "Oh my God, that feels amazing! It's cool but not cold."

"Sun warmed." He grinned and shifted closer.

They sat side by side in silence for several minutes, lost in their own thoughts. She finally shoulder-bumped him to gain his attention. "What are you thinking?"

"Professional curiosity, I guess."

Cocking her head to the side, she waited to see if he would elaborate, glad when he did.

"I wonder why the real estate agent hasn't disclosed who the owners are yet. I also wonder why they hired more than one security system designer for everything."

She glanced around, pressing her lips together as her gaze moved over the surrounding gardens to the outer wall. "What do you suspect?"

He turned and looked at her, and she felt he was calculating how much to say and how much he trusted her. In the silence, she decided to share. "Harold got the contract for Roche Electrical to put your designs in place. I'm the best he has, and he gave the plans to me to work on. But after his stroke, Harry took charge, pulled me off this project, and started sending me on others. It's not that I think any work is below me, but none of the projects he had me working on were complicated or expansive."

"Do you know who he put on this project initially?"

"Yes. Himself."

Poole's brows lifted, and his jaw tightened again. "Seriously?"

She shrugged. "He is a licensed electrician and has worked on systems before. He's not as competent as I am with the designs, but he's okay with regular electrical systems. Months go by, and Harold is out of danger but decides to retire. More months go by with me just working on other projects. I asked Harry how this contract was going, and his reply was that it had stopped because the building was taking longer than expected. To be honest, I put it out of my mind. I had enough to deal with trying to assist him with managing the business because he did not have his father's acumen."

"Sounds like maybe you should've joined your father's business before now."

"I'm not one to quit in the middle of something. I never felt like I owed Harry anything, but I felt strongly that I owed Harold something. I suppose it doesn't matter now."

Poole jerked his head back toward the house. "I

think it does matter a lot. Tell me how you got back involved in this."

"About two months ago, Harry came and talked to me. He said that this project was back on track. He said the house was almost finished being built. He'd come out several times and had done some of the work. But he realized he didn't have time to get it finished. He didn't have the time nor the ability."

"I get what you're saying. The project needed to be completed, and he didn't know how to do it."

She nodded, then looked out over the lush gardens surrounding the pool. The serenity gave her a sense of peace. Turning back to face Poole, she continued. "So I came out here, and this gorgeous house was almost complete. Of course, that made it a little more difficult to check on Harry's work, but I found errors. Your design is exquisite, but Harry didn't have the knowledge or experience to bring it to life. I've spent the past two months redoing a lot of his work and re-wiring. But I also noticed it had security glass, doors, and a security perimeter wall around the estate. We did none of that. I assumed your company was involved, and you just had someone else put it in."

Poole shook his head. "It wasn't us. We could have designed everything for them, and you're right, we would have used different companies as contractors."

"That makes perfect sense since we don't do that kind of windows or outer wall and gate installments."

"But it appears the new owners wanted to keep everything separate."

She leaned toward him, lowering her voice. "You wanna know what I think?"

He looked at her and nodded. "Absolutely."

"I think they're being sneaky. I don't think it's just some rich person who wants an architectural dream house to bring his family and show off to his friends. I think it's someone who wants a place to hide out."

Poole didn't react to her words, but she'd spent enough time with her brothers and knew they were trained to hide their reactions and emotions. A flash of something moved through his eyes, and she was sure she'd hit the nail on the head.

"I hate like hell that we didn't know who the new owners are and that you've been out here alone getting the work finished. LSIWC would have stepped in to make sure you were safe. At least with it finished, I won't have to return."

His words spoke of his company, but the way they were growled made her feel like it was his personal vow to keep her safe. Sucking in a shaky breath, she nodded. "Agreed. Although, I wasn't always alone. The painters were here when I first started. Some of the concrete workers just finished recently. It's only been the last couple of weeks that I've been out here alone, and I never felt afraid when I was here. I'll kind of miss it. It's been really nice to experience this gorgeous place. It's been fun to pretend how I would design and decorate."

His jaw grew tighter when she mentioned being out here alone. She laughed to relieve the tension. "Then I would go back to my little apartment and be perfectly satisfied that I didn't live in a place like this. Can you imagine trying to clean the whole house? Then there's the outbuildings, guest houses, and that doesn't include the pool and gardens."

"Doubt they do it themselves," he grumbled.

"Yes," she said with a dramatic flair, snapping her fingers. "Jeeves... I'm going to LA for shopping. Make sure the house is spotless when I return!"

Laughter bubbled up from his chest, and her heart warmed seeing his smile aimed toward her.

"Is that what you do with your house? Order your staff around?" he joked.

"Oh, yes." She waved her hand around and shook her head. "My place is only a tiny rental. And seriously? I'm pretty sure my whole rental would fit into the space of the owner's bedroom here, but I turned it into my own special place. For now. And, while I don't have a separate sitting room, I like to chill when I get home after work. A good book to read. A glass of wine." She shrugged, realizing how narrow it made her life seem.

"What's your favorite wine?"

She blinked at his question and laughed again. "I'm such a wine dork. I know nothing about wine other than it's made from grapes, and I drink what I like. The lighter and sweeter, the better!"

His wide grin took away the fear that he found her lacking. That tidbit of knowledge lodged inside her heart as she smiled in return.

9

A grin stretched across Poole's face as Tricia's words hit him. The last time he'd been alone with a woman had been two months ago, and the encounter failed to kindle the warmth he now felt. He'd crossed paths with a woman at a local winery as she traveled through California on a wine tour. Her undeniable attractiveness grabbed his attention, but he soon learned she was a pretentious wine snob with little to add to a conversation. He'd nearly walked away from boredom with her endless dissertations on wine, but his prolonged dry spell clouded his judgment, and her overt flirting tempted him when she invited him back to her hotel room.

It didn't take long to wish he hadn't taken her up on her offer. The sex was perfunctory, and it was apparent they were both ready to say goodbye when it was over. As he'd made a hasty exit, she'd said she would look him up the next time she was in the area. He knew it was an empty gesture, and he wouldn't take her up on another invitation even if she did, having no intention of repeating a hollow experience. He'd been less discriminating when younger and in the military, but older now, he preferred to be interested in the woman before having sex.

Tricia was a breath of fresh air, a stark contrast to his previous encounter. Her presence had sparked interest in his perusal of the house. He loved hearing everything she had to say about her family, career, or vivid decorating ideas. He'd never imagined sitting on the side of the pool with a fully dressed woman, submerging their feet in the cool water, to be worth postponing his paid-for trip to Vegas. Yet here he was. A soft chuckle escaped his lips. His inner voices were no longer battling. It seemed that talking to Tricia had silenced them. He couldn't help but revel in the tranquility that had settled as they sat beside each other.

He stared at her profile as she looked out over the gardens. Her nose turned up slightly at the end. A freckle dotted her cheek next to her right eye, and his finger itched to reach up and touch it.

"God, this water feels so good," she moaned as she kicked her feet, causing splashes.

"Let's get in."

His words slipped out before he'd thought them through. But now that they were spoken aloud, he didn't want to take them back. Her wide-eyed expression revealed she was surprised, but she didn't object. Or at least not initially. "Come on," he cajoled, not wanting to think of reasons they shouldn't enjoy their time together. "Underwear stays on. It's just like bathing suits."

Deciding to give in to the impetuous idea, he stood, and his hands went to the bottom of his shirt. Whipping it over his head, he tossed it back several feet away from the pool. Next, his fingers landed on his belt buckle. He caught the blush on her cheeks. "Come on, Tricia. Don't let me have all the fun."

She stood with her lips pressed together, but her hands hesitated at the bottom of her shirt.

"I'll wait," he volunteered. "I'll turn my back, and you get in. Then I'll follow." He turned his back toward her without giving her a chance to object and waited. The sound of clothes rustling met his ears. Suddenly, his cock reacted, and his breath caught in his throat. The desire to cool off and have a little fun might not be such a good idea since she'd be able to see his erection. A splash sounded before he could devise an alternate plan, followed by a squeal.

Chuckling, he stripped his jeans and tossed them to where his shirt lay. Keeping his boxers in place, he turned around and jumped in quickly before searching her out, hoping the water in her eyes would keep her from seeing him clearly.

As soon as his body hit the cool water, he dove low and swam to the other end of the pool. Coming to the surface, he shook his head, sending water droplets flying. She was in the shallow end, her face lifted to the sun before lowering to gaze at him. The bright smile on her face shot straight to his chest, warming him as much as the beams of sunlight peeking through the palm fronds.

He swam toward her, his long arms making easy strokes through the water, and he stood in front of her in no time. "Was I right about this being a good idea?"

She nodded, her smile still in place. "I thought the water might be too cold, but it's heated, isn't it?"

"I'm sure it is. Until the owners move in, it's probably turned down to a temperature that doesn't use too much electricity, but the sun has kept it warm. Once they occupy their estate, they could easily use this pool even in winter."

She had moved to where only her head was above the water, but it was easy to see she wore a white bra and white panties. Her modesty was refreshing, and he didn't want her to be embarrassed, so he stayed several feet away.

She bounced up and down on her feet but went no deeper. Tilting his head to the side, he stared before asking, "Do you know how to swim?"

"Yes. Well, sort of. I know how to dog paddle."

Brows lifted, he didn't hide his incredulity. "You never took swimming lessons?"

"I did when I was a kid. I learned basic strokes and safety, but we didn't live near a pool once we moved from Nevada to California. My brothers had some friends who had pools and would go swimming all the time." She shrugged. "I guess I never spent much time in the water."

He took her hands and slowly walked backward,

drawing her closer. When she stiffened, he vowed, "I'll keep you safe."

She stared intently, and he hoped she could see his genuine oath. Finally, she nodded but tightened her grip as they moved into deeper water. He slowly pulled her closer, willing to stop if she indicated. But instead, she focused on his face as he walked them into the deeper water. He lifted his hands to settle hers onto his shoulders and then slid his hands down to hold her waist firmly. He hoped this would make her feel more secure but also had the advantage of bringing her closer to him.

Soon, her facial muscles relaxed, and she even laughed as he walked around the pool with her attached to him like a spider monkey. His cock protested the closeness to her core without being able to slide in, and he kept his hips from pressing inward. It made for an awkward position, but to keep the smile on her face, he battled his cock's urges.

Her gaze dropped to his shoulder before lifting to his face again. "Tell me about your tattoo. I assume it's not a coincidence that you have a lighthouse tattoo and work for a company called Lighthouse Security."

He chuckled and shook his head. "No, not a coincidence." The sun reflected off the water, adding sparkles to her eyes as he stared at her beauty. A soft smile played about her lips, and his focus landed on the little freckle by her eye. The desire to kiss her filled his mind. Clearing his throat, he forced his thoughts back to her question. "All of the Keepers have the same tattoo. There's a tracer under the skin where the beacon is. It allows someone to find our location while we're on missions."

"And the meaning behind the title Keepers?"

His bottom lip slid between his teeth for a few seconds, trying to find the words to describe what it meant to become a Keeper. "When I was with the Navy, being a SEAL wasn't just what I did... it was who I was. It defined me and others who had taken that oath."

She smiled and nodded. "Like Trent did with Recon."

"Absolutely. And for me, it was my identity for many years. Now, the same identity is with Lighthouse Security and Investigations. The original developer of LSI had the concept of forming the same camaraderie as in the military. And we're known as Keepers, based on the lighthouse keepers of old. Guiding, protecting, warning, saving. Same concept."

"You were a protector before your sister became ill. And when Rebecca died, you're still a protector, but you needed protecting as well."

His gaze narrowed, but she wasn't finished.

"LSI's lighthouse guided you to where you needed to be."

Her whisper-soft words hit him like a tidal wave crashing on the rocks. He'd never thought of LSIWC that way. After all, he was the protector. But his chest deflated as air rushed out. She was right. The Navy and his SEAL brothers had been what he needed when he joined. And they sure as hell had rallied around when Rebecca was ill and then died. He could only handle so much at one time, and the Navy no longer was the right fit for him. If Carson hadn't come along with his hand out when he did, Poole had no idea where he'd be right now.

His gaze never left her face, needing her as much as he wanted her. During their conversation, he'd guided her through the deeper water. She still clung to him but finally relaxed, giving him her trust. A gift he didn't take lightly.

He returned to the shallow end, where wide steps covered one corner of the pool. Twisting, he sat down, and she ended up straddling his lap. Uncertain if she would scramble away, he held his breath as she leaned closer, wrapping her arms around his neck, their chests now pressed together. Their breaths were shallow, and their gazes locked. Her mouth was open slightly, but the rapid blinking of her eyes made him sure she would never make the first move. He was equally unsure if he should.

What had started as a cool-off swim and a bit of fun now took on a new life as he inched forward just enough to bring his lips close to hers, giving her plenty of opportunity to move away or say no. Instead, her gaze dropped to his mouth, and she sucked in a quick breath. Their bodies, pulled by an invisible thread, gravitated closer. The world around them faded as she met him halfway, pressing her lips to his.

The touch sent jolts throughout his body, and his grip tightened on her waist, more to steady himself than her. *Rocked.* It was the only description he could think of when their mouths melded together. Her vulnerability, mixed with their desire, forged an intimate connection. He loosened one hand to slide upward to cup her head, angling her slightly to align their lips for maximum contact. She tensed for a few seconds, then her body relaxed as she pressed closer to him, and her tongue darted out to trace his lips. A shiver ran down his spine as he craved more.

When she opened her mouth, he plunged into her warmth, dragging his tongue over hers. The velvet softness unleashed a multitude of sensations. The kiss started slow and gentle. A languid exploration. Soft and yielding. Savoring the taste and texture that was uniquely her own. Their breaths mingled, feeding off the essence of each other.

Time slowed, and the world around them faded away. There was no way he would be able to keep the kiss light. Impossible. Not with the way his senses were firing, his cock was aching, and the desire to plunder was overwhelming. But the last thing he wanted to do was take advantage of her or the situation. So, as much as he wanted to strip her out of her bra and panties and explore every inch of her body, he focused on the kiss. Electric currents coursed through their bodies, sending tingles along every nerve. With this kiss, any pretense was stripped away as raw emotions forced their way into his consciousness.

He couldn't remember the last time he'd kissed like this... the truth was that he'd never kissed like this. He was breathless as she slowly lifted her head, and their lips reluctantly parted. Staring into her beautiful face, he matched her panting, breath for breath, in order to survive. The lingering taste of possibility hung between them, but neither spoke.

She blew out a long exhalation, finally whispering, "That was, by far, the best kiss I've ever experienced in my life. Nothing has ever come close."

A grin curved his lips. He loved her honesty. He loved her vulnerability. He loved her fresh outlook. He loved getting to know her. He'd love to know her better. But his cock was tired of being ignored. This wasn't the time or place, and he had no desire to take advantage of the situation. She deserved much more.

An equally long exhalation left his lips, as well. "I guess we should get out and dry off."

"We have no towels."

"We can sit in the sun for a few minutes."

"Do you have an answer for everything?"

He chuckled. "Honestly, I'd love to stay here and keep kissing you, but I'm not sure my body can handle much more without wanting it all."

She blinked, and pink tinged her cheeks. "Oh. Yeah. Right." She pressed her hands against his shoulders and stood, quickly walking up the pool steps to the patio.

He tried to keep his eyes away from her body, but it was impossible now that he'd felt her curves press against his hard planes. As he followed, her delectable ass was practically naked in the wet white panties. Then she turned and sat down on the patio, and her nipples poked through the thin silk of her white bra.

Poole decided he'd found heaven and hell in the same moment— staring at her beauty and unable to enjoy it further.

10

"There are a number of outbuildings," Tricia said suddenly, turning toward Poole.

They had sat on the warm patio, partially in the shade, turning front to back several times to dry their bodies and underwear without becoming too hot.

They were dressed once more but still dangled their legs in the cool water. Neither had mentioned the kiss, and he wondered if there would be a repeat performance or if it would be one of those life-changing moments when he was ruined for all other women because of her kiss, but they'd never speak of it again. The silence had been comfortable, and he couldn't remember the last time he'd felt this at ease with a woman outside of work. When she spoke of the outbuildings, he had to drag his mind to the estate and off the woman who'd captured his thoughts.

"We didn't do the security for them. I don't actually know if they have security like the main house," she continued.

Her words dragged his attention from her freckles to what he was supposed to be doing here. "What kind of outbuildings?"

"Several look like guest houses but are somewhat rudimentary for a place like this. No fancy bathrooms. More like the bunk rooms I used to have at summer camp when I was a kid. There's also another garage beyond the house. I know there's no security camera on it like the ones here at the house for the owners and main staff." She turned and held his gaze. "Honestly, Poole, this place is more of a compound than just an estate."

Her description was accurate, and he was glad this was her last visit.

A gust of wind whipped past them, and she shivered, blinking as she looked up when dark, rolling clouds moved overhead. He hauled his feet from the water and stood, hating for their time together to end. Bending, he offered his hand. "Come on, it looks like a storm is coming. We need to leave."

She didn't hesitate but immediately placed her hand in his. An electrical current ran between their grip, and he dragged his gaze from her face to the sky, wondering if lightning had struck nearby.

"You also felt that?" she asked, allowing him to pull her to her feet, her eyes focused on him.

"Yeah." His gaze held hers, seeing confusion pass through her beautiful eyes. Another gust of wind cut through his musings.

They bent at the same time and grabbed their boots and socks. Hustling toward the house, he pulled out his phone and looked at the weather radar. When he'd started out this morning, the prediction was for sunny skies with a slight chance of showers. Now, he stared at the new forecast of an electrical storm with high winds and hail. "Damn, Tricia, a storm is coming. It's almost on top of us."

They hurried inside, closing and locking the door behind them. "I'll grab my tool belt and the trash bag," she said, walking quickly through the kitchen. "The real estate agent will have professional cleaners come through before the owners can move in, but since I won't be back, I just want to make sure I've left the place as I found it."

As she moved out of the room, he called LSIWC again. "Hey, Jeb. The storm caught me off guard. I'm getting ready to head out now. I just want to make sure Tricia gets off safely, too."

"The electrician?"

"Yeah. I don't want to leave her unprotected."

"This storm was supposed to hit tonight, but it's come over the mountains much quicker than predicted and a helluva lot bigger. You'll head straight into it as you drive toward Vegas. You should probably find a place to spend the night and let it pass. Then you can finish the drive tomorrow morning."

"Fuck," he muttered, hating to have Tricia take a chance on outrunning the storm. "Okay, thanks. I'll let you know what I decide."

He disconnected as she walked back into the room. Her gaze stayed on his face as she approached, and her eyes narrowed slightly.

"What's wrong?"

A flash of satisfaction moved through him at the way she could read his moods. It had been a while since he'd had a long-term girlfriend, but even they had not always been able to discern when something was on his mind.

"A massive storm is approaching. Lightning. Torrential rain. Hail."

"Well, shit!" Her face scrunched as her gaze shot out the window.

"How far away do you live?"

"It takes about an hour and a half to get to my apartment." She quickly looked at him and added, "You know what? I'll just stay here and wait out the storm."

"This fucker is huge. It's going to last for hours. By the time it eases, it'll be dark. I don't want you to drive in the dark on the roads around here."

"Okay." She scrunched her nose as she cast her gaze around. "I'll stay here overnight."

"What?" His tone was sharp, and his chin dipped down as he eyed her.

She spread her arms out wide. "Look, I have leftover pizza, some water, and a safe room upstairs with a bunk. I'll be fine overnight. Then I can make sure it's all locked up tomorrow morning and head out after the storm has passed."

"Stay here alone?"

Her eyes flashed. "Poole, you seem to forget I was alone before you came by. If you weren't here, I'd be doing the same thing."

His fingers curled into fists, which landed on his

hips. "I don't doubt your abilities, Tricia, but there's no way I can just leave with you here."

"Poole, I—"

"No, I don't want to drive off and leave you. I'll stay, too. We can both head out in the morning."

They stood silently for a moment, their gazes locked on each other, scowls on their faces. Then her lips curved, and she laughed. "Okay, partner. It looks like we're going to have a slumber party."

She turned to collect the pizza box with the leftover pizza while he stood and stared at her back. And tried to figure out why her words sent a bolt of electricity through him.

Tricia's cheeks ballooned with a weary exhalation before the hair curling on her forehead puffed upward. The unexpected turn of events was a surprise, but she was used to making the best of situations. As an electrician, she was no stranger to problem-solving, analyzing, and weighing risks before proceeding.

Poole's sudden presence in her solitude caught her off guard, but she'd quickly come to discover he was a fascinating man and the most handsome man she'd ever spent time with. *Oh God... and that kiss.* Oh, yeah... the kiss that was as shocking as touching a live wire. Her body had threatened to incinerate even though they'd been in the swimming pool.

As the danger from the storm loomed, she recognized reluctance in his eyes. She hated for him to feel trapped, but if he acted out of obligation and stayed, she needed to ensure she guarded her heart. It wasn't like her to fall head over heels so quickly, but Poole had wormed his way into her thoughts, staking a claim on a part of her heart she hadn't known was vulnerable. As lightning zinged across the desert sky, she longed to lean against his muscular body and feel his protective arms around her again.

She'd tried to make a joke by announcing a slumber party, hoping the whimsy of her words would mask the trepidation in her heart. But a gnawing sensation burrowed deep—sharing a small space with him would be anything but slumbering.

"I have some snacks in my SUV. I parked next to you and can take the garbage out when I go."

She turned as an idea hit her. "You said we were getting hail, right?" When he nodded, she said, "We can pull our vehicles into the farthest garage. There's no security on the door, so we can just lift the doors and drive in. Also, since those aren't the ones close to the house for the owners, we won't have to worry if there is a little oil stain or something left on the floor."

"Good thinking."

She beamed, feeling less self-conscious. He grabbed the garbage bag, and they walked through the staff's door. A burst of wind whipped by as she stepped outside. She spied his big SUV parked next to her truck. "Wow, nice drive. Puts my little truck to shame."

"Nothing wrong with a good work vehicle with miles on it as long as it's safe." He narrowed his eyes as his gaze swung around to her. "It is safe, right?"

"Yes, *Dad*," she quipped with an exaggerated sigh, then laughed when he shot a narrowed-eyed glare her way.

"Smart-ass," he grumbled. He leaned over and peered inside. "You always keep your truck this clean?"

"I hate messes. If I have to spend a lot of time in the truck driving to sites, especially this estate, which is *way the fuck* away from everything, I want my space to be clean." She shook her head. "My parents had never demanded that I keep my room spotless when I was younger, but with two brothers who were into every sport, the house was a constant maze of footballs, cleats, baseball bats and gloves, and athletic shoes. When I'd disappear into my room to read, I loved having everything in its place. Clothes in the closet, books on the shelves. Now, even though I live by myself, I guess the neatness habit was ingrained."

She climbed inside her truck and started the engine. He followed as she drove to the farthest garage, which turned out to be larger than she'd expected and was perfect for keeping their vehicles from being damaged by the oncoming hail. He parked beside her and exited his SUV before she could get out. He raised the garage door, and she drove in and waited as he pulled in next to her. As he climbed out again, he had a small bag in his hand. They lowered the door and darted toward the house. With another gust of wind, rain splatters began to fall, and he reached over to grab her hand, holding tight.

Their hands were still clasped when they made their

way back inside. "Glad we won't be driving in this storm," she said.

Once they entered the kitchen, she stopped and turned to stare outside at the dark clouds rolling in the sky. The rain fell in sheets, making it impossible to see the garden while pelting the patio. Poole walked to the windows and stood with his hands on his hips.

"Do you think we should lower the security shades in case the hail is bad?"

He turned and shook his head. "I don't want to be stuck inside without being able to see out the windows. Plus, they're bulletproof. The hail won't break them."

"Oh, duh," she mumbled, shaking her head, feeling foolish. "I forgot about that."

Hail popped as it hit the patio, drawing her attention, and she walked over to see the ice balls bouncing on the concrete. A jagged bolt of lightning slashed through the gray, and she winced. The thunder rumbled nearby, and she was surprised the house didn't shake. Warmth hit her back, and she felt Poole's presence before he placed his hands on her shoulders. She wasn't scared of the storm, but having him at her back was comforting. And strangely familiar.

"We can check to make sure the windows are secure. I'd hate to be wrong."

She smiled and nodded. They hurried through all the rooms, but as he'd surmised, the windows were secure against hail. *If they're supposed to keep out a bullet, they'd better hold up against the weather.*

"Let's head upstairs just to check those windows, too," he suggested.

She nodded again and wondered if she would follow him anywhere. So far, it seemed as though she would. *Into the water. Deep end of the pool. Up the front staircase.* He held her hand as they ascended. She was so focused on his steady touch that she forgot to be nervous on the open-back stairs.

Again, the windows in each room were secure. She stopped on the breezeway overlooking the front driveway and placed her hands on the rail. He stopped directly behind her. She was startled when he reached out and placed both hands on either side of hers on the railing.

She barely breathed, afraid to move. She loved the feeling of being surrounded, yet their bodies weren't touching. She wasn't sure if she found that titillating or comforting. It sure as hell wasn't awkward. Though she craved to lean back and feel his muscular body behind her, she stayed locked in place instead, terrified he would see how much the simple action meant to her. She felt him move slightly, and his chin came to rest on top of her head. Now, more confused than ever, she wondered what he was thinking.

Unable to stay quiet any longer, she laughed. "Is the top of my head a good resting place?"

He chuckled, and she could still feel the vibration through her since there was only the barest hint of space between them.

"I realized I could peer out the window over your head. Somehow, my chin just decided to rest there."

She pushed back against the railing and shoved her shoulders against his chest, eliciting a grunt. Turning, she batted her eyelashes. "Oh, so sorry. I guess you were just in my way."

He pretended to growl as he rubbed his sternum. They both grinned and walked back down the stairs. He checked his phone, and she leaned over to peer as the radar screen showed the massive storm. They were just in the early phases of it, with the radar's yellow and red designations of the worst still to come.

She had lost all sense of time but caught the clock on his phone and realized it was early evening. It hit her that they'd spend hours at the pool. *We've been together most of the day.* If anyone had told her that she would meet someone at the house and spend all day with them and then look forward to continuing to spend time with them throughout the night, she would've thought they were crazy. Tricia preferred her life to be orderly and planned, and that included her social life.

"What's on your mind?" he asked, lifting a forefinger and gently rubbing the crinkle between her eyebrows. "It looks like you're thinking too hard about something."

A long breath slid from her lips. "Honestly? I can't believe that we've spent the day together. And I can't believe we're getting ready to spend the night together." As soon as the words left her mouth, she scrunched her nose, realizing they implied sexual intimacy. "That didn't really come out the way I meant, but—"

"No, I get it." He smiled as his finger traced down her cheek before dropping away. "I feel the same way. I figured I would stop by, talk to the electrician, get some answers, check the work, and hit the road."

"I never asked where you were going."

He grabbed the back of his neck and squeezed. "Vegas."

"Las Vegas?" she gasped, her eyes bugging. "You were on vacation, and you stayed here today? Why on earth would you do that?"

"Because I discovered I liked the company," he stated definitively.

She opened her mouth to speak, then snapped it shut. Pursing her lips, she thought over his answer, hating to admit she liked it a lot. "Well, I'm glad we had time to get to know each other, but I'm sorry about your vacation."

"No worries. I'll head out tomorrow after the storm has passed."

That made sense. *Perfect sense.* Yet she couldn't deny that a tiny part of her wished she could accompany him on his vacation before returning to her boring little apartment.

11

Poole balanced on the razor's edge of uncertainty, his actions swerving wildly along the curves of unpredictability. His decision to stay during the day with Tricia, explore the house, share a meal, and enjoy time in the pool cooling off—not to mention getting hot and bothered by a kiss that rocketed through him—veered away from his typical plans. And now, he teetered on the edge of another precipice as he suggested spending the night in a house with no furniture except a minuscule sofa and twin-sized bed. All in the company of a woman residing in his mind after knowing her for less than a day. Anticipation, as well as uncertainty, coursed through his veins. *Christ, if the other Keepers only knew this!* He'd teased the others for falling quickly and wondered what they'd say in return.

Of course, this is different... I haven't fallen for her. I'm just spending time with her.

With that thought firmly in the forefront of his mind, he shifted mental gears to the evening. "It'll get dark soon, but we have electricity. Do you know if the generator is functional?"

"As far as I know. Last week, the gas company was out here checking on the fireplaces, and I'm pretty sure they checked the generator."

"Good, so we won't be in the dark." He looked around. While sitting on the floor in front of a fireplace sounded good, he knew the hard tile and wood would soon get uncomfortable. "Do you want to go upstairs?"

"Sure. There's the sofa in the safe room. It's not large but would be more comfortable than sitting on the floor down here."

He grabbed the bag and grinned. "I have snacks."

"And I have the leftover pizza!" She opened the refrigerator and grabbed the box and the water bottles.

They walked through the downstairs rooms, ensuring the lights were turned off before they ascended the main staircase. He followed as she passed the safe room and entered the owner's bedroom.

Glancing over her shoulder, she smiled. "I just have to take a detour here to look out again."

He understood. After all, the room was magnificent. She stood for a few minutes and stared out the windows even though the torrential rain hindered the view.

His gaze bypassed the window but centered on the beautiful woman standing in front of the glass, appearing both small against the backdrop of nature yet a force to be reckoned with all on her own. During the day, his admiration for her had grown. She was smart, continually striving to learn more in her chosen career. She had taken her father's advice and not settled into what could have been an easy job in the family business but had worked for several companies to gain more experience.

He appreciated her honesty, quick wit, and how she never tried to make herself out to be anything more than what she was, secure in the knowledge that she was enough. And if anyone didn't agree, they weren't worthy of her, anyway.

"Even with the rain pouring and the view completely distorted, this is still an amazing house, offering so much to the family that will move here."

He remained quiet, not wanting to interrupt her thoughts.

"It's so beautiful," she said, her voice as wistful as a sigh.

Unable to refrain from agreeing, he said, "Yes, it is."

She looked over her shoulder at him, and his gaze remained on her, not out the window. She shook her head and laughed. "I was talking about the view out the window."

He repeated the sentiment he'd offered earlier. "And I was talking about you."

With those words, her eyes widened, and her mouth formed an "O," but no other words came forth. Slowly, her lips curved, and her beauty struck him straight in the chest.

"It feels a little early to go into the safe room, doesn't it?" she asked.

He looked around, then grinned. "I have a better idea."

Her eyes remained bright as she waited. He set his

bags down in the bathroom. "Put the pizza box on the bathroom counter and follow me."

He walked down the hall and entered the safe room. She was on his heels as he eyed the two mattresses on the bunks. Bending, he snagged one from the bottom.

"Where are you going with that?"

"Grab one end, and I'll show you." He could have carried it easily by himself but wanted her involved. He took the lead, and they carried the mattress back into the owner's bedroom, where they laid it on the floor near the fireplace.

Understanding dawned on her face, and he held his breath for her reaction. He didn't have to wait long.

She threw her arms in the air and hopped up and down. "Oh my God! This is perfect. We can sleep here instead of being stuck in the tiny safe room!"

"We'll have more room. We'll have the larger bathroom. And in the morning, we'll return everything as it was."

The excitement showed on her face as she beamed while hustling back to the safe room to get the other twin mattress. Securing the room again, they soon settled into the oversized bedroom with floor-to-ceiling windows showcasing the storm and a fireplace. Tricia immediately plopped down on a mattress, then flopped onto her back and stretched like a starfish on the shore. The twin mattress was certainly large enough for her, and as he stared, unbidden images came to his mind as she reclined on the mattress with her eyes closed and a smile on her lips.

Get your head out of the gutter!

Admit it, though, she's gorgeous, lying there. It's hard not to think of lying there with her.

As I said, get your mind out of the gutter.

Rolling his eyes at his inner dialogue battling again, he lowered himself onto the other mattress.

She sat up and looked at him, then scrunched her nose. "The mattress is going to be so small for you!"

"Don't worry about it. Sleeping on any mattress, even a short one, is a lot better than some of the places I've slept in."

"I'm sure as a SEAL, you had to sleep in many lousy places."

"Same as your brother, I guarantee."

She smiled at the mention of her brother, her face soft. He loved seeing her so relaxed. As the storm continued to rage outside, their conversation slowed, and she yawned widely. "What time is it?"

He checked his phone. "It's about eight o'clock."

Her eyes bugged out, and he laughed at her expression.

"Eight o'clock! Are you kidding? I can't believe I'm already yawning!"

"It's your body's reaction to it being so dark outside. Plus, it's been a busy day for you."

Scrunching her nose, she sighed. "Although, I'm no night owl. It's probably what killed my last relationship."

A strange sensation zinged through him, creating the desire to pound any man who'd known her before him. *Jealousy?* Mentally shaking his head, he thought *No way.* Before he had a chance to ask about anyone from her past, she glanced past him and smiled.

"I can't believe I'm considering this, but do you wanna know what would be amazing?"

He knew exactly how he would answer that question but wasn't sure what she was referring to. Silence seemed to be his best option.

"We were in the pool earlier, but I'd love to take a warm bath. Does that sound weird? To think about using someone else's bathroom, and they haven't even moved in?"

He'd already thought of her in the shower, but now thinking of her in the bathtub caused his cock to twitch. He shifted on the mattress, tamping down his desire. "It's not like you're going to leave it dirty. Plus, as you said, the real estate agent will have a maid service come through before the new owners move in."

"Do you think I should go for it?"

"Absolutely."

She jumped up but then sighed. "Damn, I don't have a towel."

"I brought my bag in from the truck. I have extra clothes. If you want to dry off with the shirt you're wearing, I can loan you one of my shirts to sleep in, and then you can wear it home tomorrow." His offer was sincere, but as he spoke aloud, he realized that would give him an excuse to see her again.

Her eyes brightened. "Well, you'll have to let me know how to meet up with you again sometime so I can return it."

"Oh, sure, sure!" He had a feeling that his enthusiastic response gave evidence to his desire.

But she was already scrambling up, heading into the bathroom as soon as he handed the shirt to her. She closed the door behind her, and he heard the water running. And running. And running. Becoming worried, he stood and walked over, knocking on the door. "Tricia? Are you okay?"

The water turned off, and he heard the sound of splashing. "Yes! Sorry! I just wanted it really full of hot water. It's amazing!"

He stood with his hands gripping the bathroom doorframe, his head bent forward, resting against the door as he tried to ignore his cock's eagerness. He could still hear her splashing, and imagining her luscious curves naked in the water made him wish for things he shouldn't. *It's going to be a long fuckin' night.*

Just when he thought she must be a prune and was about to knock on the door again, he heard the water running through the pipes. A little later, she popped out, and the expression on her face was worth his cock's discomfort. Her eyes were bright, and her skin glowed pink. And her bare legs, which he'd seen in the pool, now held his attention.

"That was so amazing! My apartment has a small bathtub, and the water doesn't get hot enough for me to fill it full. That was almost like being in a real hot tub!"

He stood, struck dumb at the sight of her, wearing one of his Go Navy T-shirts, the hem hanging down to her knees. He didn't even want to think of what she might be wearing underneath. He feared he might need to find a separate room to take care of his screaming erection. Clearing his throat, he mumbled, "If you're finished, I think I'll head in there and shower."

Her smile was sweet as she nodded. "Absolutely."

He started walking past her, then stopped, and she turned her head to look at him. Only a few inches remained between them, and she didn't step away. Instead, she leaned closer, placing her hand on his arm and squeezing. And just like in the pool, her gaze dropped to his mouth.

Longing filled his chest, and thoughts of "Can we? What if? I want…" swirled in his mind. With a growl, he bent and closed the scant distance, stopping when there was just the barest whisper of space between their mouths. "Tell me what you want, Tricia."

The wait was only a few seconds, but it seemed interminable. Then her lips curved slightly, and she lifted on her toes, sealing her mouth over his. Once again, the touch of their lips sent jolts of electricity through his body.

12

Almost never impetuous, Tricia molded her body to Poole's as the electric current coursed through her veins the instant their lips touched. A sigh of contentment escaped, quickly claimed by him when his arms tightened around her, drawing her closer. Time froze as the storm outside raged. She didn't care about the job. Or the winds howling outside. Or that she'd only known him less than a day.

He embodied everything she'd yearned for in a man. He possessed the qualities she admired from those she loved and respected the most... her father and brothers. His strength was a physical attribute and an essence that resonated from within him, commanding and earning respect. His intellect was an asset, and he was unthreatened by her unconventional career choice. And his kindness was an instinct, keeping her safe without undermining her independence.

The men who had played pivotal roles in her life had set the bar high. And while she'd hoped that she might find a man who sparked all of her desires, she'd harbored a sliver of doubt while not resigning herself to lowering her standards. But Poole certainly checked all her boxes.

Despite the whisper of caution fluttering deep within, reminding her of their fleeing encounter, she quickly silenced it. She didn't care. This didn't have to be forever. If she could just have him for tonight, she'd carry that memory with her forever, even if it ruined her for all other men.

"I know I just took a long bath, but would you like company in the shower?" she mumbled between their kisses.

His tongue caressed her lips, tangling with hers before he lifted his head and replied, "Oh, you'd better believe I would!"

His arms tightened around her, and he lifted her slight weight easily. Her feet dangled as he carried her back into the bathroom. She hated to lose any contact when he set her feet on the floor, so she pressed tightly against him as his mouth continued to plunder hers. Shuffling toward the shower, they separated just long enough for him to lean in and flip on the water.

It only took a second for her to jerk off his T-shirt and stand naked before him when he turned back to her. A gasp left his lips, and he stared wide-eyed. After several seconds, she blushed and ducked her head, starting to cross her arms over her breasts.

"No. Don't be self-conscious." In two long steps, he pulled her against his body again, trailing kisses from her forehead, over her cheek, sucking on her lips, then continuing down her neck.

Finally lifting his head, he mumbled, "My God, you're beautiful. The most beautiful woman I've ever seen."

She blushed even harder and shook her head. "You don't have to say that, Poole. I'm kind of the girl next door, and that's good enough for me. But I'm hardly beautiful."

"Don't ever say that again." His voice held a slight edge, capturing her attention. "I won't have anyone say anything against you, even yourself. Sure, you've got the girl-next-door vibe, but you're fuckin' beautiful."

He stepped back and jerked off his boots, socks, jeans, shirt, and boxers so quickly she could barely appreciate each part of him revealed before there was another part to admire. And when he was naked, his cock was already at full mast. "Talk about beautiful," she managed to say, even though it was hard to breathe with all the male magnificence in front of her.

She couldn't believe she'd stripped so quickly, even before he had. But her entire soul screamed at this being what she wanted. Right now. Right here. With him.

His body was delicious. Smooth skin over thick muscles. Piercing eyes that seemed to see deep within. Wavy hair that had dried unruly when they'd finished their time in the pool. A trim beard that she suddenly wanted to experience between her thighs.

He stood utterly still, and she realized he was giving her every ounce of control even though it must've been agony for him to do so.

She stepped up to him, then stopped when they were a foot apart. Smiling, she reached down and linked her fingers with his, then moved past his body and into the shower, tugging him easily after her. She glanced toward the back of the shower wall, entirely made of a glass window, bare to the outside storm. It was strange being naked in front of a window. She felt no embarrassment. No one was out there, and even if there had been, the view was only visible from the inside. Suddenly, she was filled with unbridled abandon, feeling completely free.

He turned so the water spray hit him, and she spied the body wash he'd grabbed out of his bag. They lathered each other, their hands gliding simultaneously over soft skin. He smoothed over her breasts, circling her nipples, and then he gently turned her around and soaked her back.

As he paid particular attention to her ass, she began to giggle. "Sorry. I guess I'm kind of ticklish."

He nuzzled her neck and growled, "I love every inch of you. Especially the parts that make you laugh."

He turned so the water rinsed her clean before he slid his fingers between her legs. Her head dropped back, and she groaned as one of his thick fingers slid into her sex, hitting the spot that caused her to shake and cry out. He bent, taking a nipple into his mouth, tugging lightly with his teeth. It had been so long since she'd had sex, and her orgasm hit almost immediately. Too turned on to be embarrassed, she cried out his name as her fingers dug into his shoulders.

She'd never had shower sex before but didn't want

to leave this glass enclosure without feeling all of him inside her. With his gaze still locked on her, he stepped back, and she felt the loss of his touch, not only on her skin but deep inside her chest.

He reached out of the shower and bent to dig his hand into his jeans on the floor, pulling out his wallet. Standing with a condom wrapper in his hand, he held her gaze. "I need to know this is what you want, Tricia."

"Absolutely," she vowed. "This is exactly what I want."

She let him take the lead since she had no idea how they would make this work. He rolled the condom on his impressive erection, then lifted her in his arms and pressed her back against the glass wall. She wrapped her legs around his waist, and while he held her with one hand, he placed the tip of his cock at her entrance with the other.

She was ready, but she gasped when he thrust upward, seating himself fully. He jerked his head back, eyes wide.

"It's okay, it's okay," she promised. "It doesn't hurt. I'm just full. You're... well, you're big all over."

His worried expression morphed into a smile that quirked up on one side. Then he leaned in to kiss her as their bodies began to move together. The position may have been new to her, but adjusting to the rhythm didn't take long. The movement forced her breasts to press and rub against his chest, her nipples tingling as she felt the electric jolts moving throughout her nerves, centering between her breasts and her core. It also didn't take long for her to know that she was going to come again.

His breathing pattern changed, and she hoped he was as primed as she. Holding on for dear life, she felt him tense underneath her as her channel grabbed him, and her orgasm pulsated. His face turned red, and he grimaced, the veins in his neck standing out. He held her gaze, their mouths barely apart, before he roared his own release.

She clung to his shoulders as he continued to thrust until every last drop must've been wrung from him. Uncertain her body could move without being held up by him, she wrapped her arms tightly around him before burying her face against his neck.

They clung together for a long moment as the water continued to flow all around them, hitting the glass and swirling at their feet. He slowly pulled out and set her feet on the shower floor, maintaining his grip until her legs would hold her up. His gaze stayed on her as they panted in unison.

"Wow," she barely managed to say. "That was... that was... wow."

He chuckled, then shook his head to sling water all about. "You can say that again, darlin'." He disposed of the condom and gently maneuvered her back under the water, rinsing their bodies.

She looked over her shoulder to the window. "I'm glad no one can see my ass." She giggled.

"No one but me."

His words held a hint of possessiveness that caused her sex to clench again. He flipped off the water before she could say anything, and they stepped out onto the floor. He reached into his bag and pulled out another T-shirt, drying her off before using it on himself.

"I'm afraid that's not gonna get you very dry," she said, staring at the damp material in his hand.

"Let's turn on the fireplace, and we can dry off in front of the fire."

Her eyes widened, and she nodded. "I like the way you think!"

They left the bathroom and entered the bedroom. He flipped the switch on the wall next to the fireplace. She held her breath, anticipation mounting, then cheered when the flames roared to life. The crackle of the fireplace immediately radiated its warmth, and she lifted her arms, fingers wiggling toward the heat.

After pulling out a comb from her purse, she ran it through her hair, then tugged on the T-shirt he'd given her earlier. Sitting on one of the mattresses close to the fire, she stretched out like a purring cat, sighing with contentment.

Having returned to the bathroom to don a pair of sweatpants, Poole walked back into the room. Her gaze dropped to where they hung low on his hips, showing off the delectable, muscular V that now led to what she knew was a spectacular cock.

So mesmerized by his physique, she hadn't noticed his hands were full until he bent and set the pizza box and the bag of snacks onto the mattress.

"I wish this was more."

"No, it's perfect. Remember, it's imperative to have ridiculous snacks at slumber parties."

Grinning, he dropped down on the mattress next to her, and they ate cold pizza, peanut butter bars, and trail mix, washing it down with water.

Throughout their impromptu feast, her smile remained a constant presence on her face. Gazing into the eyes of the man staring at her, she couldn't imagine a better partner to spend a stormy night with, locked away in a dream house. Parting tomorrow would suck, but she'd take tonight if that were all she could have of him.

After they finished eating, she scurried around, cleaning up every crumb. She didn't regret their decisions but couldn't stand leaving the mess for the morning to clean up. When she went into the bathroom to use the toilet, she wiped the remaining water droplets from the shower glass and the tub. She didn't have a bag like he did, but she stacked her jeans, socks, and boots next to her purse. Looking around, she was satisfied that she would have little to do in the morning. *Except get dressed and say goodbye.* That thought sat in her gut like a rock. *I just met a great guy, fell heavily into lust, and have no time to see if anything else could develop!* Sighing, she opened the bathroom door and stepped into the bedroom.

Poole had pushed the two mattresses together to make a larger bed and was now lying on his side with his elbow crooked and his head resting in his hand. His eyes were locked onto her as she walked closer. Her mouth felt like the desert as she stared back. Sucking in a ragged breath as she moved toward him, she wasn't sure where he wanted her to sleep.

He patted the mattress beside him, and she eagerly dropped to her knees before rolling to her back, maintaining the thread between them that their gazes created. They had no blankets, but the fireplace cast heat over the room as well as light.

"How's the slumber party going?" he asked, lowering his head and sliding one arm around her waist.

A chuckle slipped out. "I'd give it a nine out of ten."

His eyes widened, and a gasp slipped out. "Only a nine?"

"We had a fire and snacks, but the only thing we haven't done is tell ghost stories."

"Ghost stories?" His voice held incredulity.

She rolled to her side to face him, her fingers tracing the contours of his jaw. "When I was little, slumber parties always involved ghost stories."

"And when you got older?"

She pressed her lips together, but the edges curled upward slightly. "When I was a teenager, my friends and I used to talk about kissing. Who we'd kissed. Who we wanted to kiss. I didn't do a lot of kissing, so it was mostly who I wanted to kiss."

"I like kissing more than ghost stories."

"Well, you did ask me to rate the slumber party so far," she countered.

His fingers tightened around her waist before dragging her closer until their bodies pressed together. "Okay, how's this? There once was a ghost who discovered a sweet electrician, and when he kissed her, sparks flew from their lips. He discovered her kisses gave him the life force needed for shower sex. And now, the ghost thinks more kissing will give him the necessary jolts for sex on a mattress in front of a fire, in a spectacular house in the middle of a storm." He leaned forward and kissed her lightly, sliding his tongue over her lips. "How was that?"

"If we have sex in front of this fireplace, the slumber party definitely will go to a ten. Maybe higher," she panted, her lips seeking his again.

"Good. Then let's find out how high we can go." With that, Poole's lips devoured hers before he rolled on top, gently pressing her back into the mattress.

She'd thought nothing could top shower sex, but having his body surrounding hers as he lay on top... *Oh yeah... the best slumber party ever.*

13

With an abrupt jolt, Poole was pulled from sleep, his eyes snapping open as his body jerked. His senses, sharpened by years of instinct and training, rapidly assessed his surroundings. A thin veil of emerging daylight suggested pre-dawn. Rain was no longer hitting the windows, indicating the storm had passed as predicted. *Our makeshift bed is on the floor. Tricia is curled up next to me, still sleeping.* A wave of warmth washed over him at the sight, urging him to close his eyes and tighten his arms around her, inhaling her scent and continuing to memorize everything about her.

Yet something had jolted him from sleep, and he couldn't ignore the hairs on his neck standing on end until he discerned what it was. Sliding gently from her side, he stood and looked down as she blinked her eyes open.

"Poole?" Her voice was a soft question, sleep-roughened and filled with confusion.

"I need to check something. I thought I heard a noise. Stay here, I'll be right back." He kept his tone steady despite the adrenaline surging through his veins.

Darting into the bathroom, he pulled on his jeans and retrieved his gun from his bag, letting the reassuring weight of his weapon settle in his hand. Concealing it in his waistband, he stalked through the bedroom. His gaze landed on Tricia, still sprawled on the mattress with sleep-tousled hair in messy curls about her face. He offered a brief, tight-lipped smile. Ignoring his body's desire to lie back down with her, he walked past the safe room and turned the corner. He walked to the end of the hall and turned the corner, stopping on the landing that offered a vantage point overlooking the grand entry foyer and the expansive windows that revealed the front drive. His body tensed as he took in the scene unfolding outside.

A monstrous black SUV with black-tinted windows had stopped in the front circle. The doors opened, and four men poured out of the vehicle. All dressed in black, their silhouettes hardened by combat gear and the unmistakable outline of rifles slung over their shoulders.

Fuck!

Firing on all synapses, he started to turn when another SUV came to a stop closer to the front door. Two more guards emerged, followed closely by two men in dark suits. Neatly trimmed black hair. One with a mustache and one with a full goatee. Even from a distance, he couldn't miss the aura of power and danger that radiated from them. He had no doubt he was looking at the property owner, and he'd bet his paycheck that the men were linked to the cartel.

Fuck!

Another surge of adrenaline coursed through him as he spun around and sprinted back to the bedroom. His voice was a whisper, laced with urgency as he burst into the room. "Tricia, get up!" His gaze flew to the place where the mattresses lay on the floor, but she was missing. His heart lurched before he spotted her walking from the bathroom, fully dressed and holding his bag.

"The bathroom is cleaned out, and everything's in your bag." Her face was alert but not anxious. She shrugged. "When you said you heard a noise, I thought it must be the real estate agent, although I can't imagine why she's here so early on a Sunday! But we can explain. We'll just tell her we got caught in the storm—"

"Good job, but it's not the real estate agent. I think the owners are here, and it looks bad. Grab the bag and all your shit, we're getting into the safe room."

She blinked and then leaped into action just when he thought he would have to waste time giving her more directions. Snagging his bag's handles and her purse, she looked over her shoulder into the bathroom before hustling out of the room. Thrilled that she followed orders without question, he raced past her to double-check the bathroom. It was spotless. *Thank fuck she's a neat freak.*

Twisting around, he discovered her already heading down the hall. Grabbing the two mattresses under each arm, he was thankful they were thin and lightweight as he wrestled them toward the safe room. She popped out of the doorway and clutched the end of one. She managed to shove it inside, and he followed.

"What do you need me to do?" Her words were quiet but firm, giving off the barest hint of fear.

"Let's just get in and secure the room."

He couldn't believe how fast she'd been able to move. In less than a moment from when he clapped eyes on the men driving up, they were in the safe room. The fact that she liked things neat had served them well, possibly saving their asses.

The door clicked behind them, locking them into the safe room. She sat on the couch, perched on the edge, her hands clasped in her lap. He quickly shoved the mattresses back onto the bunk beds, then sat down at the desk and flipped on the computers.

"What do you need me to do?" she repeated, her voice shaking.

Glancing to the side, he spied her pale face and wide eyes, fear now oozing through the calm facade. He'd been so impressed with her jumping into action to rush into the safe room without question, he'd forgotten she wasn't in his line of work and had no idea what was happening.

As the screens came to life, revealing scenes from the security cameras around the compound, he turned and faced her, reaching out to lay his hand over hers.

"I must've heard the sound of an approaching vehicle. I went out to see if it was workmen or the real estate agent coming early, but it was an SUV full of armed men—"

She gasped but remained quiet.

"Another SUV pulled up, and a couple of suited men climbed out with more guards. I have no idea who they are, but my experience tells me they reek of cartel."

Her wide eyes now bugged as another gasp slipped out. "Cartel? You mean, like a... drug cartel?"

"That'd be my guess."

"Oh my God! But why are they here?"

"Remember what we were surmising about whoever wanted this property? Added security? Staying hidden? Not wanting anyone to be able to find this place?"

Air rushed from her lungs. She visibly battled to breathe steadily, but she remained silently nodding.

"We're safe in here. I'm calling my people and let them know what's going on."

"But if they had this estate planned out... if they designed the house... they know about the safe room. We'll be trapped in here!"

"There's no way they're staying at this house. There's no furniture, no food, no accommodations. My guess is that they're just here to check and see that it's ready, and then they'll leave."

"What if they try to get in here?"

"We have it locked. They won't be able to get in."

"They'll assume someone's in here—"

"They'll assume the electronics aren't working and no one is here."

She jerked her head up and down. Her fingers were

cold, and he tried to warm them as he wrapped his hands tighter around hers.

"Tricia, look at me."

She held his gaze, and he continued. "We're going to be fine. We're going to get out of here. But for now, I need you to do exactly as I say. I have some work to do, so I'm just going to have you sit there quietly and let me take care of things, okay?"

Again, she jerked her head up and down. He wished he could offer her more comfort but preferred to provide her protection right now.

"And Trish?" He waited until he had her full attention. "Thanks to you and your desire to be so neat, if they come into the house, they'll never know we were here."

Her face remained wary, but her lips curved slightly.

Turning back to the computers, he brought up the outside camera and watched as the armed guards from the first SUV dispersed around the drive. No one proved they were expecting trouble as they maintained casual stances and their weapons remained slung over their backs.

He grabbed his phone and hit the emergency number for LSIWC, knowing someone was always on call during the weekends and evenings. The phone only rang once before it connected.

"You've got Adam. What's your situation, Poole?"

"The storm came, and we stayed the night at the house. I'm here with the electrician. Visitors just arrived. Armed guards. Looks like a cartel. Maybe the owners. Jeb was checking to see who actually bought this place, but yesterday, there was no urgency. That's changed now."

"On it. Patching Jeb and Carson in now."

Within ten seconds, both Jeb and Carson were also on the call.

"Are you and the electrician secure?" Carson asked.

"House is clean. Vehicles are in a far garage, not close to the house. We are secure in the safe room upstairs. My eyes are on the security cameras."

"I'll get patched into your security," Jeb said.

"I'm calling everyone in," Carson said.

"We don't need a full assault or rescue. We've jammed the safe room door so no one can get in. As soon as they leave and everything's clear, we'll get out of here."

"Hop can get to his bird, and I'll come with him," Adam volunteered.

"I'll let you know as soon as I get in," Jeb said.

"Right now, the guards are walking outside, and it looks like one guard and the two men in suits are coming to the front door. You should be able to get a match on the face very soon."

"Keep this line open," Carson said. "I'll inform you when Hop and Adam get into the air. Abbie and Natalie will coordinate with the maps and satellite views."

Disconnecting, he kept his gaze riveted onto the screen. Tricia stood and silently stepped behind him, leaning forward, her gaze also on the screen.

"I feel like we're in the middle of a military mission," she whispered.

Their voices couldn't be heard outside the safe

room, but he was glad she was quiet. "Right now, my boss will organize a team to get close. We have a couple of pilots, and some of my co-workers will fly nearby in case they're needed."

Her hand landed on his shoulder, her fingers gripping, and he turned to look up at her face. "Poole, what's happening?"

"I don't know for certain, but as soon as one of my co-workers can get a positive identification on this man." He touched the screen, pointing at the suited man who appeared to be in charge. "Then we will know more of what we're dealing with."

"I know you don't want me to ask a lot of questions, but what can I do to help?"

He was impressed as hell with how she handled their situation. But right now, he couldn't think of anything for her to do other than stay calm, yet to say those words might come across as demeaning.

"It's best if I just stay quiet, isn't it?" she asked.

A burst of air left his lips, and he nodded. "Right now, yes. But stay alert, and if you know of something about the security or electricity in this house that I might not have thought of, then jump in."

That was the right thing to say because she immediately turned her sharp-eyed gaze back to the camera image on the screen. One guard who had entered the house stayed by the front door. Another one walked with the two men dressed in black suits. They stood for a moment in the foyer, twisting their heads as they looked around.

They moved into the room Tricia had called the

receiving room and went straight into the office. Poole was able to follow their movements with the various cameras.

"The place looks good, Ricardo," the goateed man said.

"The building inspectors have finished, and the occupancy permit was issued, boss."

"And the security?"

"I'll check with the companies we used and make sure it's all ready."

The boss scoffed. "My wife will only care about the decorator."

Ricardo replied, "She gave me the names of three she could work with. I vetted all of them and have it down to the one we can trust the most. As soon as I get your okay, I'll start ordering the furniture you and your wife want."

"Good, good."

The room was flooded with light, and the goateed man stood in front of the embankment of glass. "Magnificent. This will be perfect."

They moved out of the office and sauntered through several downstairs rooms with their armed guard tagging along. Once in the kitchen, the boss walked to the sliding glass door overlooking the patio. He jerked his head, and Ricardo hustled to open the door, sliding it to the side. He and the boss stepped onto the patio overlooking the swimming pool and gardens.

Poole and Tricia could no longer hear the conversations once the men had left the office.

MARYANN JORDAN

"There's only audio in the receiving room and office. Everywhere else just has video," she said.

"Yeah... I remember."

She winced. "Shit, I'm sorry. Of course, you know."

"It was from the specs from the real estate agent. He must have given the instructions."

"Poole, what's happening?"

He shook his head, knowing she was curious, but if what he suspected was true, it was best that Tricia knew as little as possible. His fingers balled into a fist, and the urge to pound something was strong.

"You're tense."

He craned his neck, his gaze locking on her hand that rested gently on his shoulder. She had discerned the coiled tension coursing through every taut muscle with her light touch. He was on the brink of pushing her away, giving in to the instinct to protect her from the unfolding chaos. But the precarious situation they were in wasn't her fault. That realization only fueled his anger and overwhelming frustration. *I was here playing house and banging her in the shower when I should've ensured we were safe.*

Her fingers slipped from his shoulders, and she sighed as she retreated to settle on the sofa. As much as he needed to formulate a plan, he missed the comforting sensation of her touch. He couldn't read her emotions with her head bowed and face concealed. He wanted to assure her that they would be fine, but the grim reality was that he couldn't make that guarantee.

If he was here alone, he could stealthily evade the guards, making it to his SUV. And if escape by vehicle

134

proved impossible, he'd survive in the desert until Hop or one of the other Keepers could rescue him. But with Tricia thrown into the volatile mix, stealth would be impossible. He needed to keep his head on the new mission he hadn't counted on when he'd gone to bed with her last night.

14

Tricia could sense there was more to the situation than what Poole revealed. She was cognizant of the severity of their predicament. She grasped the probability that these men were from a drug cartel. She understood that yesterday's suspicions about ordering the various security systems from different companies might indicate that her fears were true. Yet what gnawed at her was Poole's unwillingness to impart more information to her.

They were locked in the safe room, but how secure were they really when the very person they were hiding from would have been the person who asked for a safe room to begin with? Now that the men inside the house had vacated the office, they could only follow their movements but had no idea what they were discussing. And certainly not since they'd walked out onto the patio.

Trying to steady her heartbeat, she forced herself to a rational perspective. *Poole is right— the men can't possibly stay here without furniture, food, and supplies. They must just be checking on things, and then they'll leave.*

"Poole?"

"Yeah?"

"We can just wait them out here, right?"

He turned his gaze toward her, and she held her breath, hoping he would answer.

"That's the plan right now."

"So they're just checking on the place, and then they'll leave."

He offered a curt nod, then turned his gaze back to the computer screens.

She knew he was worried, but this version of Poole was not what she'd grown used to. Granted, he'd been rather curt when she first met him, but since then, he was engaging, witty, fun... and hell, that didn't even include the mind-blowing sex they'd had last night... twice. *I've known him a day... what the hell do I really know about what he's like?* She dropped her chin. *God, I had sex with a man I just met, and we're now stuck here.*

She rarely dated, finding some men assumed she was a beer-drinking, bar-hopping, good-time easy lay just because she was in a male-dominated career. She'd never been able to understand that perverted concept. But then, she also found that some men weren't interested because she didn't fit their pencil skirt, high-heeled, perfect hair, and makeup image of womanhood. When she was younger, she occasionally met someone for a how-do-you-do-let's-fuck night, but the following day found her out the door usually faster than even they'd managed. A couple of relationships held the promise of something longer but never lasted.

Staring at Poole, she'd never met anyone like him. Confident. Smart. Good heart. Fun. But damn, she also never expected them to be trapped together in a do-or-die situation. Not that she was opposed to having more time with him, but the whole hide-so-we-don't-get-killed vibe was unexpected.

Standing, she walked behind him again and peered intently at the computer screens. The men outside had guns slung over their shoulders, but they appeared relaxed, walking and chatting in pairs. The guard inside the house was now out by the pool while the two men in suits walked back into the kitchen. They stood next to the counter as they talked.

"I wish like fuck we knew what they were talking about," Poole said.

Staring down at him as she stood to the side and slightly behind him, clarity washed over her. He was a protector. Every fiber of his being was wired to ensure her safety at all costs. Yet, considering his given occupation with an investigative company, his innate curiosity would compel him to discover these men's identities and intentions. Dragging her tongue along her bottom lip, she sucked in a deep breath and let it out slowly.

She lifted her gaze, her mind whirling with thoughts circling as fast as a merry-go-round. She stared at the wall behind the computer for a moment, then slowly turned as she cast her eyes around the rest of the room, visions of the house blueprints flooding her mind.

Closing her eyes, she imagined each space on each floor in a way that the typical homeowner would never think. Finally, a slow smile curved her lips. The entrance to this room was at the back of the shelved linen closet. At the top of the closet was another trap-door to the attic.

Hurrying back to the sofa where she sat, twisting her body so that she faced Poole as he sat in the desk chair, she asked, "How important is it to know what they're talking about?"

His attention shot straight to her face, and his brows lowered. "I'm sorry? What exactly are you asking?"

"I assumed at first that you just wanted to be able to see them so that you knew what they were doing so you could protect us. Then I thought you just wanted to know when they'd leave so we could get out of here. But it dawned on me, as an investigator, you want to know who these guys are, right?"

He hesitated, so she jumped in and continued. "Don't give me a bullshit answer, Poole. I might not be a hotshot investigator, but I'm not stupid, and I'm sure as hell not helpless."

"Tricia, I never said you were stupid or helpless. I don't know what kind of situation we're in, and my first responsibility is to get us out of here safely."

"I understand that. But if you knew that they were talking about drug dealing, selling, smuggling, or what-ever cartels do, you'd want to know that, right?"

"Are we speaking hypothetically?"

She huffed, frustrated at his ambiguous replies, and waved her arms. "Yes, fine. We're talking hypothetically."

"Then yes, knowing what they're discussing would be nice. As an investigator with a company that has ties to the FBI, I'd like to be able to turn over any information I discover. If these guys are cartel criminals, then I'd love nothing more than to shut them down. But since I can't hear them, and I have you to be responsible for, that takes a back seat to us just making sure we know when they leave so we can get the fuck out of here."

He held her gaze for a moment longer. Then he rolled the chair a little closer, reached up with his hand to cup her jaw, and she leaned into his palm without hesitation or overthinking. "Tricia, are you okay?"

She nodded and remained silent while allowing the warmth of his hand to penetrate her cool cheek. Finally, when she'd drawn strength from his touch, she asked, "What would you say if I told you that I could get close and hear what they were discussing?"

He turned, giving her his full attention as his brows snapped down and his eyes narrowed. "What the fuck are you talking about, babe?"

Everything blanked in her mind for a second except hearing him growl the word *babe*. It was a throwaway word used by many guys in a bar, on a date, or when they're banging a stranger and can't remember the woman's name.

But she knew it was also a term of endearment. Her dad still called her mom "babe," and the little smile her mom would get on her face always made Tricia long for the time when she'd hear the word *babe* growled at her by someone who cared. She swallowed deeply. While she'd only known him for a day and knew she was very much in *lust* with him, hearing his deep voice growl the word, even if he was kind of pissed, still reverberated through her.

"Tricia?"

Jerking, she returned to the matter they were discussing, wondering if she'd lost her mind as it traveled down strange paths due to all the stress they were experiencing.

"Sorry. I... um... sorry."

"What were you talking about?"

Clearing her throat, she plunged ahead. "You're an expert with the security you designed, but I had to be all over the house while checking Harry's work. I was crawling around, seeing much of the house electrician's work, HVAC systems, and plumbing. In the linen closet, right outside our door, another trapdoor leads into the attic. It's tiny. In fact, I remember thinking then it was a stupid place for it to be. But from there, it's possible to move through some of the spaces between floors where the air-conditioning ducts didn't take up the whole space."

Poole said nothing but held her gaze, and she tried not to squirm under his intense perusal.

"That's good information, Tricia, but I'm not sure it's pertinent. Right now, I want to focus on safely getting us both out of here."

"I understand, but the offer is there."

"Babe, I don't think it's missed your attention that I'm a big guy. You've already said that the space was really small. It was great of you to think of it, but I don't know that it'll be something I can use."

She pressed her lips together tightly, then released them, dragging her tongue over her bottom lip. "Poole, I wasn't suggesting that you'd be the one to do that. But I'm small enough and could—"

"No! Fucking hell, no!"

"But—"

"We're not having this discussion," he said, jerking back in his chair. "There's no way in the world I'm going to put you at risk on an unofficial investigation to scout for information."

"Whether it's official or not, you're here."

He sucked in a deep breath, then let it out slowly. "When we get out of here, I'll tell the FBI liaison everything we saw. In fact, I have somebody already patching into this security camera, so we'll have faces we can identify."

She opened her mouth to speak again, but he stood, his size filling the small space. With his hands on her shoulders, he bent low until his face was directly in front of hers. "Not going to happen, Tricia. I don't want you in any more danger than you already are. We'll ride this out. We're going to stay in here until they're gone. My people will be nearby in case we need them, and we'll give out info to law enforcement once it's all over with."

With his face so close to hers, it was hard to think of anything other than the desire to kiss him. But she forced her mind to stay on his words, understanding he was right. The most important thing was that they could get away safely.

But while she had only known him for a day, the more she learned about him, the more she knew he was a take-charge person, and if he was an investigator, one who even knew, much less worked with, the FBI, he would want to know what was happening.

He let go of her shoulders to turn back to the security camera visuals on the computer, and she walked over and sat on the sofa, her hands once again clasped in her lap, wishing she could do something.

15

An hour trickled by with no sign of the men leaving. Sweat broke out across Poole's forehead at the thought of one of the guards venturing to the far garage and uncovering his SUV and Tricia's truck. The last thing he wanted was for the arrivals to discover somebody else was on the property.

If they could remain concealed in the safe room until the gang left, he could ensure Tricia reached her truck and got the hell away. Forget fucking Vegas— he'd follow her back to her place to make sure she got there safely.

Glancing to the side, he watched as she pulled out the cheese crackers he'd left in his snack bag. Her actions were meticulous as she arranged the crackers on a paper plate as though she needed to do something with her hands.

The absurdity of their fucked-up situation filled him, yet he was grateful he was here. If she'd decided to work all day yesterday, was caught by the storm, and spent the night alone, she would've been a vulnerable target when the visitors arrived. That thought sliced through his gut.

Lending her his T-shirt yesterday, he'd hoped to see her again if she wanted. He'd never anticipated them sleeping together, but something about the enigmatic woman made him want to be around her for a lot longer than just a night of pleasure.

She'd captivated him with each shared anecdote, every revealed facet of her life. And she was the first woman he could remember that he wanted to see again.

Lust? Absolutely. Friendship? Hopefully. Anything more? He had no idea but really wanted the opportunity to explore what they'd started.

He couldn't believe her audacious suggestion to crawl through the ductwork confines to navigate to where she could hear conversations. Granted, if he were a much smaller man, he probably would have loved doing that so he could've caught the bastards with whatever they were planning.

He'd been in earlier contact with LSIWC and knew that Carson had brought Landon on board, but he hadn't heard anything in almost thirty minutes. Finally, his phone vibrated, and he looked down, snagging it.

"It's Rick. I'm fucking sorry, man, but it's been a shit show here. How are you guys?"

"We're fine. We're safe. What's going on?"

"Our area of California took a hit from the power company. Fuckin' blackout. Which normally wouldn't be a problem, but the backup generator went out on us. Teddy got someone in almost immediately, and we're up and running now, but I have to tell you that I'm sorry as fuck this happened. Carson is pissed as hell. I thought he was going to have an aneurysm. He can't tolerate incompetence and was about to take the generator installer's head off."

"No worries. I knew you guys were working on something. What have you got for me?"

"I'm here with Jeb. He's feeding me the information but still analyzing and collating. First of all, your intuition was spot-on. The first man who walked in, the suited man with the goatee, is Tomas Munez. The other man with a mustache and wearing a suit is Ricardo Cordova. Carson has pulled in Landon, but he's just now being caught up to speed. He was out of contact on another mission, and it took a while for us to get to him. Neither Tomas nor Ricardo are wanted by the FBI, although they have ties to the Sinaloa cartel. Tomas's wife is the sister of a cartel leader. DEA and FBI know them but haven't gotten anything on them. Neither of them bought the house. At least officially. A California lawyer, Manuel Sanchez, purchased the property three years ago. He put in for a building permit two years ago, and the house has been built over the last eighteen months. His wife is in real estate, and I bet you can guess who is the agent representing the buyer."

"Keep it all in the family, right? Or should I say, all in the cartel?"

"You've got that right. Again, there's nothing on the attorney or his wife, but he's a contract lawyer who never came across the FBI's radar. Landon is now getting some agents to look into him and his wife."

"The only audio I have is when they're in the office. All of the cameras in the house are visual only. If his family is going to occupy the estate at some time, he probably wanted to maintain privacy in the family areas."

"The number one priority is to get you and Ms. Burrows out of there safely."

"Agreed." Poole looked over at Tricia and gave her a pointed stare, knowing she could hear part of their conversation. She lifted a brow, then turned back to the plate of cheese crackers, staring down at them as though they were the most interesting item in the room. But he had no doubt she was soaking up the information.

"What I can't figure out is why they're still there. It's been over an hour, and everyone seems to be waiting. Even the guards outside."

Jeb jumped in. "Yeah, we've been watching it. The armed guards outside seem completely at ease. But with no furniture in the house, no one can be that comfortable."

"They must be waiting on another arrival," Poole surmised, hating to give voice to the scenario he'd been thinking of as he watched the men inside the house. "I really want them to move the fuck on so we can get out of here."

"Where are your vehicles?" Carson asked.

"Tricia had the idea of putting them in one of the far garages just before the storm hit since hail was in the forecast. There were no security locks, so opening and closing the door was easy. Great for the storm, but it'll be a fuckup for us if any of them happen to discover it."

"Hop and Adam have taken the bird and are close. They'll land out of sight from anyone at the estate or anyone coming from the road. Landon called in an agent to provide them with a vehicle. Everything was more difficult due to the whole power outage fuckup from the electric company... goddammit," Carson growled.

Poole knew the boss was furious. Of all of them, Carson always kept his cool. The only other time he'd ever seen him lose it was when his wife, Jeannie, was in trouble. "Boss, we're doing okay. We had some food and water and slept last night. We're tucked away where they can't get to us."

"Poole?"

He smiled, hearing Abbie's voice. "What do you have for me, Abbie?"

"There are a lot of outbuildings in that compound that I can see from the satellite images. Natalie is here with me, and we're looking at ways that you can get from the main house to the garage, even if it has to be tonight under cover of darkness."

Natalie grumbled, "Vehicles aren't gonna do you any good if the assholes haven't left by then."

"If we're still here by the time it gets dark, I can get us out of the compound and over the wall. Once there, Hop and Adam can get to us."

"I hate like fuck that you may have to sit there for hours until the end of the day," Carson said.

"Boss, it's nothing that we haven't done before." He

knew that wasn't true as soon as his words left his mouth. It wasn't anything that the Keepers hadn't done before, but Tricia was an entirely different matter. She came in yesterday to take care of the shoddy work her boss had left and was now caught up in this situation.

"Landon was hoping that the security included audio. He's having Jeb hang onto all the video, of course, but the audio would've been great to have found out what those fuckers are doing."

"Ah-hmm."

He looked up as Tricia cleared her throat, giving him a pointed stare. Shaking his head, he ignored her silent suggestion and said, "Let us know what you need from us. We'll stay here, but be ready to move at a moment's notice. And I will have my eyes on these security cameras because I need to know if they head to the car garage or if somebody decides to find the safe room."

"We've got a secure channel from your computer to LSIWC now that our generator is running. Keep in touch, and we'll also have you patch in to Hop, Adam, and Landon."

"Will do." Disconnecting, he looked toward Tricia, and before she could open her mouth, he shook his head. "Don't even go there."

She huffed but walked over and handed him a bottle of water she'd filled from the tap and a small paper plate filled with cheese crackers.

They ate in silence, then his phone vibrated again. "Hop, what have you got?"

"We've landed about six miles from the compound. Natalie is sending us satellite intel so we can keep an eye on what's happening there. Are you sure you don't want us bringing in some firepower for a great distraction?"

"Like the idea, but no. The last thing I want is for anyone here to make any connection to Ms. Burrows. The best thing that can happen is that they finish their business here and get on the road. Then she and I can leave without anyone being the wiser."

"Sounds good. Just know we're here."

"Makes this situation a helluva lot better knowing you and Adam are close by." Disconnecting, he laid his phone on the desk, then scrubbed his hand over his face. A soft touch landed on his shoulders, and he opened his eyes to see the computer screen reflection of Tricia standing behind him, her hands kneading the muscles in his neck. Unable to stifle his moan as her hands worked magic, he finally reached up and clasped his hand over hers. Pulling her to the side, he guided her around and down on his lap.

She sat, her face so close, her eyes peering into his. She licked her bottom lip but remained silent. Thoughts slammed into him, but none were on the situation developing on the screens. Desire flickered along his spine, the pull to bring her close and let his tongue follow the trail over her now moistened lips. He wanted them to be far away from the estate, ensconced in their own little world with no one to intrude upon their time. He wanted to trace his fingers over her body, from her freckles to her toes.

Dragging in a ragged breath, he let it out slowly. Pushing away all other thoughts, he knew he needed to focus on the security feeds because this whole damn situation was on him.

"I don't want to distract you," she said. "But I can't help but be curious about what's going through your mind. This situation is so bizarre that I can't tell with just a look."

He held her gaze, then leaned forward to touch his forehead against hers. "Babe, there are so many things going through my mind right now, it's embarrassing."

Her head tilted to the side. "Embarrassing? I don't understand."

"Embarrassing that we're even in the situation. I could have insisted we leave yesterday afternoon instead of sitting by the pool. I could have checked the weather report earlier and then known to turn down your pizza offer so we could get on the road. As we talked yesterday, and both felt that the multiple security companies working on this property pointed to something nefarious, I should've known for us to get the fuck out of here. And I hate like hell that you're stuck in the middle of this situation as we wait to see when these fuckers will leave."

"Oh, I see. You're upset because you're not all-knowing and all-powerful."

"Never claimed to be those things, but as many missions as I've been on, I sure as hell should've been more prepared."

"Poole! You weren't here on a mission. I was never part of a mission. It's not like you fucked up a mission! We simply met in what should've been an innocuous situation that's turned bad. That's no different from somebody at a store when an active shooter shows up. If you and I met in the grocery store next to the vegetables, and a trigger-happy nutjob entered, you wouldn't beat yourself up that you didn't know about it ahead of time, even if tomatoes and cucumbers are exploding all around us."

Her words sank in, and his lips quirked on one side despite his desire to maintain a serious expression. *But fuck, if she didn't make sense.* "A vegetable-shooting, trigger-happy nutjob, huh?"

Her lips curved in return. "I think that's an apt description. Who knows what those guys are," she said, twisting to jab her finger toward the computer screen. Turning back toward him, she clutched his face and held him close. "You can't blame yourself for situations that happen outside your control. And even if you have regrets, I don't. Yesterday was the most fun I've had in a long time."

Their gazes held as a low-humming current ran between them. "Yeah?"

She nodded slowly, her gaze dropping to his chest. "Yeah."

He missed seeing her eyes but was more curious about her thoughts.

"I'm not very spontaneous. One-night stands when I was in college seemed easier. Nowadays, I'm more cautious. And not a lot of men... *good* men have come my way." She shrugged. "Last night was special." She jerked slightly, then added, "Not that I expect anything! It's just that I wanted you to know I don't regret it at all. It was special, and I'd hate it if you regretted our time."

"I promise you, Tricia. I don't regret it at all."

She smiled, her whole face beaming with beauty. "Now, all we can do is figure out what's next, right?"

"I have a few ideas of what I'd like to do, sweetheart," he said.

"I like the sound of that."

"Not talking about sex, Tricia, although that would be my top choice."

She laughed and shook her head. "It would be hard to have sex and keep an eye on the computer screens simultaneously."

"You're right, having to stare at these fuckers is a real cockblock."

They chuckled, and when their mirth slowed, he peered deeply into her eyes. "I want to see you again." She blinked, and he realized he was not being clear. "After this is all over."

She smiled. "Well, I do have to give your shirt back."

"I would've been a gentleman and given you that shirt anyway. But when I gave it to you, I hoped you would offer to return it so I could see you again."

"I'd like that. You're the first man I've met in a long time who I'd like to spend more time with than just the rather unusual first date we've had."

"I would never call yesterday our first date, but now that I think about it, I guess it could be. Although I'd much rather take you out, show you off, and still have us end up naked in front of a fireplace."

Laughter erupted, and he loved how her whole body seemed to smile. He leaned forward, desperate to feel her lips on his when his phone vibrated again. She jumped up and moved out of the way.

He grabbed it, hitting connect. "Natalie? What have you got?"

"There's another vehicle traveling your way. It's several miles out, but the only other vehicle in the area. Black SUV. Black-tinted windows."

"So maybe that's what they've been waiting on. They've got a meeting here."

Adam came onto the line. "We can come in closer."

"Okay, I'll have you do that, but stay back and out of sight unless I signal that we're in trouble."

"Poole? It's Landon."

"Yeah?" Seeing Tricia staring at him, he mouthed, "FBI."

"I've been looking at the feed that Jeb is sending to me. If they meet in one of the rooms that have audio, we'll be golden. If not, just take care of yourself, and we'll try to figure out what the fuck they're doing."

He sucked in a deep breath and stared at the screen, seeing Tomas and Ricardo still standing in the kitchen, leaning against the counters. It made sense for them to be there since no other room had furniture. With the counter, they could sit on, lean against, or use it as a desk if needed. "My guess is they're going to be in the kitchen, which means video only."

"Whatever happens, happens," Landon said. "If we can just identify them, that'll get us closer to figuring out what's happening. Stay safe."

He disconnected and stared at the screen, wishing Tomas and Ricardo would move back toward the front.

The audio might pick up even if they were just close to the receiving room or office. But so far, the two men gave no indication they were ready to leave the kitchen.

Looking over at Tricia, he admitted, "This is the first time I can remember wishing I was a much smaller man."

16

Tricia's audible swallow sounded in the tight space. She reached for the water bottle, taking a much-needed gulp. Her gaze remained steadfast on Poole while he communicated with his co-workers. He was no longer keeping her out of what was happening but instead had them on speaker so she knew what was transpiring. The situation was surreal, like a scene ripped from a TV drama or blockbuster movie where badass security men and women worked to bring down the villains. *But that's what they're doing, isn't it?*

She was out of her depth, trying not to let the whirlpool of circumstances pull her under. Yet she clung to the idea that she could assist. When he said he wished he was a smaller man, he referred to her idea of making it down to the crawlspace to get underneath the kitchen to listen at the air vents. *At least he acknowledged my plan had merit.*

"Poole?"

"Yeah, Tricia?"

"Do you remember looking at the blueprints for this estate when you were developing the security system design?"

His eyes shifted from the computer screen over to her. Cocking his head to the side, he stared. "I'm assuming that's a rhetorical question?"

Inclining her head, she agreed. "Yes, it is. But I wanted to emphasize that I've been living those blueprints for several months."

"Living?"

"I've had other jobs that I've worked, but I've been to this estate at least once a week for the past two months, reviewing all the work that Harry screwed up. I've been in the attic. I've been in the crawlspace underneath the house. I've seen where the HVAC ductwork goes up, and I know there's space between." She saw him open his mouth, but she threw her hand up. "Hear me out, please."

His lips grew tight. Blowing out a breath, he said, "Okay, I'll hear you out. But only if you let me put you on speakerphone with my people. I know you've got an idea, but I think you'll hear from them that it's not good."

She ran her tongue over her teeth, considering his request. Then, slowly nodding, she said, "You're right. I'll ditch it if they say it's not a good idea."

It only took a moment for him to get the people he worked with back on the line on speaker.

"Ms. Burrows? This is Carson Dyer, I'm the founder of the company that Poole works for. He says you have a suggestion, and we have the experts here to evaluate your idea."

"I won't repeat everything about myself and what I've been doing because I'm sure you know that. But I've been working on this project for a few months and know every inch of this house. Not just what someone sees when they walk inside the front door but what is behind the walls. I know where the plumbing lines are. I know where the electricity runs to each room. I know the attic and crawl-space HVAC system and where the ductwork goes. In the past two months, I have crawled into every open space available, ensuring the security cameras and wiring were exactly where they needed to be and were functional."

"Ms. Burrows? My name is Abbie. I have the blue-prints of the estate in front of me."

"Hey. Please call me Tricia."

"Okay, Tricia. Now that I have the blueprints up, what are you suggesting?"

"I know the number one objective is for me and Poole to get out of here safely and unnoticed. But I also understand it would be very helpful if you could hear the conversations from the men meeting in the house. Believe me, I'm not looking to be a hero, but I can get to where I can hear what they're saying."

"Okay, keep going."

"There is a trapdoor to the attic in the linen closet just outside the safe room door. It's in a strange place and not very large once the shelving is in. But I'm a slender woman and would have no problem getting into the attic. Once there, I can go down the space available

159

for the HVAC ductwork between the second and first floors. That's only about fourteen feet. Once there, I can follow the space for the ducts until I am into the crawl-space, about another sixteen feet or so. From there, I can get close to one of the vents in the kitchen. If I had my phone, I could record what they say. Then, all I have to do is make my way back up to the safe room, where Poole and I will continue to wait them out and then leave when they leave. Or… um… if they leave soon, then I could just get out through the crawlspace and meet him on the outside."

Poole sat with his thick arms crossed over his chest, his brow lifted. She had no problem reading his expression. It screamed, "My people will decimate your plan, considering you don't know what you're talking about and have never done anything like this before."

There was mumbling on the other end of the line, but she could not discern what was being said. After another minute, his lifted brow lowered until he was scowling as he stared at the phone.

"Tricia? It's still Abbie. I've followed along with what you said, and I think you're right…it could work."

She smiled until Poole rambled, "What the fuck, Abbie? You can't seriously be thinking that this is a good plan."

"Poole, I said it *could* work. That means we haven't evaluated what she suggested, just that it's feasible. I didn't say she *should* do it."

"Well, I can tell you, she shouldn't," he bit out. "It's too dangerous. She's a master electrician, not a master spy."

"Poole, nobody is suggesting she actually undertake to try to find out what they are saying."

She recognized the voice of his boss and waited to see what they would say.

"Tricia? One of the things we evaluate is the level of danger combined with the possibility of success. I know you're not used to doing this, but—"

"Actually, Mr. Dyer, I am. When crawling on top of the building, underneath it, or through it, I have to evaluate what I can do, where I can go safely, and whether it will work. I might not be used to listening to somebody's conversations, so the result is different. But I can certainly evaluate the feasibility and probability of success."

"Very good, Tricia," Carson said. "Then I'm going to ask you to evaluate the plan you just proposed."

Realizing they were taking her seriously, it also struck her that there was much on the line, and to over-inflate her possible success would have more than just her own disappointment to contend with.

Blowing out a long breath, she considered what needed to occur. "The space I'm talking about traversing is large enough to squeeze through. I'm not going to get stuck, and I'm not going to fall. The risk level is much less than if I had to stand on a roof, for example. I also feel that I can get close enough to a vent that even if I'm not right in the room where they are, I can catch at least some of what they're saying. Although, I think the biggest risk would be that my phone microphone wouldn't be strong enough to catch everything.

That would suck if I went to all the trouble and didn't get a good recording."

"We can help with that," Abbie quickly interjected.

Tricia thought Poole was going to explode. She leaned over and placed her hand on his arm. "What could you do, Abbie?"

"Poole has a high-intensity microphone that can pick up voices from a distance. He'll be able to see where the meeting is taking place and can guide you to the right junction or location in the crawlspace. If you're near an air vent, then you'd be able to record their conversation."

"And if one of the outside guards happens to look inside the garage, finds our vehicles, and sets off a fuckin' alarm, how the fuck can I get her out of there if she's behind the fuckin' walls?" he growled.

"I'm watching the guards outside," Natalie interjected. "They've all gathered in the shade, and it looks like they're just shootin' the shit."

"Now, maybe. But what about when the other vehicle gets here?"

"I'd be in the crawlspace. I can get to anywhere in the house quickly—"

"Going down is a helluva lot easier than coming back up," he argued.

She pinched her lips, knowing he was right about that. Finally, she nodded. "That's true, but I can shimmy up fairly quickly. If everyone is watching all around, and you can communicate with me, then we won't be taken by surprise."

"And this could all be for nothing. They could meet in the office where we've got audio."

"If they do, I'll come back quicker."

Now, it was Poole's time to pinch his lips. His jaw was tight, and she watched as a muscle ticked in his cheek. She leaned forward and pressed her hand to his leg again. Gaining his full attention, she whispered, "It's important, isn't it?"

"Maybe to the FBI, but the only important thing to me is your safety."

There was silence from the phone, and she had no idea what was happening with those who had been listening.

"Poole? It's Landon. I'd love to hear what's going on in that meeting, but there's no way I'm making this decision for a civilian. Ms. Burrows, I'm grateful for your idea."

Poole held her gaze with a blend of admiration and fear. It was one thing for him to risk his life in the service or as a Keeper, but the idea of her placing herself in the heart of danger left a chill running through his body. His breath hitched in his throat as he imagined her crawling through the confined spaces, fragile and vulnerable amid the unknown. His heart pounded relentlessly against his rib cage. He admired her audacity, but the potential for harm darkened his thoughts.

Finally, he inhaled deeply, his chest expanding as his lungs filled before he let the air rush out. "Okay. But, I swear, Tricia, you do exactly what I say every inch of the way. If you can't promise, then this is a non-starter."

She nodded. While glad she could do something to

help, it hit her that this was a big deal. *Oh fuck.* Her fingers tingled as her nerves threatened to revolt from what she'd agreed to do. Steeling her spine, she lifted her chin and nodded again. "I promise."

Poole left his phone on an open call to hear what the others were saying. Then he stood so quickly her hand fell off his thigh, and she watched as he crossed the room in two steps and grabbed his bag. He started digging inside, and she waited, knowing that her part of the scheme would take place once she was on the move. Until then, she wanted to soak up everything he and the others had to tell her.

He turned around with a small case in his hand and popped it open. Holding a small earbud, he said, "This is a transmitter. It stays in your ear. I'll be able to talk to you. And my co-workers will be able to if needed. I don't want a bunch of voices coming at you, trying to tell you too many things, so they'll go through me unless there's a reason they can't."

She nodded and looked at the small earpiece in her palm.

"You can speak, and we'll hear you."

She fit it into her ear and shook her head slightly, satisfied it would stay in place. She practiced speaking, and they had one of his co-workers talk frequently to ensure she could hear.

She nodded again and waited.

He pulled another item from the case and said, "This is a video camera and a microphone. We won't worry about the visual from you, so that won't matter. I want to put it on you so you don't have to worry about it. He pulled out a chain, looped it around her neck, secured it to the camera microphone, and clipped it to her shirt. "It'll stay in place. You won't knock it off or lose it. Once you get close, it'll be able to pick up sounds through the air vents."

She continued to nod, wanting to assure him that she could handle what she suggested, but uncertainty began to creep in. *He said it perfectly... I'm a master electrician, not a master spy.* But it was too late to turn back, and she was determined to see it through. An image of her brothers ran through her mind. *They knew the risks and took them anyway because the outcome was worth it.* Blowing out a breath, she kept her gaze on Poole.

Finally, he pulled out another small chain and, from the end, dangled a lighthouse charm. Her brow furrowed as she looked at it and then at him.

"Put this on, and don't take it off," he ordered. "With it, my co-workers will be able to find you, no matter where you are. They'll be able to see where you if something goes wrong, and we get outside and separated."

She leaned forward as he fastened it around her neck. Maybe because it resembled a beautiful piece of jewelry, it felt special as it nestled against her chest.

Then, with a suddenness that left her breathless, he reached out and captured her in his firm grip. His hands were warm and calloused from years of labor, yet he cradled her face gently. His touch was both urgent and tender. His gaze held hers for a moment that stretched with a silent communication that spoke volumes of his worry, desire, and unspoken promise. Then he leaned in and kissed her.

It wasn't just a good kiss... it was a symphony of sensation. Raw emotions were conveyed through their touch. The kiss was fierce and intense, passion and desperation. It tasted like hope, and goodbyes, and promises. The world seemed to fade, blocking out the harsh reality.

Finally, pulling back, their gazes once again holding on to each other as tightly as their hands clung. She'd never experienced anything like the kiss he'd just bestowed. A goodbye. A beacon of hope. A light in the darkness. Swallowing deeply, she offered a little smile before stepping away from his embrace, afraid she wouldn't leave if she lingered.

Walking swiftly to the door, she waited as he checked the location of the two men and the guard inside the house. None had come to the second floor, so he unlatched the electronic locks on the door. She slipped out, then turned to see that he held the door open, watching. They both looked up to see the small trapdoor in the ceiling. She climbed the shelving like a ladder, then pushed the door up and to the side.

She scrambled through the opening, then turned and looked down, seeing his face peering up at her. Smiling once again, she replaced the small wooden door, now obscuring him from her sight. Abbie had insisted on sending a copy of the blueprints to her phone, but she didn't need them. It was memorized and reviewed numerous times over the past few months. Keeping low, she stepped on the two-by-fours in the attic, moving toward the back part of the house. Finding the chute that went straight down, the soft

HVAC duct did not take up the entire space. Someone much larger than herself would've had difficulty, but she climbed down, using the two-by-four supports as a ladder, just like the shelves.

Occasionally, her shirt caught on a protruding nail, but she moved with caution and so far had not injured herself. There was little air movement in the shaft, and sweat dripped down her face. She was afraid of using her sleeve to wipe, terrified of dislodging the earpiece transmitter or the video camera clipped to her shirt.

"Status?" Poole asked. Then, as though he wanted to make sure she understood, he quickly said, "How are you?"

"I'm fine. I'm waiting to see where I'm supposed to go."

"I've just been informed that the SUV has arrived. So far, the guards outside have done nothing more than stand up and move around a little. But no one is actively searching for anything outside."

Hearing that her and Poole's vehicles were still undiscovered, she breathed a sigh of relief.

"Okay, they've stopped outside the front. The driver is behind the wheel, and two armed guards have left. In this car, there's only one man in a suit, and they've just escorted him inside. My people should be able to get an ID on him soon."

She crouched at the junction of several air vents, wishing she'd thought to bring a bottle of water with her. She swiped the dripping sweat from her brow using her fingers but had little room to do anything else.

After only a moment, Poole radioed, "They're heading into the kitchen."

"Okay. I'll get as close as I can to a vent."

With that news, she hastened past the first floor, afraid of taking too long to get where she wanted to go. Finally, she came to a plywood trapdoor leading to the crawlspace. Praying she didn't run into snakes or scorpions, she slid the door open and, using the light on her phone, only spied sand and dirt about four feet below. Dropping down into the crawlspace, she shone the light around in a full circle, breathing another sigh of relief that there were no creepy crawlies to be seen.

It took her a moment to orient herself before she crouched and hurried past the HVAC system, ducking under the plumbing pipes and coming to the area closest to the kitchen. Moving to the soft ducts, she pulled aside a small section that led straight to a vent in the floor. Suddenly, voices met her ears, and she jumped, almost hitting her head on a pipe, realizing the men were standing directly over her.

"We are honored you could come to meet with us today."

"This is a beautiful estate, Tomas. Once you and your family move in, you'll have to have me over for a more formal tour."

"I would be honored, sir."

Will you be able to maintain the pipeline through here?"

"Absolutely, sir. As you can see, we are off the grid. Self-sufficient out here with water, and backup generators, and it's our expectation that we will be able to handle all the shipments necessary."

"Your idea of using drones as well as helicopters instead of

just trucks interests me. You will not be able to carry as much per trip, and I have concerns about this."

"I understand, but, sir, transporting the product with trucks is becoming harder and harder. It's slower, more cumbersome, and has a much higher rate of being stopped by the authorities."

"And using airplanes?"

"They have to have runways and are more likely to end up on the radar. Helicopters and drones can go short distances, land in easier places, and while they cannot hold as much as a truck, we can take multiple trips to keep up with the demand."

"I'm putting a lot of faith in your ability to make this happen."

"I understand. You won't be disappointed. We'll be fully operational very soon."

17

Poole listened to the conversation unfolding in the kitchen. Landon and the Keepers would undoubtedly be thrilled with such a clear indication of what would be taking place at the compound, hungrily absorbing every detail. The emerging information confirmed the property had been bought and constructed with the idea that Tomas and his family would live there while using it as a drug-running point for the cartel.

Right now, Poole didn't give a fuck about the drug-laden plans unfolding before them. His sole focus was on the woman currently tucked underneath the house in the crawlspace, risking her life to provide them with the information.

From their very first encounter, he'd been drawn to her as a magnet pulled toward an iron core. But it wasn't fleeting. The more time he spent with her, the more he wanted to learn about her. He was frustrated with her heroics, coming from a civilian world where her only experience in a mission came from movies and television. Yet, here she was, playing the hero.

The Keepers and I are used to this! Gritting his teeth, he focused on the video feed from her location to ensure she was safe amid the clandestine chaos.

The meeting didn't last as long as Poole had dreaded, a silver lining to the cloud hovering over him. The faster the men left the house and the estate, the faster he could breathe a sigh of relief. He gripped his phone as he listened in on the conversation, then finally set it on the desk out of fear that he would crush it. *Come on. Come on. Shut the fuck up and get out of there.*

His silent plea echoed in his head before it was finally answered. The meeting appeared to conclude as farewells were offered. He remained quiet until the men walked back through the house, and he saw them step through the front door, handshakes ensuing.

"Fucking phenomenal," Landon said, and Poole could hear the glee in his voice.

Poole knew that his friend was talking about discovering what was happening at the estate and how the FBI and DEA would now have it on their radar, but what he thought was fucking phenomenal was Tricia. "Are you okay?"

He held his breath until he heard her reply, "Yes. Are they gone?"

"All the men have left the house, but don't do anything now because they're still talking on the front patio." After several long minutes, the man who had arrived last was escorted by his armed guards to his SUV and pulled away, driving down the lane. Holding his breath, waiting until the other men left, Poole's heart fell into his stomach when they turned and walked back into the house. He could hear the cursing from the other Keepers but knew he needed to hold on to his shit to keep Tricia in the loop. "The two original men have come back into the house. Stay where you are, and don't move around. We don't want to give them any reason to suspect noise from anywhere."

"Okay," she whispered.

He knew she was scared by her barely spoken one-word response. He couldn't wait to put this behind them and hold her in his arms again, not caring what that said about how he felt about her so quickly. His eyes stayed glued to the computer screen of the two men in the foyer continuing to talk. Suddenly, they turned and started walking up the staircase. He bolted to his feet, ensuring that the door to the safe room was secure and that they could not get into it from the outside. The room was also soundproof, but he whispered, "They're coming upstairs. Stay where you are."

"Oh my God! Poole! Are you going to be okay?" she whispered, panic clearly sounding in her words.

It didn't pass his notice that she asked about him first, and a little jolt of warmth mixed with a dose of irritation moved through him. "I'm fine. I'll be fine."

He turned and, in two steps, was back at the computer screens, watching as the men walked down the other hall, spending several minutes as they looked in each room. Their demeanor emitted no warning vibe. By all appearances, Tomas was perusing the house his family would be moving into. No suspicion or concern was evident on their faces or mannerisms. As they crossed the breezeway and made their way to the other wing, he watched as they bypassed the safe room, looked into the smaller bedroom, and then entered the owner's bedroom. He was sure he and Tricia had taken everything of theirs out of the room, and he'd even given it a final view before they left. Nonetheless, his heart was in his throat as the two men walked around the large bedroom, entered the bathroom, and came back out.

Poole wasn't worried about the footprints on the carpet, considering the cleaning service wouldn't be in for a final cleaning until all the workers finished. As the men walked back down the hall, his breathing shallowed as they stopped outside the linen closet. Ricardo pointed at the door and opened the closet. Tomas and Ricardo were right outside the safe room door. He pressed his back against the door, even though he knew the lock from the inside would keep them out. He watched from across the small space as they pressed the button several times to gain entry, but it didn't engage. The two men talked, and then Ricardo threw his hands into the air. Tomas and Ricardo turned to walk back down the hall, still talking, but neither appeared upset.

Poole continued to hold his breath, and it didn't leave his body until the two men returned to the first floor. Knowing Trish would be concerned, he radioed, "They couldn't get into the safe room. Stay where you are. I'll bring everything down as soon as they leave, and we'll meet outside."

"Okay," she whispered.

Tomas and Ricardo stood outside the front door, but Poole jumped into action. Making sure everything was secure in his bag, he threw her purse in with his things and shifted the bag onto his shoulder.

He grabbed his phone. "As soon as they leave, I'm going to get to Tricia."

He looked around the safe room, seeing no evidence that anyone had spent time there. Then, keeping his gaze on the screen showing the front of the house, he breathed a sigh of relief when Tomas and Ricardo moved to their SUV, along with the armed guards that had come with them. Both vehicles loaded, and the engines started. They circled in the front and headed down the lane. Poole stayed in place, his body twitching to get to Tricia, but not trusting any movement until he saw the SUVs leave and heard from Natalie. A moment later, he could see them pull through the security gate.

"Okay," Natalie radioed. "They're going down the road toward the highway. If you want to leave the safe room and get to Tricia, I'll let you know if anything different happens."

Glad to have the all-clear, Poole let out a huge sigh. "Thanks, guys. Without you all, this could have gone FUBAR in an instant."

"Thank *you*," Landon said. "I'll be in touch."

"Poole," Carson added, "Hop and Adam are close. Get to Tricia, and then we'll coordinate from there."

He powered down the computers in the safe room, flipped off the lights, and stepped through the door into the linen closet. Peering upward, Poole stared at the small trapdoor and shook his head, still awed that Tricia had not only volunteered but had managed to pull off monitoring the cartel meeting. He moved into the hall, ensuring everything was secure, and hustled down the steps. "Status?"

"All vehicles are several miles down the road by now," Natalie reported. "The first is at the highway, and I guess they are heading to a private airport. The last two are south of you, about three miles away, and still proceeding."

Adam came on the line. "Hop and I are at the back, near the main house. We're coming over the wall."

He acknowledged, but his concern focused on the woman in the crawlspace. "Tricia? Are you okay?"

"I'm fine. Should I replace the small piece of air duct that I pulled away?"

"Don't worry about it. I don't give a fuck if the air conditioner works or not! I want you out of there. Where are you? Where can you exit?"

"At the back of the house, on the patio side, a panel should shift to the side and allow me to get out of the crawlspace. I'm closest to that, so that's where I'll go."

"I'll be there. Don't be surprised if I have a couple of friends with me."

"As long as I see your face, I'll be good."

His heart leaped at her words, and he couldn't help but grin, not caring if the other Keepers heard and wondered about their relationship. He hustled around to the back of the house, heard a noise, and looked up, seeing Hop and Adam approaching.

"Good to see you, man," Adam said.

Offering a chin lift, he replied, "Good to see you, too."

"We noted the extra security that LSIWC didn't put in."

As glad as he was to see friends, he only wanted to lay his eyes on one face. Poole dumped his bag onto the patio and looked behind several floral shrubs, finding the panel that allowed access into the crawlspace. Dropping to his knees, he shifted the door to the side. It was pitch black inside, and tension raced through his body. "Tricia? You in there, babe?"

He didn't see or hear anything for a second, and his heart stuttered. Then her beautiful face popped into view, a wide smile curving her lips.

"Hey!" she called out. "Are we good? Is it all clear?"

Chuckling, he leaned forward so that he could grasp her forearms. "Yeah, babe, we're good." She crawled forward, and he assisted, noting the layer of dusty sand on her clothes, a smudge on her cheek, and sweat dripping from her face, plastering her shirt to her body. And she looked beautiful. Absolutely fuckin' beautiful.

As she climbed to her feet, she tilted her head back, smiled at him, and noticed they weren't alone.

"Oh. Hi!"

Hop and Adam grinned, and Adam handed her a bottle of water.

"Oh God, thank you!" she gushed in gratitude. Unscrewing the top, she drank thirstily. "Thank you! Thank you! I hadn't realized how hot it would get in there or how long I might have to stay."

"Not a problem," Adam assured. "That was quite a feat you performed. Pretty fuckin' amazing."

She shrugged but grinned. "I was glad I didn't have to do much crawling behind walls, but because I didn't trust the wiring my boss put in, I've had to traverse this house inside and out for the past couple of months. I knew I'd be able to do it again."

Hop clapped Poole on the back. "She's badass. I like her."

Not wanting her to be spooked by his enthusiastic friends, he growled, "Just glad it's over."

She finished her water and turned her gaze up to him. "What's next?"

"You're finished here, right? No more return visits?"

She barked out a rueful chuckle and nodded. "Absolutely finished. When I return today, I'll tell my boss it's *done*. He'll sign off on everything. Then it'll go to your boss."

"Good. Because I don't give a fuck what your boss says, I don't want you back here."

Her eyes widened, and she shook her head. "Don't worry! I won't come back here for anything." She grinned up at him. "Anyway, I'm getting a new job, right? Time to dump Roche Electrical!"

He slung his arm around her shoulders. "That's right. You now get to join Burrows Electrical and Security Systems. I was honest when I said your dad needs to check with Carson because I can promise that Roche Electrical will not get any more contracts from us."

By now, the four had walked back down the lane to the garage. She looked over and said, "I was so nervous they'd find our vehicles. Thank God we stored them to keep the hail from causing them any damage."

Poole nodded, knowing how close they came to being caught by drug cartel members. "Thanks to your brilliant suggestion to use this garage that wasn't close to the house."

They raised the garage door, showing his SUV and her truck safely tucked away. He looked down at her, and she pressed her lips together, fiddling with her hands as though suddenly nervous. He wanted to pull her close, but with the other Keepers there, he hated not knowing what she would be comfortable with.

Turning to Hop and Adam, he said, "Guys, if you give me a couple of minutes, I'll drive you back to where you've got the helicopter."

"No problem," they said in unison before turning to Tricia.

Adam shook her hand and said, "You were really cool under pressure back there, Tricia. It was good to get the intel you provided, but amazing for someone unused to what we do to step up and jump in."

She beamed, her eyes bright. "Thanks."

Hop stepped up and thrust out his hand. "If you're ever in our area, give us a call. My wife would love to meet you."

"Oh... um... sure," she replied, glancing toward Poole. Her smile remained in place, but he could see uncertainty in her eyes.

The two Keepers moved to the far side of the lane near the garage. Poole dug around in his bag, pulled out her purse, and handed it to her. "I grabbed this from the house."

"Oh, thank you! And here... I need to give you this." She unfastened the miniature camera and the earpiece transmitter, handing them to him. She reached behind to unclasp the lighthouse necklace, but he stopped her.

"No, keep that on." She cocked her head to the side, peering up at him, and he shrugged. "I don't mean it in a creepy way like we're going to figure out every place you go. But I'd really like it if you keep it, even if you're not wearing it. If you just had it as a remembrance of me, I'd consider it an honor."

He wasn't sure what she thought, but her brilliant smile gave him his answer. "Thanks, I'd love to."

Their gazes locked, and the intensity of the moment amplified in the awkward silence that stretched between them. She dropped her chin, seeming to find solace as she stared at her boots. He wanted to know what she was thinking, but fear kept his mouth shut.

Finally, she lifted her head and held his gaze once again. "You know, Poole," she began softly. "When the world is spinning out of control, things get said that don't always hold up in the harsh light of day. If the idea of seeing me again doesn't hold the same appeal now that the danger is over, I can return your Navy shirt by mail. I don't want you to feel trapped or obligated or—"

"No!" The world barreled out of him as his hands reached out to her. Holding her shoulders, he shook his head. "What I said earlier about wanting to see you again wasn't an empty promise. It was sincere. It still is.

As for the T-shirt... please keep it. I like the idea that you're wearing it."

She smiled again as they pulled out their phones and traded phone numbers. He looked over at her older truck and sighed. "Are you gonna be okay getting home?"

She laughed and nodded. "Oh yeah. I've been down this road so many times, I could probably drive it in my sleep."

"Well, okay," he said reluctantly, opening her driver's door.

She stepped close but didn't climb in. Turning, she looked up to stare into his eyes. "I hope you have a good time in Las Vegas."

"I wish you were going with me." Those words slipped out before he thought about the implications, but realized the sentiment was true. He'd love to have more time with her, and a vacation at a resort in Vegas, where they could both have fun, seemed like the perfect thing to do.

She laughed, her smile wide. "Sounds nice, but I have to talk to my boss, then I have to talk to my dad, then I have to figure out what I'm going to do. But maybe you can call me on your way back from your trip. We'll get together if you still want to see me."

He hated saying goodbye but knew it was time. He barely opened his arms when she rushed forward, plastering her front to his.

"I really loved meeting you, Poole," she said. Her arms tightened around his waist.

"Me too. This is been an adventure I hadn't planned

on, but I can't tell you how glad I am we met. And I was serious... I want to spend more time with you."

She looked up, and he bent to take her lips in a kiss. It only took a second for the jolt to fire through their bodies again. If Hop and Adam weren't outside the garage waiting, he thought he would have fallen into a fantasy by having sex against his SUV. Or in the back of his SUV. Or anywhere near his SUV.

Finally, they reluctantly separated. She climbed behind the steering wheel, cranked her truck to life, and backed out of the garage. With a wave, she headed down the lane. He climbed in the driver seat, and Adam settled in the passenger side. Pulling out of the garage, Hop shut the garage door before climbing into the back seat. At the end of the drive, Poole found Tricia's truck waiting. She rolled down her window and shouted, "I have the security button to close the gate behind you."

He felt foolish that he hadn't even thought of that and waved. As he passed her, he watched as the gate to the estate closed. Then he turned in one direction to take Hop and Adam back to their helicopter, and she headed down the lane toward the highway.

"I was telling the truth when I said she was a badass," Hop said.

"Yeah."

"Seems like a really nice girl," Adam added.

"Yeah."

A moment passed, and then Hop and Adam started laughing.

"Do you wanna tell me what the fuck is so funny about the situation?" Poole growled.

"It's just that you were going to Vegas and thought this was a quick stop. Who knew a day later you'd call the pretty electrician 'babe.'"

He opened his mouth to refute, then clamped it shut. The truth was, he didn't want to deny anything they said. Tricia was badass. And she was nice. And he liked spending time with her. And as far as he was concerned, he was going to spend more time with her— preferably when they weren't hiding from danger.

18

The hum of his SUV's engine was the only soundtrack as Poole drove several more hours after dropping off Hop and Adam. His thoughts were on Tricia, and the lure of listening to music, an audiobook, or a podcast held no interest.

By the time the skyline of Las Vegas came into view, thoughts of Bennett falling a few months earlier when he had provided a security escort for a beautiful scientist in Vegas. Initially, Bennett hadn't wanted to go, grumbling about the blaring lights, teeming crowds, and air of superficiality. But Poole couldn't deny the allure of a free vacation, even if the destination wasn't his ideal choice.

Arriving at the Aria Hotel, he retrieved his bags with little enthusiasm, handed his keys to the valet, and then walked through the grand lobby. At the desk, the receptionist pleasantly clucked over his first missed day on the reservation, but he acknowledged his delayed arrival with a nonchalant shrug.

His original plans revolved around an early visit to the gaming tables, having dinner and drinks, and then attending a show. Now, he scanned the sweeping expanse of the sleek, modern lobby, and a sigh of indifference escaped. The glass, chrome, marble, and wood did little to pique his architectural interest. Exhaustion weighed on him, snuffing out little interest in anything other than going straight to his room.

Exiting the elevator, he walked down the plush carpeted hall until he came to his door. Once inside, he stared at the continuing modern theme with sleek furniture. The California king was the only furniture in the room with any allure.

"Jesus, am I an old man already?" he muttered as he discarded his bag onto the floor and headed into the bathroom, the desire to scrub off the day's accumulated sweat— the residue of the nerve-wracking episode with Tricia. The spacious shower reminded him of the steamy encounter from the previous night. *How could that have been just yesterday?*

The intoxicating image of her sweet body as they discovered each other had never left his mind... another reason he knew he wanted to spend more time with her. No one-night stand had made him long for more. And he hadn't been this interested in a woman in a long time. Tipping his head back, he sighed. His Vegas vacation was losing its glitter and neon lure before it began.

Giving a mental shake, he grabbed clean clothes and stepped into the shower. When scrubbed clean, he thought he might be ready to hit the tables, but walking back into the bedroom, he could only think about

Tricia. Snagging his phone from the nightstand, he sent off a text. **Are you home yet?**

When he saw the three dots appear, his chest depressed with a sigh of relief.

Yes! Getting ready to talk to Harry and then call my parents.

Don't spend much time on Harry—he's soon history. I hope you have a good conversation with your parents.

Have fun in Vegas! Now I wish I'd taken you up on the offer!

He dropped his chin, stared at his bare feet on the plush carpet, and groaned as he was filled with the desire for her to be there, too. **Wish you were here with me.**

She sent a sad-face emoji, followed by **Call when you're on your way home. I'll wear your shirt.** She ended that with a happy-face emoji.

The image of her in his shirt was a siren's call straight to his cock. Needing a diversion, he finished dressing and took the elevator to one of the less crowded restaurants at this time of day. He decimated the large steak and potatoes, even ordered dessert, and finished the beer he'd ordered with his meal. A few women in the restaurant tried to catch his eye, but he wasn't interested. The only woman who interested him right now was hours away, getting ready to change her life—a new job, a new place to live, and hopefully, there would be room for him.

Finished with dinner, he bypassed the bar, ignoring more open-invitation glances sent his way. He walked to the entrance of one of the casinos, hesitated, and then decided the gaming tables weren't capturing his interest. *Tomorrow... I'll come back tomorrow.*

Taking the elevator to his floor again, he ignored the couple in the corner kissing, unable to keep their hands off each other. *If Tricia were here...*

Once in his room, he stripped, climbed into the bed, and pulled the covers up. It should have been more comfortable than two twin mattresses pushed together where his feet didn't dangle over the edge. But because Tricia wasn't there with his body spooned around hers, the California king just didn't feel right. *Jesus!* After only one night, he missed her in his arms.

He tossed and turned before finally falling asleep with dreams of a wavy-haired, dark-eyed woman who kissed with her whole being and created electrical sparks throughout every nerve. And he wasn't surprised when he woke up later, his cock hard as a rock.

"You were there today? On a Sunday?" Harry asked.

"Yes, because I wanted to get the damn job finished!"

"Well, I'm not paying overtime for that."

"I didn't ask you for overtime, Harry. I just wanted you to know I was out there and went through everything yesterday and again this morning. You can let the security company know the job is done. I assume that's what you want to have happen so you can get paid."

Tricia heard the familiar noise on the other end of the phone— the sound of his chewing a pastry from the shop across the street. That was how she knew he would be at the office today. He'd tell his wife he had to work on Sunday to get caught up when he really had a thing going on the side with the owner of the pastry shop. He got free pastries, and the shop owner got... *ugh, I don't want to think about what she's getting from him!* Next came the slurp of the large coffee he would drink to wash down the massive pastry.

"Of course, that's what I want," he grumbled. "Of course, I want to be paid. I can't pay you if I don't get paid."

"Well, when I left today, it was all taken care of." She abruptly ended her call and tossed her phone onto the truck seat beside her. Conversations with Harry typically left her with a gnawing headache, and today would've been no different except for two things. She had resolved to leave Roche Electrical after she spoke to her dad and gave him the good news. And she'd met a man she was drawn to. Gorgeous, intelligent, thoughtful, a real hero, and out-of-this-world sex that sent a warm flush coursing through her veins.

As the tires of her old truck ate up the miles that stretched before her, she spent reviewing every moment since she heard Poole's voice while standing on top of the step ladder. Tempted to pinch herself to assure she wasn't dreaming, she knew the memories were real. She had the beard burn along her chest to prove it.

What had started as an attempt to tick off another finished job had turned into meeting the first man who sparked a flame within her. The intimacy was a surprise, but everything about their time together felt right.

Her two closest friends would sleep with a man after dancing and two drinks at a bar. Not that she judged, but random hookups had never made her comfortable. Marla would always say it was just physical but then became frustrated when the one-night stand didn't call again. Brenda always claimed that Marla had no clue what a true *one*-night stand meant. Tricia often observed their banter, complaints, and candid comparisons, content to remain on the sidelines.

A chuckle escaped as she envisioned their reactions if she disclosed the time she spent with Poole. She snorted. Marla would want her to call him immediately so he wouldn't get away, and Brenda would pry for intimate details. Scrunching her nose, she shook her head. "And that's why I'll keep my night with Poole to myself!" she muttered aloud.

With Poole, she knew a lot more about him than the typical bar pickup, and the only risk was to her heart because she wanted to see him again. *Maybe I'm more like Marla than I realized.*

Once home, she headed straight to the shower to wash off the dirt from the crawlspace but couldn't get the image of her previous shower out of her mind. Big shower stall. Wide windows. Glass walls. And Poole. His muscles had muscles. And his hair. Long enough to grab and even droop over his forehead. As she ran her soapy hands over her body, she imagined them as his hands. Turned on and frustrated, she slipped her fingers inside and came faster than usual when she took care of herself. It wasn't the same, but it took the edge off her overpowering need to be with him.

Once dressed, she reheated the hamburger and french fries she'd grabbed on the way home. Now, her mind turned to the events after the amazing sex with Poole. She spent time analyzing her impetuous adventure of getting to the crawlspace just to listen in on a drug cartel's meeting. *A drug cartel's meeting! Damn! Did that really happen?* When Poole told her about his job, she understood that it was more than just security systems, but it hadn't dawned on her what it could look like. But seeing it in action was truly like a movie or TV show.

She plopped down on her sofa, lifted her feet onto the small coffee table, and looked around the small apartment. Renting while working for Roche Electrical for the past two years made sense. She added very little touches to make the apartment feel more like her home. Knowing it was temporary always kept her from truly making it hers. She longed for the day when she could buy her own house and paint and decorate however she wanted. Sometimes, when visiting her parents, she'd spend time looking at real estate in the area, dreaming of the day when she'd be a partner with her dad.

As though he could hear her thoughts, her phone rang, and she looked down to see her dad's number. Answering, she laughed, "I was just thinking about you and Mom."

"Then great minds think alike because we were just talking about you."

"What's up?"

"Your mom reminded me that you would be working this weekend, and I just wanted to see how you were doing."

"Well, you wouldn't believe me if I told you what all happened this weekend."

"Hang on just a minute," her dad said, and she could hear voices in the background. He chuckled. "Your mom wants to hear all the news, too. Why don't you come over and have dinner with us?"

She didn't hesitate to agree. Her parents lived a couple of hours away, but she didn't care if she was late for work tomorrow on a Monday morning anyway. Hell, if Harry wasn't going to pay her for working over the weekend, then she would go to work on Monday morning when she wanted! "Sounds perfect. Tell Mom I'll bring the wine."

That evening, her parents sat at the kitchen table with their mouths hanging open as she enthralled them with the tale of her weekend.

"I can't believe that happened to you!" her mom nearly shouted.

"I have to admit it was crazy, Mom, but after spending time with Poole, I felt comfortable that he did everything he could to ensure I was safe."

"But to let you go down through the house into the crawlspace!"

"It felt like the right thing to do, Mom." She looked toward her dad. "You understand, don't you?"

Her dad nodded slowly. "Even though I hate the idea that you were in danger, yes. All of my children have had the same instinct to protect."

She hadn't thought of it that way, but thinking of her brother Trent still with the Marines and Marcus, who'd died in the service, she couldn't think of anything nicer her father could've said. Glancing at her mom, who'd already lost one child, she realized that her cavalier response to a dangerous situation would have hit her mother hard.

Downplaying the situation, she said, "I was never in danger. Poole had the FBI and some of his friends nearby." She was stretching the truth slightly, but it seemed to give her mom a bit of relief.

"Well, I'm glad you're not going back there!"

Her mom hopped up and served the pie while Tricia talked to her dad. "There's more that I haven't told you." Seeing her mother gasp from the kitchen, she rushed, "No! It's not bad. It's just about work."

Looking at her dad again, she explained. "Poole told me that his company, Lighthouse Security Investigation, didn't know Harry had taken over for his father. He wanted to know why I was reviewing the work, and I told him that Harry's work was shit. He said they're getting ready to vet all their contractors again and will make some changes. He also told me that Roche Electrical would lose their contract with them. So that brings me to my future."

Her dad's eyes sparkled, and he leaned forward, the piece of apple pie balancing on the end of a fork as he halted it on the way to his mouth. "I can't wait to hear what you've got to say, sweetheart."

"I'm going to be leaving Roche Electrical. I've learned everything I can, and now that the exclusive contract with a major security and investigation firm will be jerked from Harry, there's nothing else for me to learn there, anyway. I think it's time for me to come home." From the kitchen, her mom rushed in and plopped down into the chair, squealing. "You'll come back and work with your father?"

She smiled at her mom before turning her gaze back to her dad. "If you're ready to have me, I think I've learned all I can to be an asset to Burrows Electrical. And if you're ready to change the name to Burrows Electrical and Security Systems, I'm more than ready, Dad."

"Tricia, sweetheart, that was always the plan. I never wanted you to feel forced to be in the family business, but you coming back and working with me is this old man's dream come true."

She smiled, her heart full. "Then get ready because I'm going to start the process. I want to find an apartment or house to rent—"

"You can live here until you find a place," her mom rushed.

"I know, Mom, and I appreciate that. I'd like to buy someday, but I will rent to start with. And if Dad and I are working together, I'll need my own space for downtime."

"I'll file the paperwork tomorrow with the county to change the business's name, and you'll bring your own licenses, so I don't have to do anything about that. As far as I'm concerned, tomorrow morning, you're a Burrows Electrical and Security Systems partner!"

She laughed. "Well, don't expect me to be in the

office first thing tomorrow. I have to talk to Harry and make arrangements for moving and dealing with my lease. So you start making the changes, Dad, and give me a month to settle my affairs. Maybe less, if I'm lucky."

"I think that's cause to celebrate," her mom said, jumping up and hurrying back into the kitchen. She returned with vanilla ice cream and began scooping it onto the pie.

Tricia had a bite and then said, "By the way, there's more."

"Oh, I don't know if my heart can take more tonight." Her mom laughed.

"Poole told me that he liked my work and that if I was going to work for you, that was good enough for him. We'd have to be vetted, but he wants you to contact Lighthouse Security Investigations West Coast and start the process of becoming a contract for them to install the elite security systems they do."

"Are you kidding?" Her dad stared wide-eyed, his jaw slack.

"It would be a lucrative contract, Dad."

"I have no doubt!" He leaned back in his seat, shaking his head. "Your mom was right. I'm unsure how much more of this good news I can take!"

She laughed and reached over to take his hand in hers. "It's what we planned on all along, but now, with a contract with an elite firm that could really provide some money."

"I'll contact them as soon as I get the paperwork for the name change."

"I think they'll be ready for it, Dad, so don't put it off. In my adventures over the weekend, I had a chance to chat over the phone just a little bit with the boss. Nothing was said about it, but I think with Poole's backing, he'll be expecting your call."

Her dad dove into the rest of his apple pie, seeming to relish each bite as his grin stayed on his face. Her mom turned her and held her gaze for a long moment, causing Tricia to squirm, wondering what she was thinking. Finally, her mom said, "You keep mentioning Mr. Poole—"

"He says his friends just call him Poole."

"Hmm. Okay. So you keep mentioning Poole as though spending time with him... well, it's almost as though *you* speak of him as a friend."

"I know it might seem rushed, but I consider him a friend... or someone I want to get to know more."

"Do you think you'll see this *friend* again?"

She wanted to play it cool but could feel blush pinken her cheeks. "Yeah, I think I'll see him again." She shrugged, aiming for nonchalance. "When Burrows gets their contract, I'm sure I'll have a chance to work with him since he helps design the systems."

"Hmm," her mom mumbled, a little smile curving her lips.

Her mother stopped fishing for information, and Tricia was glad when she let the subject drop. After saying her goodbyes, her mom walked her to her truck and offered a heartfelt hug. "I haven't seen you this happy or excited in a long time, Tricia. Whether it was from the excitement of what happened this weekend, coming home to work with your dad, meeting some-body you thought was special, or a combination of it all, it's just nice to see the beautiful smile on your face."

Filled with happiness, contentment, and her mom's good cooking, she climbed inside her truck. By the time she got home, it was dark. There was no garage to park her vehicle in, but as she got out, she was glad for the parking space close to her apartment. Looking at the magnetic vinyl sign claiming Roche Electrical on the side of the driver's door, she grinned. She couldn't wait to pull it off when she returned them tomorrow morn-ing. Clicking the key fob to lock the doors, she jogged around the side to her front door. And that night, when she closed her eyes, she saw Poole's eyes and his quirky smile in her dreams.

19

Harry Roche sat at his desk, grumbling, "Where the hell is Tricia? Has anyone seen her today?"

One of the electrician journeymen popped his head around the corner. "She worked over the weekend. I think she's coming in late today."

"Is this what I'm squandering my money on? Everyone taking advantage of my good nature? If you work on the weekends, you still gotta be here on Monday mornings!" Harry's voice boomed through the office.

No one answered as his words echoed off the worn-out machinery and tools strewn around. Rubbing his stubbled jaw, he swiveled in his chair to face the cluttered desk and reached for the phone to call her. A new job request had come in, and he needed his most skilled electrician to take it.

Just as he was getting ready to call Tricia's phone to tell her to get to work, a knock sounded on the doorframe of his office. He jerked his head up and observed a tall figure looming in the entrance— a man with thick jet-black hair and a mustache. The man's black suit fit him well, and Harry knew it wasn't bought at the same suit discount store he used.

"May I help you?" An optimistic glint appeared in Harry's eyes as he wondered if a lucrative contract might come his way. He mentally added a few zeros to the imagined estimate he would quote.

"We've interacted before, but our exchanges have been limited to the telephone. I am Ricardo Cordova. I represent the client who will be living at the estate represented by Pence Realty."

A rush of adrenaline propelled Harry to jump to his feet, hastily brushing the pastry crumbs off his shirt while ignoring the unflattering strain of the buttons across his portly stomach. "Yes, yes, please come in. It's good to meet you in person, Mr. Cordova. Um... I've done everything you asked. Just exactly the way you requested."

"I trust you have." Ricardo's gaze swept across the small office, his stern expression unchanging before settling back on Harry. "I'm here today to evaluate the progress of the security system installation."

"Oh." Harry breathed a sigh of relief. "Well, you can rest easy. I've had my best electrician on the job site."

"My associate wants to know when the work will be done."

Harry blinked in confusion. "Um... my electrician was just there and said everything's fine. She says we're all done."

Ricardo inclined his head slightly and held Harry's

gaze. Harry tried not to squirm under the intense scrutiny. He swiped at the beads of perspiration dripping down his forehead but could do nothing about the sweat pooling under his arms or the river trickling down his back.

"The client and I were just there. Everything seemed to be in order, except for the safe room upstairs. The door latch to enter did not work. We were unable to see the room."

Harry's brow knotted in disbelief, and he shook his head. "I don't understand! She's my best electrician. She said she was just there, and it was all good." He looked around, desperate for Tricia to miraculously appear so she could take the heat if something wasn't right. "She's not here for you to talk to right now, but she said it was all working fine when she left."

"She? A woman?"

"Oh, yes, sir, Mr. Cordova. I trained her myself, and she's the best."

"If you trained her, why didn't you complete the job?"

"Well… uh… she… she needed the experience, and I did the overseeing. I can assure you, it's—"

"You say she was just there?"

"Yes, yes. She wanted to check over a few things and is very conscientious. So she was back there this weekend."

Ricardo's brows lifted slightly, but his expression remained stoic. "When was she there this weekend?"

Harry's chin jerked back, strangling in his too-tight

shirt. "Um... well, she said... she said... I don't know when she arrived, but she... uh... was there yesterday."

"On a Sunday?"

Harry nodded and smiled, assuming Ricardo was impressed. Puffing out his chest, he grinned. "Yes, indeed. My employees will work any day of the week necessary to get the job done and get it done right."

"I see. Well, if she's as conscientious as you say, we must have simply not located the correct latch to enter the safe room." Ricardo turned to start out of the office.

Harry started to exhale in relief when Ricardo stopped and looked over his shoulder.

"Do you have many women electricians who work for you?"

"Oh, no, sir. We just have the one."

The man's smile didn't reach his eyes. Rather, the cold, predatory glint from his white teeth contrasted starkly against his tanned skin and dark mustache, triggering an unsettling image in Harry's mind. He remembered an illustration from a children's storybook from his past. A fierce, hungry wolf prepared to devour innocent Little Red Riding Hood. The eerie image had haunted his childhood dreams, and right now, he wished it was Tricia in place of him, facing this intimidating stranger. Now, staring at the man still looming in his doorway, he wished he hadn't agreed to work on this project, but the hefty paycheck had been too enticing to resist.

The money he was taking under the table for this client would set him up for an early retirement. Hell, it would set him up for life. Making money without

POOLE

having to work too much was right up his alley. "Patricia Burrows," he blurted. "That's her."

The man's eyes narrowed so subtly that Harry wasn't sure if the information he offered irritated or pleased the wolf.

"I'll be in touch." Ricardo's words hung in the air, leaving a chilling promise behind.

A bead of sweat slithered down Harry's flushed face. As soon as Ricardo walked away, Harry collapsed into his chair, relief and apprehension mingling within. Looking at the remains of his half-eaten pastry, he had no appetite for more as queasy unease filled him.

Ricardo maneuvered his sleek black vehicle out of the parking lot. His fingers drummed on the leather-bound steering wheel, betraying the turbulent thoughts swirling in his mind.

He initiated a call using the car's built-in system. Not waiting for the standard greeting, he bit out, "I don't trust him. He relegated the task to an employee when he had explicitly committed to doing the work himself. I want one of ours back on the estate to evaluate the entire system. And I want to know if someone was there when we were."

His dark eyes flicked briefly to the rearview mirror, capturing an image of Harry's business receding in the distance. "And dig into Patricia Burrows. He indicated she was there yesterday. If she poses a threat, we will take care of her."

His tone hardened as he continued. "And when the matter is concluded, I also want to deal with Harry Roche. But not until we have extracted everything useful from him that we can."

So what did you do today in the big bad city of Las Vegas?

Hit the gaming tables for a little while. A very little while.

?? Did you lose all your money??

Not even close. I gave up early.

Why?

Just no fun alone.

I have a hard time imagining you alone. I see you with a long-legged blonde hanging over your shoulder, cheering you on as you drink martinis.

I think you have me confused with James Bond.

Oh yeah, that's right... I'm the super spy!

Very funny. Are you at home?

Yes.

Tricia's phone immediately rang, and she laughed when she spied Poole's name on caller ID. Connecting, she quipped, "Did your thumbs get tired of texting?"

His deep rumble of laughter sounded so familiar that she was instantly hit with déjà vu and wished he was there with her.

"No, smart-ass. More like I wanted to hear your voice instead of just seeing your texts."

She sighed while grinning. "That's sweet."

"What can I say? I'm a sweet guy. Plus, I wanted to see how your day went."

Now, it was her turn to laugh. "Well, I did exactly as I planned. I slept late since I had worked over the weekend. And when I got to work, Harry was in a pissy mood. So I decided to rip the bandage off and immediately told him I was putting in my two-week notice."

"How did that go?"

"Oh, about as well as you'd expect. He fussed, fumed, blew up, and blustered. He acted like he had spent so much time training me when, in reality, his dad had me training Harry! I brought his company up in level of work and professionalism, but you'd think I had bitten the hand that fed me since birth." She barked out laughter. "Oh, and get this... he accused my father of nepotism by hiring me! And he has never worked for anyone other than his dad's company. Ugh! Anyway, the unpleasantness is over."

"Did you say anything about the house or contracts from LSIWC?"

"No. He knew I redid his work and was there over the weekend. Anything between Roche Electrical and your company is not my concern. But hopefully, my dad will check with your boss to get on a list to be vetted to work with your company."

"Good. That's exactly what I hoped would happen."

"It was kind of weird with Harry, though. I got the feeling that he kept wanting to say something, but then he got mad about me leaving and just sputtered and fumed." She shrugged. "I don't know. He was always a hard one to figure out. Part lazy. Part sneaky. And sometimes just downright mean."

"Then I'm glad you don't have to stay there much longer. If you did, I'd have to pay him a visit and kick his ass."

Laughter barked out. "That's also sweet in a slightly more violent way. But don't worry. I can take care of myself. If growing up with two brothers didn't toughen me up, then working in a male-dominated field certainly did."

"Well, you can never have too many people on your side for a good ass kicking."

"True!" She sobered, then added, "That's another weird thing. I told him I'd give him my two-week notice, and he told me as far as he was concerned, I could go ahead and leave. It was almost as though he wanted me gone... like he was afraid of me staying. If he thought I would argue or beg for another chance since I needed a paycheck, he was unpleasantly surprised because I took him up on it! I cleaned out my locker, collected my last paycheck, then talked to my landlord to let him know I'd be moving out soon."

"That is good news. It sounds like you had a busy day."

"I did. Very productive, and I'm excited about moving back. Since I'm not working for Harry, I thought I'd start looking for a new apartment soon."

"Why don't you come here?"

"What? Where?"

"Since you're not working, you could come to Vegas."

"Are you serious?"

"Absolutely."

She was tempted. God knows she was tempted! But she squeezed her eyes shut and sighed heavily. "You have no idea how much I want to take you up on that offer, Poole. But the truth is, I'm not exactly rolling in money. Once I get moved out, I'll get my security deposit back from this apartment, but to go into a new apartment closer to my dad's business, I'll have to pay the first and last month's rent and the security deposit. Not to mention moving costs. I'd give anything to see you before the end of the week, but I just don't have discretionary vacation money right now."

There was a hesitation, and she already knew what he was thinking. She rushed to add, "Don't you dare offer to pay. Anyway, let's keep getting to know each other before we jump into a Vegas vacation together."

"Okay," he agreed, his voice sounding like a grumpy toddler not getting the last cookie. "But I warn you, I don't know that I'm going to make it a whole week before I see you again."

"I don't wanna ruin your vacation."

"When I made plans to come here, we hadn't met. Now that I know you, I want to spend more time with you."

"Instead of gambling and possibly winning a fortune at the tables? Instead of eating mediocre and overpriced food for tourists? Instead of pretending to be James Bond and having a beautiful long-legged blonde hang over your shoulder?"

"Yes, yes," he said, with an exaggerated, defeated air.

207

"I'd rather spend time with you than any of those amazing things you just mentioned."

Laughter rang out as she was unable to contain her happiness at the idea that he wanted to spend more time with her. Since they'd said goodbye, she had wrestled with the idea that her feelings for him were unreciprocated. Now, having heard that he was interested in getting to know her more kept a smile on her face.

They talked long into the night, the conversations flowing freely. They meandered through various topics, and her heart warmed at the realization that he chose to stay cooped up in his hotel room just talking to her over the myriad of Vegas vacation distractions.

But she wasn't going to complain. Instead, she savored every moment of talking to him, giving her a chance to learn more about the man who'd captured her desires.

20

Poole had no doubts. It was official—he was D.O.N.E. Utterly and unequivocally done.

His day had started with the best intentions, rising early to swim laps in the hotel pool. But his invigorating solitude soon turned into a chaotic playground for excited and somewhat unruly children, who exhibited better behavior than their parents.

Determined to escape the growing crowds, he'd entered the casino before lunch. But his desire to try his luck at the gaming tables was countered as his gaze fixated on the weary faces of people who seemed to have been there all night. Their glassy eyes and unsteady steps showed the bitter reality of losing most, if not all, of their hard-earned paychecks. It was depressing as fuck.

He settled into one of the casino restaurants for lunch, but Tricia's comment about overpriced, mediocre food for tourists was true. Needing to get outside, he attempted a leisurely stroll along the famous Las Vegas Strip, but the throngs of tourists clogging the sidewalks rendered it impossible to gain any enjoyment.

His mood plummeted as the day progressed. Retreating to the hotel, he headed straight to his room and changed for the evening. Entering the casino once more, he hoped for the crowd to be more invigorating, but the allure of gambling didn't hold his attention like he assumed it would. Hungry, he stood at the entrance of one of the exclusive restaurants but abruptly halted, having no desire to sit by himself at a table or endure the company of a stranger.

Navigating through the lobby, he wondered what the hell had happened to him. The memories of the last time he'd been to Las Vegas filled his mind. He'd come with his SEAL buddies, fresh from a tough mission, ready to cut loose and live wild. Winning a few thousand dollars at the tables, he indulged in a few exotic shows and met a beautiful, willing woman in the bar for a few hours of fun. By the time he and his buddies left, he'd considered it a successful vacation.

Now, everywhere he turned, he felt like an impostor —a single man in Vegas having a great time. Only he wasn't. Well, he was single, but he sure as fuck wasn't having a great time.

Determined to salvage the evening, he headed into one of the more sophisticated bars, grateful for the opportunity to eat dinner while sitting at the bar counter. The allure of a solitary meal was cut short as he was soon joined by a woman whose appearance fit

Tricia's playful description of a beautiful, long-legged blonde in a shiny, second-skin dress that might as well have been a layer of latex paint.

She laughed too loudly, talked too much, leaned too close, and when her flirting didn't even get a drink offer from him, she went for the kill and said, "Do you want to fuck?"

She was interested in whatever he was willing to give, but not one thing about her captured his attention, made him want to know more about her, or wanted her anywhere near his dick. He turned her down flat. "No," was the first and last word he directed toward her.

She attempted to leave in a huff with an indignant pout on her lips, but her grand exit was marred when her latex dress stuck to the barstool. A comical, fart-like noise escaped when the material finally pulled loose. He didn't even try to cover the laughter that burst forth. The only woman he wanted for company was Tricia, and he had a feeling that she would also have laughed just as hard over the latex faux-leather mishap.

Finally, he returned to his room by nine o'clock with no desire to see any famed shows. He stripped and showered, trying to ignore the way the stream of hot water once again made him think of Tricia in a glass-walled shower, giving her trust and body to him. *Am I ruined for all showers from now on?*

Stalking into the bedroom, he stopped at the edge of the bed, turned, and collapsed on his back, bouncing slightly as he stared blankly at the ceiling. Four more days of vacation stretched out before him, yet the prospect of spending them in Las Vegas held zero appeal.

A new idea began to form, and the more he thought about it, the faster his heart raced. Tricia wasn't working, and he had more days off. He could spend it with her, get to know each other more, and help with her transition. A smile spread across his face, and he twisted around to snag his phone from the nightstand.

"Hey, you," she answered almost immediately, but her sleepy tone rang through loud and clear.

"Hey, back." He grinned, breathing easier than he had all day. "Were you asleep?"

"No, no," she teased. "For a single woman to admit she was in bed asleep by nine-thirty? That'd just be embarrassing to admit that I have no life."

"If I was there, would you be so bored?"

"God, no, Poole! If you were here, I might be in bed, but I wouldn't be asleep!"

He blinked at her words, his cock instantly reacting. Before he had a chance to follow up, she continued along a tamer route.

"Was today more enjoyable?"

"Fuck, no," he admitted easily.

"Oh, I'm sorry! Really, I am."

Her sympathetic words hit him. She gave no evidence of being jealous that he was on vacation while her life was in upheaval in the middle of changing jobs. She wasn't questioning who he'd been with or what he'd done. He inwardly scoffed. *Why should she? We're not together. We've known each other for less than a week and spent only one day together.* She was behaving more rationally than he because all he wanted to do was see her again. Now, he had no idea if his idea would be met with derision or enthusiasm.

"It's okay. Being here by myself just really isn't a lot of fun. But I've come up with a solution for making me happier." There was a silence before he heard a soft sigh.

"Oh, Poole, you know I can't come to Vegas right now—"

"I know."

There was another hesitation before she said, "Oh, how embarrassing. I'm sorry... I just assumed... oh, never mind. What's your solution?"

"Since you can't come to Vegas, I thought I'd leave early and come to you." There was another hesitation, only this time his stomach dropped as he waited to see what she would say.

"Really?" she finally shouted, not bothering to hide her excitement.

Air rushed from his lungs, and he chuckled. "Yeah. If you'd like."

"I'd love it!" Her exuberance came through loud and clear.

Elation filled him, along with a huge dose of relief. "I can leave in the morning and be at your place by lunch."

"Are you sure? I feel like you're cutting your vacation so short."

He'd never been a man afraid to show what he was thinking, or even his emotions, and wasn't about to start now. "Look, Tricia. I know we just met. I know the twenty-four hours we spent together were wild and crazy, rushed and weird. But I really want to see you again. And being here alone just isn't what it's cracked up to be. I'd much rather spend some time with you."

"Well, if you're sure, then I am too! It's kind of embarrassing how much I've been thinking about you. I feel like a teenager with a crush instead of a thirty-something-year-old who should know better."

"What's wrong with a crush?"

"Please don't take offense at the description, but crushes are often one-sided. By this age, I know I was hit with lust at first sight, but I wasn't prepared to be hit with feelings of *Gee, I really wanna get to know this guy*."

His chest swelled. "So you really wanna get to know me?"

"Oh, come on! Don't play coy. You know I do."

"Good! Because I sure as hell would hate to think I'm the only one with the one-sided crush."

With plans settled for the next day, he finally said good night. Filled with energy, he packed his bag and set it by the door. Deciding he'd skip breakfast and grab a bite on the road, he fell into bed, finally excited for the last days of his vacation.

By eleven o'clock the next day, he pulled into an apartment complex and found Tricia's building. And damn, if she wasn't walking toward him, dressed simply in jeans and his Go-Navy T-shirt tied at the waist. Casual, sexy, beautiful. Her hair waved about her shoulders, loose curls framing her face.

He climbed down, and the urge to smile at her

battled with the need to scowl when he realized she was outside her *first-floor* apartment. But when she squealed as she rushed toward him, his smile stretched across his face when she flung herself into his embrace. She fit against him perfectly, her face nestled against his neck, her lithe body held tightly against his.

She leaned back and peered up at him, but before he could kiss her, she asked, "Why were you frowning and smiling all at the same time when you first saw me?"

He barked out a laugh. "You don't miss much, do you?"

She shrugged, and he continued. "The smile was because I couldn't wait to see you. The frown was me realizing that you live on the first floor. And your front door isn't facing the parking lot. It's around to the side. You know that's the worst security, right?"

She twisted her head and looked behind her before a sigh left her lips. "Yeah, but when I first moved here, I didn't have a lot of choices in affordable apartments. A small college is nearby, so college students occupy most of these apartments. I was lucky to get one when I moved in." Crinkling her nose, she turned and looked back up at him. "But it's not for long! I've already got a few places to look at that are closer to my parents."

Tucking her under his arm, they started toward her apartment. "How's your morning so far?"

Her eyes sparkled. "Because this place was furnished, I don't have a lot of my personal belongings here. It hasn't taken too many boxes to pack up."

"Well, I'm here to help. Put me to use."

Brows lifted, she shook her head. "You should be very careful with what you offer. You might just become my pack mule."

Bending, he kissed her lightly before mumbling, "Give me half a chance, and I'll be anything you want me to be."

"Right now, I'd like to kiss you in a way that would get us arrested if we continue to stand out here. So come on in."

He reached down and grabbed her hand, allowing her to lead him around the corner of the building to her front door. Entering, he could easily see how the apartment would appeal to college students. Small. Spartan furnishings. Besides a brightly colored blanket and several throw pillows, the living room gave little evidence of personality. Then he spied a two-photograph frame next to the television. Walking closer, he studied the image of a man and woman with their arms around two boys and a little girl. All smiling. All happy. The second picture was much more recent, with the couple now older and a bearded man standing next to Tricia.

"That's my family," Tricia said unnecessarily, her voice soft.

He would have known her even at a much younger age and recognized the new photograph as missing her brother. The smiles were still in place, but he didn't miss the sadness buried deep but not quite hidden in her parents' eyes.

"I sometimes think of my life like those two

photographs... before, with Marcus, and after his death."

His breath hitched in his throat as he nodded, then looked from the pictures to her face. "I know what you mean. There was life with Becky, life when she was ill, and life after she died. It's all part of my history but very separate. Very distinct."

"Yes," she whispered, nodding, her eyes filled with warm understanding. "And right now, I want to be alive with you, making new memories."

He wrapped his arms around her again. Time slowed as their eyes locked, and the world around them faded into the background. Anticipation hung heavy in the air as his arms tightened and hers snaked around his neck. Their breaths mingled as they inched closer.

Then, with a purposeful movement, she lifted on her toes and dragged her fingertips over his cheek. Her touch sent an electric current coursing through his veins, heightening his senses and leaving him longing for more.

"You mentioned wanting a kiss," he whispered against her lips.

Her answer was to plaster her lips to his. The current sparked along his nerves, sending his thoughts fleeing as the blood rushed south. Not wanting their connection to be just about sex, he shifted back slightly, allowing the kiss to linger. Finally pulling back, he said, "I want to take you out to eat."

She blinked, her confusion evident. "Out? Now?"

"Yes, because if we don't go out, I'm taking you to bed."

Eyes brightening, she was about to speak, but he hastened to add, "That can come later. Right now, I want to take you out. Talk. Learn more about each other. And make this thing between us not just about lust."

If it was possible, her eyes twinkled even more. "I'd love to go out with you. There's a great diner down the road beside a little lake. They serve breakfast all day."

"God, I'm starving. That sounds perfect."

Half an hour later, they sat inside the diner near the back, overlooking the sparkling water glistening in the sunlight. She grinned and said, "Do you realize this is only the third day we've been together at the same place?"

"Weird, isn't it? But what we have feels natural." As he was driving to see her today, it had crossed his mind that maybe his excitement wouldn't last. Perhaps the allure was more a figment of his imagination. Maybe he could see her and not be enthralled. But he'd pushed past the doubt and decided there was only one way to see if their initial attraction was genuine. And the minute he laid eyes on her, he knew from his perspective it was.

And trained to read people, he'd wondered what he would discover when he looked across the table at her.

Her unwavering gaze held his. Her lips curved, and her eyes shone. She tucked a lock of hair behind her ear and pressed her lips together to keep from smiling even wider. Finally, losing the battle, her smile spread to her whole face. Putting his doubts aside, he knew her feelings were real.

"That's a lovely thing to say, Poole. And for what it's worth, I feel the same. It's just natural between us."

Warmth spread throughout his chest. "Did you tell anyone else? About us, I mean."

She nodded. "Yes, I did. When visiting my parents the other day, my mom noticed how often I mentioned your name. And she wondered if I was going to see you again. That night, I lay in bed and allowed doubt to creep in. But I don't think that's a bad thing. I was logically trying to figure out how on earth I could be so excited about a man I just met."

"Well, you must admit, how we met was unusual. But I don't think it's any different from the start of anyone else's relationship. Two people meet, and they click. It might have started as an initial spark but lasted longer than five minutes."

She threw her head back and laughed. "Yeah, I have to say that the first twenty-four hours we spent together was a testament that what we had wasn't just an initial spark."

The server brought their food, and they dove into the meal with gusto. He was a big guy and could put away a lot of pancakes, scrambled eggs, sausage, bacon, and potatoes, and he was glad to see that she didn't mind eating. The server returned with a basket of fluffy biscuits, butter, and jam.

She groaned, her eyes bugging out as her lips curved around the fork filled with pancakes and syrup. "This is so good," she managed to moan.

She may have been talking about their food, but the sound hit him straight in his dick. Now, he wasn't sure that going out in public before enjoying more of their time together alone was a smart idea. He hated to have to walk out of the restaurant with his cock leading the way.

"Can I ask a question?" she asked.

He looked up, grateful for anything to get his mind off her lips and the sounds of pleasure she made. "Sure, but for the record, Tricia, you don't have to ask."

She dipped her chin in acknowledgment. "What can you tell me about your work? When we first met, I assumed you just designed security systems. I know you said you also did investigations, but seeing what happened on Sunday morning at the house, well..." She shrugged. "It was pretty evident that you do some super TV-spy kind of things."

"You liked my toys?"

"Oh, I like your toys," she quipped, glancing down at his crotch.

"Fuck," he moaned, unprepared for his joking words to be turned back on him and cause his cock to twitch again.

Laughing, she said, "I'll be good. Since I was worried about our kiss in my parking lot, I won't get us kicked out of here before we finish breakfast with my sexual innuendos!"

"Good, because I am hungry... for both breakfast and you!"

"Now, who's going to get us kicked out?" Their laughter slowed, and she sighed. "I am curious about your work, but assume there's a lot you can't tell me, right?"

"Well, I can give you the short version." He waited, and when she nodded, he continued, "I told you some about the security, but the investigations are both on our own and with government contracts."

"That's how you're tight with the FBI?"

"Yep, that's right."

"Do you usually travel with your handy-dandy spy kit of miniature cameras, ear radios, and whatever else is in your bag?"

A deep chuckle erupted. "I have some standard equipment that I usually have with me at all times."

"And this?" Her fingers moved to the chain around her neck, and she pulled the lighthouse charm pendant from underneath her shirt.

His lungs seized as he tried to suck in air, staring at the small silver lighthouse charm dangling between her fingers, knowing it had been resting against her chest. For the Keepers, the symbol of the lighthouse is everything. And seeing it on Tricia was like a brand against her skin, still proclaiming her as his to protect.

She tilted her head to the side and realized she was waiting for him to speak. Clearing his throat, he said, "Those are given to people in particular circumstances, sometimes with an active mission, and then we take it back if needed. But for most of us, it's been given to someone special, and they keep it."

"I was going to joke about wearing your class ring on a chain around my neck like my parents said they did in high school. But now that I've heard you say what it means, I just want to hold on to it."

He reached across the table and wrapped his hand

around hers, the pendant now clutched in their grasp. "I want you to hold on to it." He glanced down at their mostly finished plates, then held her gaze as he asked, "Do you want to get back to your place?"

She sucked in a quick breath before her lips curved. "Oh, yeah. I can't think of anything I want more."

21

They returned to her apartment, and as soon as his SUV stopped in the parking lot, she bolted from the passenger side and met him on the sidewalk, her hand quickly finding his. Leading him to the front door, she felt the heat from his body as he pressed close. Fumbling with the keys, she finally unlocked the door just as he reached around and shoved it open. She tossed her purse onto the table and heard his booted foot kick the door closed behind them.

Turning, they stood, their eyes locked in a magnetic embrace, and the anticipation built as her gaze dropped to his lips. Heart pounding, she lifted on her toes as she leaned closer, her hands landing on his chest. Their lips touched softly, and his arms banded around her. As he pulled her closer, she slipped her arms from between them to around his neck.

The kiss deepened, and she was filled with longing, desperate for more of everything he had to offer. The electricity that seemed to build each time they were together kept them pressed tightly. His taste was intoxicating as their breaths mingled. His tongue delved in, and she welcomed it with a swipe of her own. Her insides quivered, every cell tingling. *How can I get this hot with just a kiss?*

He bent and lifted her in his arms without losing the intensity of the kiss. She was barely aware of swinging her legs around his waist but wanted to hold on as he started to move. He walked past the kitchen counter, and she didn't need to give directions to the bedroom in her tiny apartment.

The entire ten seconds it took to get to her bed, their heads angled, noses bumped, and lips devoured each other. When they finally parted, their gazes held, and time stood still. Her desire was undeniable, but her breathing labored as she waited to see what was in his eyes. And what stared back was the same longing reflected.

When he hefted her slightly, she read his intent and loosened her legs from around his waist, letting them slide slowly until her feet rested on the floor. She shifted backward only slightly, just enough to grab the material of her shirt at the hem, then dragged it upward, never taking her eyes off him except for the second it took the material to pass over her head. She dropped her shirt unheeded to the floor, letting it slide from her fingers.

His gaze caressed her body from head to toe and back again. "Jesus, Tricia, you're gorgeous."

The air rushed from her lungs. Emboldened, she unsnapped her jeans and shoved them down her legs.

"Shit," she cursed, stumbling and looking down to see she hadn't taken her shoes off first.

He chuckled and spanned her waist with his hand. Lifting her, he swung her around and plopped her down on the side of the bed. She blushed at the sight of her jeans tangled around her ankles. "I guess I'm not very good at seductive stripping, am I? Good thing you probably got to see some shows in Vegas."

He simply knelt and untied her shoes. Pulling them off, he tossed them aside, followed by her socks and then her jeans. He remained kneeling and placed his large hands on her thighs while his gaze lifted to her face. "You are real and honest and beautiful. Your cute *strip-trip* was perfect. And for the record... I didn't go to any Vegas shows."

"No?" she whispered, her hands clutching his shoulders as he leaned closer.

"No. Why would I want to see a half-naked, overly made-up, plastic showgirl when all I could think of was you?" His hand glided up her legs, his thumbs stroking close to her sex.

"Oh... oh..." Her breath was shaky as her body reacted to the need coursing through her veins. Even though she was garbed in only her bra and panties, she felt overdressed and overheated. Reaching behind her, she unsnapped her bra and let the satin fall from her breasts, loving how his gaze zeroed in on her erect nipples.

"Oh man, Tricia. You are so fuckin' beautiful," he groaned as his hands gently spread her legs, and his thumbs slipped underneath her panties. In the same movement, he leaned forward, his mouth capturing a nipple. He sucked deeply before kissing across her chest to the other.

Her head dropped back as ecstasy flooded, but the desire to watch him had her dip her chin, keeping him in her sight.

"Lie back," he ordered gently as his lips moved lower, skimming her tummy.

Ready to follow whatever instructions he wanted, she leaned back, propping first on her elbows, then sliding the rest of the way to the mattress. He hooked his fingers into the waistband of her panties, and soon, they landed on the floor with her other clothes. He leaned in and sniffed her sex, and they groaned simultaneously. Lifting her legs over his shoulders, he dove in, licking her folds.

She gasped and reached down to curl her fingers around his thick, luscious hair. He inserted a finger, tweaking the spot that had her crying out as his mouth suctioned around her bud, tugging slightly. Her short nails scratched along his scalp, her chest heaved, and her hips lifted, instinctively rising to where the pleasure was centered. It took very little for her insides to tighten and then uncoil as her orgasm sent electric shocks through her core. Barely aware that he'd gently lowered her legs before crawling over her body, she eagerly kissed him, tasting her essence on his lips.

Unsure she could move, she lay with her gaze cemented to him as he stood and stripped quickly. Grinning, she said, "I noticed you removed your boots before you took off your jeans. That makes you a better stripper than me."

He chuckled as he fisted his erection and then rolled the condom on. Bending again, he crawled over her body, centering the tip at her entrance. "I've been thinking of this since we said goodbye last weekend."

"Me, too," she squeaked, hating that her voice wasn't sultry as her anticipation ratcheted upward.

He grinned, and her gaze landed on his dimple. From what she could tell, he didn't give a fuck if she squeaked, squealed, or squawked.

She expected him to thrust hard, but instead, with the utmost control, he slid in slowly, allowing her to feel each inch of his glorious cock as it stretched her channel. Neurons fired, synapses popped, and the electricity from the slow friction was unlike anything she'd ever experienced.

Once fully seated, he held his upper body off her with the strength of his arms. Then he slowly lowered until their chests barely touched. Muscles bunched and stretched underneath smooth skin, and she'd never felt more turned on in her life.

"What do you want?"

For a few seconds, she thought he was teasing, but with her eyes wide open staring into his, she could tell he wanted to give her anything she wanted. Even though he was on top, in a position of power and control, he returned it to her. Her fingers dug into his shoulders, and her heart seized.

"You. I want you. Fast or slow. Hard or easy. I just want all of you inside all of me."

He didn't move, and she wondered if he was disappointed in her answer. But then, slowly, his lips curved, and the little quirk appeared along with the dimple. Dragging his cock out slowly, he thrust harder, and her back arched, wanting to meet him with each movement.

She gasped at the fullness, but he stole her oxygen as he erased the tiny distance between them, sealing his mouth over hers. Now, her breasts rubbed against his chest with each movement, their tongues tangled as his hips pistoned with the movement that must have made Eve glad she was a woman when Adam figured out he was a man.

Fucking or making love, she didn't care about labels. She'd learned when the military police showed up at her family's door to tell them her brother had died that tomorrow is not a guarantee. She wanted Poole and was sure that her insta-lust was turning into deeper feelings, but she didn't give a damn if it seemed too soon to anyone else.

He lifted slightly, his lips full from their kissing, and halted the movement of his body. Staring down, he said, "Are you okay? I feel like your mind is racing."

"You've mistaken my mind for my heart. My mind is on board with everything we're doing. My heart is racing, trying to catch up with the feeling of you deep inside me." She lifted a brow and added, "Please, I'm begging you. Don't stop."

His nose nuzzled along the side of hers until his lips landed at her ear. "I have no intention of stopping until you feel me with every fiber of your body."

She opened her mouth to offer a witty response, but

his hips thrust again, and his cock swelled even more inside her channel, dragging against her inner walls. No response left her lips. No response was needed. She wrapped her legs around his waist, her heels digging against his ass, and continued to meet him until she truly had no idea where he began, and she ended.

Giving over to the sparks shooting through her body, she dug her nails into his muscles as she tightened, quivered, and then felt her orgasm flood her senses.

He'd given her two orgasms, and she prayed he was close. Not because she wanted the sex to be over but because she desperately wanted to give him the same pleasure he'd given her. Boneless, she forced her body to tighten around him, giving all she had. His smile disappeared along with his dimple as his body shuddered. He lifted his head, the muscles in his neck and back taut, and then, through gritted teeth, he roared out her name as he powered through his own release.

He flopped on top of her and buried his face in her neck. She loved the weight of him, feeling comforted as his body surrounded hers. But considering how much larger he was than she, it didn't miss her notice that he kept his elbows tucked at either side of her, managing to keep his full weight from crushing her into the mattress.

They lay, bodies wrapped around each other, and heartbeats pressed together, slowly beating a normal rhythm instead of sounding like galloping horses racing to the finish line. It took a moment for awareness to dawn, but she wanted to catalog the experience. The feel of silky skin over thick muscles. The sweat-damp hair along his forehead. The sheer size of him— athletic and fit, yet he didn't sport a tight six-pack. Instead, he looked like a real man who sometimes liked his pizza and beer. She loved that most of all. He felt... real.

Feelings were developing, making it hard to hold back. She never equated sex with love, but then she'd never had sex with Poole. He was different from any man she'd ever met.

His body finally shifted to the side, taking some of the weight off while still surrounding her with his arms around her. His eyes opened, and they stared for a long moment, neither speaking. She wasn't even sure what she would say to him. *You are the greatest lay I've ever had. I want to know you more but don't want to scare you off. Give me all your secrets, and I'll share all of mine.*

"Girl, I can tell your heart has slowed, but your mind is going a hundred miles a minute. And from the guy who's just been buried deep in you and would like to be buried deep in you a lot more, I'm terrified. Can you put me out of my misery and tell me what you're thinking?"

A giggle tried to slip out, but with some of his weight still pressing on her chest, it came out as more of a chortle. His arms tightened around her, and they rolled to lay side by side, facing each other. "I was just thinking how much I like you, but I don't wanna seem clingy."

His lips curved, and his smile lit something deep inside her.

"As far as I'm concerned, Tricia, you can cling all you want."

She tightened her grip on him as another giggle slipped out. "I like spending time with you, Poole. I don't know if what we're doing is just something easy for you, but I'm thrilled you're here."

"Babe, I left Vegas because you were all I could think about. Right here with you is where I want to be. And that's not because we're in bed. That's because I want to be with *you*."

She smiled, then leaned forward and rested her head on his shoulder. He slid his cock out, and she instantly missed the fullness.

"Let me take care of this, and I'll be back."

True to his word, he returned to her bed after a quick trip to the bathroom, his arms pulling her to his chest.

Staring into his eyes, she ventured, "Why does this feel so real?"

"Because it *is* real."

And with those four little words, she smiled, pressing her body against his. It was scary how much those words meant to her.

22

"You just have to let the FBI, DEA, or whoever build a case against the men in that house?"

Poole looked over at Tricia as her hands dramatically waved in the air, and he hid his grin. "Yep. LSIWC is no longer involved unless something changes. We might get called in since we designed the house security. We'll certainly provide them with the necessary surveillance access. I suppose the family will move in since that's what they indicated, but the feds will watch to see if they run drugs through there."

She huffed loudly with just as much dramatic flair as she had when waving her hands around. "So you just have to sit and wait?"

"Believe me, we have plenty of cases to work on. Private investigations. Security designs. Security missions. We have enough to keep us busy and in the money."

She was quiet for a moment, but he didn't doubt her mind was still pondering the situation with the estate.

"But doesn't it drive you crazy to know that there will be drug dealers in that house and not do anything about it?"

Poole sat on Tricia's sofa as she reclined on the other end, her legs lying across his lap with his large hand gently massaging her calves. The empty pizza box and two empty beer bottles were on the coffee table. She was neat but didn't mind letting go when the situation called for it. And post-sex pizza and beer called for it. That was another thing he loved about being with her. "And what do you think I should do?"

Her face scrunched as she flung her arms out again. "I don't know. Put on your Superman suit and fly there to capture them."

A chuckle erupted at the image. "Sorry, babe, but my Superman cape is at the cleaners. Without the cape, I'd just look like a guy in an adult onesie."

Her eyes bugged out for a two-second count before she burst into laughter. He loved the sound and tightened his grip on her leg.

"How would you even know about a onesie, Poole?"

"Hey, I've been to a baby shower."

Her eyes bugged again. "No way!" Then they narrowed. "Who?"

Now, he laughed at her suspicious expression. "Don't worry. I have no baby mamas out there. When my boss and his wife had a baby, our office manager, Rachel, insisted we throw them a baby shower. And she also insisted that we Keepers bring appropriate gifts since most of us were clueless. She had onesies on the list."

"Is that what you brought?"

"Hell, no. I had no idea what it was, so I went for something I understood. I got the car seat with the highest safety rating."

She sat up so quickly that his hand fell off her leg. "Poole! A onesie would only cost a little bit. You bought an expensive car seat?"

"Tricia, the cost didn't matter. What mattered was making sure their baby was safe when traveling."

She stared at him, her gaze never wavering. He watched as she blinked away the gathering moisture. Lifting his forefinger, he trailed a gentle path over her cheek. "What's wrong, babe?"

Swallowing deeply, she shook her head. "Nothing. That's what's scary."

"Scary?"

She nodded. "I was scared of this," she said, her hand waving between them. "I was scared of feelings developing, even though I've only known you briefly. I was scared that everything you did and said was so wonderful and would turn out to be fake or false or… I don't know… maybe too good to be true. You told me earlier that this thing between us is real. I need you to know it feels real to me, too."

He jerked his feet off the coffee table, plopping them onto the floor. Snagging her around the waist, he lifted as he twisted and fell back on the sofa with her lying on top of him. Clutching her cheeks, he dove his fingers into her hair, pushing it back from her face so he could stare unhindered into her eyes. "What I feel isn't casual, Tricia. After last weekend— getting to know you, sharing what we did that night, then watching you put your fear aside to step up and volunteer to do something that most people would never consider, and do it just because you felt like it was the right thing to do... I want more of you. I want to see how far we can go. You've knocked all interest in another woman out of my mind."

She pressed her hips downward and slid her legs to either side of his thighs. His erection swelled, and she grinned. "Can you show me again how real we are?"

His hands brought her face closer to his. "Fuck yeah, babe." Then he sealed his mouth over hers, and on the too-small sofa in her tiny-ass apartment, he proved to both of them that they were as genuine as two people could be.

"Are you sure you want to do this?"

Poole glanced to the side as Tricia twisted her hands together in her lap. His shoulders shook in silent mirth, seeing this strong woman filled with nerves as he drove them along the highway. For the past two days, they spent most of their time together making love— in the bed, on the sofa, against the shower wall of her minuscule shower, which was a herculean feat in and of itself. They talked and ate between sex, getting to know more about each other's minds and lives, as well as their bodies. And everything he discovered just fed his fascination about her.

Now, against her bout of nerves and protestations,

they were on the road to visit her parents before checking out a couple of apartments for her to consider moving into.

He reached over and placed his hand on hers, stilling the kneading fingers. "Yes, I'm sure." Squeezing her hand, he asked, "I want to know why you think it's not a good idea."

"You can't imagine my mother."

"Tell me."

"I never bring a guy home to meet my parents."

"Never?" His voice was steady, but it was hard to hide his surprise..

"Well, not since Johnny Ludley in high school. He was my sort-of boyfriend."

"What the hell is a *sort-of* boyfriend?"

"You know, he was my boyfriend when it suited him, and he conveniently forgot when he was interested in someone else."

"That's not a sort-of boyfriend, Tricia. That's an asshole."

"We were only seventeen years old, Poole."

"First of all, by seventeen, a boy should know how to act like a man. Second, if he wasn't a full-fledged asshole, he was an asshole-in-training."

Laughter rang out, filling his SUV. He grinned, loving the sound as it wrapped around his heart. "That's better. Keep telling me why this isn't a good idea with your mom."

"My dad will be cool, but my mom... well, it won't matter to her that we've just met. Literally *just* met! As soon as she sees your gorgeous face with that adorable dimple, talks to you, and finds out that you're a stand-up guy who treats me well, she'll plan to invite you to dinner." She jerked her head to stare at him and rushed, "Please, I don't want to scare you away. I don't want *her* to scare you away. She might go overboard, but that's not me, I promise."

"I know that's not you, Tricia. You're cautious and a planner, and unless you're trying to crawl through a building so that you can listen to drug dealers, you're not impetuous. But it's perfectly fine if your mom sees us together and goes overboard."

"I don't want it to scare you away," she repeated, her voice soft with doubt slithering through each word.

Squeezing her hand again, he said, "It won't. To be honest, if your mom likes me well enough to start asking me to be around, then I know I'll have her seal of approval. You can put the brakes on your mom, but I gain the knowledge that she cares about you and wouldn't want you with another Johnny Ludley."

Tricia laughed again and shook her head. "No, she wouldn't. She told me that he married a girl he met in college, cheated on her, divorced, married the girl he cheated on her with, and then was shocked when she cheated on him! The last I heard, he's on wife number three. Or maybe it's four."

He blew out a heavy breath. "Yep, I was right. He was an asshole in training who became a full-fledged asshole."

Her mood seemed to ease, and soon, she directed him into the driveway of a house in an older neighborhood. The yards were large, many with picket fences surrounding them, including her parents' house. He looked at the single-floor ranch house with the attached two-car garage. "I love older homes," he said, appreciating the mid-century architecture. "Did you grow up here?"

"Believe it or not, yes. As a teenager, I wanted one of the big, two-story colonial homes that so many of my friends had. But my parents said, 'One day, you kids will be gone, and we want a place full of memories that can also carry us into our older years.' I didn't get it then, but I do now. Mom has trouble with her knees, and I can rest easy knowing they don't have to contend with stairs."

Parking, he twisted in the seat and reached over to cup her cheeks. Her brows dipped in question, and he leaned over to place a soft kiss on her lips. "You're a good daughter, Tricia. And a good woman."

Her face gentled at his words. "Come on, big guy. Let's get the introductions over so my mom can start falling for you."

"Hang tight. I'll come to get you." He slid from his seat and walked around the front of his SUV. Opening her door, he assisted her down, and after she retrieved the cake they'd picked up to bring, he carried it so that her hands would be free to greet her parents.

As soon as they started up the walk, the front door opened, and her parents walked out, faces stretched wide with smiles. Her mother was an older version of Tricia, beautiful with silver starting to streak through her brown hair, framing her face. Laugh lines only added to her beauty. Her father was tall, also with silver in his hair, and his eyes twinkled in the way Tricia's did when she was happy. They engulfed her in heartfelt hugs, and it wasn't until she stepped back that he was introduced to Jack and Susan Burrows.

"Mom. Dad. This is Frederick Poole."

He shook their hands, noting their warm greetings. "My friends call me Poole, but my family calls me Frederick."

"Well, if it's all the same to you, I'd like to call you Frederick," Susan said, her smile wide.

"Absolutely," he agreed easily, not bothered at the implication despite Tricia's bug-eyed expression shot toward him over her mother's head.

The next few hours passed just the way he hoped they would. Tricia's parents were as real and down-to-earth as she was. The conversation was easy, and laughter abounded, and her mother invited him to stay for lunch.

"Told you," Tricia whispered as they walked into the eat-in kitchen.

He leaned over and whispered, "Yeah, but that means I have her seal of approval."

"Like that was ever in doubt," she said, rolling her eyes as they sat down at the table.

As the meal finished, Jack held Poole's gaze and said, "Frederick, how about you and I take a look at some of my electrical equipment in the garage." He recognized the man-code for wanting to talk privately, and the two of them were soon looking over some of the newer security equipment her dad had bought.

"I can't tell you how excited I am that Tricia is ready

to join the family business and take us into more avenues of work with her background in security systems."

"She's also happy about the change, Jack. She's ready for the move."

Jack smiled, his pride in his daughter's achievements evident. He held Poole's gaze and then looked down at the equipment table, his hands rubbing over some of the tools. Poole could tell something was on the man's mind, and normally, with someone he didn't know well, he would let it progress. But this was Tricia's dad, and he wanted the man to be comfortable enough to talk to him. "What are you worried about, Jack?"

Jack looked up and shook his head slightly, his eyes warm. "Straight to the point. I like that." He pressed his lips together, then let out a sigh. "My daughter told me who you work for and that I should call your boss. As you probably know, there's not a lot of information out there about Lighthouse Security Investigation, but its reputation speaks for itself. I read up on everything I could. I also trust my daughter. I haven't made the call yet even though I know if we were fortunate enough to get a contract with your boss to provide security system installations, that would be lucrative."

"But something is holding you back?"

Jack rubbed his fingers over his chin but kept his gaze on Poole. "It's not that I mind getting a contract based on who my daughter is dating. I know how businesses are run all over the world. Often, a handshake on the golf course or who is seeing who is how deals are made. You and my daughter have just met. You're new.

You seem like a good man, and I hope the relationship continues as long as my daughter is happy. But it's a risk for me to take a chance on a business contract that could get jerked away if something goes wrong between you and Tricia."

Poole nodded slowly, respect moving through him. "Jack, I understand where you're coming from, but you have nothing to worry about. I'm building a strong relationship with Tricia, but I understand your reservations. You have my assurance that the business LSIWC would do with Burrows Electrical would have nothing to do with my relationship with Tricia. You'd earn a contract on your own merit and keep it on your own merit. Believe me, my boss does not take his business lightly, nor would he take his partnership with his contractors lightly either."

Jack once more held his gaze before his lips curved slightly. "I appreciate you putting my concerns to rest, Frederick. I've already put in for a change in name to our business license with my daughter added on. And I'll make the call to Lighthouse tomorrow."

"My boss will be expecting you."

They shook hands and sauntered back into the house. Encountering Tricia's anxious expression, he made a beeline for her. He bent to kiss the top of her head and whispered his reassurances, "It's all good." Met with her radiant smile again, he wondered if his heart would ever grow accustomed to the sudden leap it performed at the sight of her happiness.

When it was time to say their goodbyes, it was easy to accept their gracious invitations to visit again. As he assisted Tricia back into his SUV, he was anxiously ready for their next endeavor. Four prospective apartments awaited their inspection, and he was glad that all of them were closer to him than her current abode.

The first three options they inspected fell short of both of their expectations. Too small. Too old. She shared his opinion, and he was glad she wasn't willing to compromise her safety or comfort. He didn't want her to live in another tiny-ass box or one that wasn't secure. The thought of her living in a less-than-reputable neighborhood rankled him.

The final listing was farther away from her parents but closer to him. He wrestled with a twinge of selfish hope that it would outshine the previous disappointments due to its proximity to him. It might seem irrational since he and Tricia were new, but his desire for her to live closer made it easier for them to continue to get to know each other. He knew he shouldn't influence her decision on where to live this early in their relationship, but damn, he really liked the idea of her being closer.

"This listing is an hour away from my parents," she said.

Considering she'd been living for over an hour away in her last apartment, he wasn't certain how she felt about the distance. "Did you want to be closer?"

She slowly shook her head. "No, an hour is really fine. I guess it's just that I gave up an apartment an hour and a half southwest of them and might be taking an apartment an hour to the east. Maybe it doesn't make sense to make this change."

"What would you say if I told you I was glad you were looking at something closer to where I live? It would only put you about forty minutes away from me. Would that freak you out? Would that make you wonder if I would be a clingy boyfriend?"

She snorted, then laughed. "Somehow, you don't seem to fit the image of a clingy boyfriend."

"What about a boyfriend of the non-clingy variety?" The words slipped out unbidden, and while a blush crept over his face, he had no desire to take them back.

She glanced over at him. "Is that what you are?"

He flipped on the blinker, pulled off the main highway, and parked on a side road. He turned and looked into her face, seeing a mixture of doubt and hope moving through her eyes. "It's what I want to be."

"Oh…" she said, her lips twitching.

"Look, Tricia. I know labels can sound silly at our age, but here's the deal. I don't want to date anybody else. I don't want you to date anybody else. I want us to be exclusive until we've taken this relationship as far as it can go. And from what I've seen in the time we've been together, I think it's got a good chance of lasting. So yeah, I consider you to be my girlfriend."

Her lips twitched again, her eyes now sparkling. "Are you going to be clingy?"

Chuckling, he said, "It's been many years since I've had a girlfriend. Chances are, I might be pretty clingy."

"Okay." Still grinning, she added, "Let's go see this apartment that will bring me closer to you."

It only took another ten minutes to drive, but he could feel her excitement rise the minute they turned into the complex. The apartments were new, two-story, two-bedroom townhomes with lush grass and land-scaping. The amenities included a swimming pool, tennis courts, and a gym. When the complex manager gave them the tour, Tricia could barely contain her enthusiasm as she looked at the open floor plan, new appliances, and a bedroom that would be large enough for a king-size bed. The manager left them so they could look around more on their own.

She met him in the middle of the kitchen and reached out to clutch his hands with hers, barely able to contain her excitement as she bounced on her toes.

"What do you think, babe? You look nervous."

"I'm nervous because it's nice. It's a little pricey, but it's still in my budget. And it's so pretty, and there's so much I could do with it. I have pieces of furniture in storage, and my parents are giving me some. But I feel like I could start over here and make this place my own."

"I love it for you," he said, wrapping his arms around her and pulling her close. "The security is decent, and we can add more. I also see this as a place where you could be happy, and I don't mind telling you, I see it as where I'd spend a lot of time with you here."

"Does it make me sound clingy to say that I can imagine seeing you spending a lot of time here, too?" she asked with a smile.

"When two people meet, and something clicks so that they want to explore it more, I don't think there's anything clingy about that. I think it's just fucking lucky. And in my life, I never discount luck."

She tilted her head to the side, her eyes warm. "Trent says that. He says it doesn't matter how prepared you are, there's always a bit of luck."

"I think your brother and I will get along just fine."

"You will. Marcus was so easygoing, and you would have loved him. Trent has the oldest child's quiet maturity but can sometimes seem standoffish. You would've gotten along with both of them, and yes, I can't wait for Trent to meet you."

"Are you going to take this place?"

"Yes! The office manager said it would be ready immediately, but I need a mover to get my stuff from storage. Plus, I have a couple more nights in my old place to clean it up before I move out."

Bending, he halted when his lips were a whisper away from her. "Then, babe, welcome to your new home," he said before sealing his mouth over hers.

23

Following their apartment hunting expedition, Poole and Tricia drove back to her place, where they spent two more days and nights getting to know each other in every way possible. And every moment he spent with her solidified in his mind that he wanted more. When the time came to say goodbye, their separation cut deeper than he'd anticipated.

Standing at her doorway with her in his arms, he felt an insistent ache radiating from his chest as they shared a farewell kiss. A week ago, he'd embarked on his Vegas vacation with no other thoughts than to have a good time before returning to work. Yet now, an enchanting woman was in his arms and banished work to the furthest corners of his mind.

With a reluctant sigh, they untangled themselves. Sliding into the driver's seat of his SUV, he watched as she stood alone on the sidewalk, waving with a forced smile on her lips and sadness in her eyes. And he could have sworn his fucking heart ached.

Back at work the next day, he sat in the LSIWC compound, immersed in the latest revelations the Keepers and Landon had discovered about the cartel estate. He had been honest with Tricia when he said it was up to the FBI as it was their case, but the Keepers were committed to assisting however necessary.

Poole was interested in the case but no longer worried that Tricia would be associated with the property in any way. Since she'd left Roche Electrical, she wouldn't have to go back, even if the owners needed Roche Electrical to complete more work.

Leo reported on the new vetting of most of their subcontractors. Carson was pleased to find that almost everyone continued to maintain the level of professionalism that LSIWC required, other than Roche Electrical and one other company outside of Los Angeles that they decided to break ties with. "Everything Tricia told you about Harry Roche is true. He took over for his father, and while we could be lenient, considering Harold Roche had a stroke and was forced to give his business to his son, Harry doesn't have the professional know-how to do what we want. Tricia was the only employee who could handle the needs, so I'm cutting ties with Roche Electrical. Rachel is sending them the message today."

"It's a good thing she left them," Jeb added. "Harry Roche's finances in the past couple of months are a mess. I didn't take the time to dig further since we're no longer working with them, but he isn't to be trusted with our level of business."

Carson looked over at Poole. "And I know you're

curious, but Tricia's dad contacted us. Rachel has sent him the forms, and he and I've had a long conversation. I like the man, and knowing his daughter will work with him as a business partner gives me confidence. Since we've seen her work, and you can vouch, I see no reason not to offer Burrows Electrical and Security Systems a subcontract with us."

Carson hesitated, but Poole knew what he was thinking, so he spoke up. "The relationship I have with Tricia isn't casual. I want to see where it goes."

The whooping drowned out his next words, and he shook his head.

Carson's lips quirked upward. "Well, Hop and Adam returned, saying they were impressed with her. Of course, we all saw what she did, so I must admit, she's got my approval."

Laughing, he said, "I assured her dad that if anything happened with my relationship with her, it would not have any bearing on their business working with ours."

Carson tapped the table with his knuckles as he nodded. "I had no doubt that's how you'd feel, but it's good to have it out in the open."

"I can't wait to meet her," Natalie said. "She really kept her cool."

"Me, too," Abbie chimed in. "She was amazing at the Munez estate."

Jeb and Ian walked in, both men's expressions hard. Jeb let out a string of curses as the others turned to them. He looked at Poole, his face full of regret. "I'm fucking sorry, man, I missed something. I only spent a cursory amount of time looking at Harry's business since we knew Tricia was leaving, and we would be cutting ties with him, anyway. I focused on our other vendors. I had Ian look at Harry personally."

"What came up?"

"His business finances were a mess since his dad left and turned the business over to him. But in his personal bank account, he's got some serious big-ass money coming in."

"Can you tell where it's from?" Carson asked.

"It'll take more digging to find out, but at least one of the large payments came from Manuel Sanchez, the attorney married to the real estate agent... Carolyn Pence."

Recognizing the connections, Poole growled, "Fuckin' Harry is in bed with the cartel. And he had Tricia working out there alone!"

"They've probably been paying him off to get the work done and keep his mouth shut," Ian said.

Carson looked down at his phone and said, "Perfect timing. Landon's got info for us."

Landon came across the screen, the lines emanating from the corners of his eyes, making him appear older than his years. "My friends at the CIA identified the third man at the Munez property as Juan Guzmán. His family is climbing in Sinoloan Cartel leadership. He fuckin' flew illegally into the US on a private plane from Mexico and then flew right back. Of everyone in his family, he's the one who appears to have his eye set on finding new routes to transport drugs. Getting Tomas Munez to transport through his estate will be a feather in his fuckin' cap."

"What does DEA say?" Poole asked.

"They want your surveillance, and I told them we'd work out a deal. Looks like things have moved fast. The house has been given an occupancy permit. My contacts say that Tomas plans on moving in quickly. Probably not his family right away. He'll likely settle his guards and get the product route set up. My guess is that Ricardo Cordova will live there and oversee the route. Munez's wife and two kids are still in Los Angeles. Big-ass house there. The estate won't be their primary residence, so it's perfect to use as a drug route."

"I suppose DEA wants to let them get things set up and running before going in," Adam surmised, sighing heavily. "I know they need to, but I hate seeing the drugs being moved."

Poole looked over at his friend. Adam was as loyal as any Keeper, but was quiet and more introspective. Over a few beers one night after a long mission, Adam had opened up to Poole about his sister's drug dependence. They never spoke about it again, but Poole could feel intensity rolling off Adam.

"DEA is probably looking to get someone on the inside," Landon continued. "But as for you, they only want access to the surveillance."

Carson filled Landon in on what they'd discovered about Harry Roche, gaining his immediate interest and promise to have an agent assigned to Harry.

Poole leaned back in his seat and scrubbed his hand over his face. Even when the security system was accessible by the homeowner, LSIWC would secretly maintain the ability to access it. By the time Landon finished his report, Poole heaved a sigh of relief. "I'm just glad Tricia is away from Harry Roche and managed to stay off everyone's radar."

Tricia cast her gaze around her tiny apartment, surprised at the paltry number of boxes required to pack her belongings. When she began working for Roche Electrical, she knew it was only temporary and chose a furnished apartment. Judiciously, she'd stored some of her nicer pieces of furniture acquired after college in the back of her parents' garage. Plus, her parents wanted to give her a few pieces of family furniture, which she'd accept eagerly.

She only brought her kitchen items, clothes, toiletries, books, and television. Other than that, the small apartment had been furnished with the basics.

Now that everything she owned was in boxes stacked in the middle of the small living room, she couldn't suppress the smile. The sight signaled change as it was time to enter the next phase of her life. She embraced the anticipation of new adventures. Thoughts of Poole and moving on with him stretched her grin even wider. He was arriving tomorrow with his SUV to help haul her belongings despite her assurance that her old pickup truck could accommodate her boxes. He was adamant about sharing the experience of the move with her, and considering she wanted to see him, her protestations fell to the side.

She'd maintained a steady line of communication

with her parents, who were ecstatic at her decision to join the family business. She'd even managed to have a conversation with Trent, who confessed his relief at her career shift.

"Good for you, Sis," he declared. *"That was never my or Marcus's path to take. Dad was cool with what we wanted to do with our careers, but I know he's excited to have your name up there with his."*

Then he shifted his focus to who she was dating, grilling her about Poole's line of work and his personality. She laughed, knowing that their mom would be unable to keep her lips sealed as she spilled the beans about Tricia's new man.

Her stomach rumbled, and she decided to run out for a sub since she'd already cleaned out her refrigerator, other than a small container of milk and orange juice. A knock on her door drew her curiosity since she rarely had visitors. Peeking through the security hole, she was surprised who stood on her stoop. Unlatching her door, she opened it. "What are you doing here?"

Harry looked back at her, then pointed out toward the parking lot. "I came to get the Roche Electrical signs you've had on your truck."

She jerked slightly, scoffing. "I gave those to your secretary when I picked up my last paycheck."

"She said she doesn't have them. Those cost me money, and I need them back."

Planting her fists on her hips, she glared. "Harry, I assure you that I don't want those magnetic signs proclaiming Roche Electrical plastered to my truck when I'm no longer working for your company. I don't have them." She punctuated the last sentence with as much vehemence as she could politely muster.

"Well, they've got to be somewhere. Maybe you pulled them off the doors, tossed them into your truck, and forgot about them."

"I didn't forget about them because I handed them to your secretary!"

"At least take a look to make sure you didn't just think you did."

The last thing she wanted to do was stand on her door stoop and argue with her idiot former boss about cheap-ass, magnetic business signs. Turning, she grabbed her keys off the small table by the door. "Fine. I'll prove to you that I don't have them in my truck."

Not waiting, she marched past him. She wasn't surprised to see his vehicle parked next to hers even though he was in another tenant's parking space instead of the clearly marked visitor's space. Pissed, she made it to her truck and threw open the door. Standing back, she waved her hand and said, "There. You can plainly see the signs are not here."

Turning, she jumped at seeing him stand so close. Trapped between her open door and his body, she tried to scoot by, a feat that would've been easier if his stomach wasn't so large. As he leaned closer to look inside her truck, his hand suddenly came up, and she felt the stinging pinch in her arm.

"Ouch! What...?" Her whole body jerked back against her open truck door as she looked down to see a hypodermic still in her arm. Harry jumped, scrambling backward a few steps, eyes wide as though surprised at what he'd done.

"What the hell?" she yelled, swatting at the needle, knocking it to the ground as wooziness hit her. She struggled to keep her knees locked so she wouldn't fall and looked at his pale, sweating face. "Wha...ha...you...dahn?" she slurred, unable to keep her body upright.

His mouth opened and closed like a fish out of water, but his words made no sense as he caught her before she tumbled to the ground. Barely aware of being shuffled around, she managed to keep her eyes open just long enough to see she was lying in a back seat before her world descended into black.

24

Tricia's mind awakened to a whirlwind of blurry images, like puzzle pieces slowly coming together. Her heavy eyelids fluttered open, and the world appeared askew, tilting her perception. She lay on the hard surface for a moment, trying to make sense of her surroundings. A peculiar sensation coursed through her body as if her limbs and head were detached from her core. The hard, cold surface beneath her cheek offered little comfort.

Gradually, her vision cleared, revealing her hand on the floor, and with a determined effort, she commanded her fingers to wiggle. That act served as a link between her brain and her disjointed body. Hand, then arm, then feet, and legs. Each movement aided the connection until she felt whole.

Awareness dawned like a flickering light illuminating the recesses of her memory. She managed to push against her flattened palm and hoist upward. The room materialized before her eyes— bare, stark, with a concrete floor. Sitting up fully, she could now discern garage doors.

She blinked several more times, and her body jolted upright as the recollected events assaulted her memory. The unwelcome Harry appeared at her door, complaining about his signs. His careless jab of a hypodermic needle into her arm. *Oh God, he drugged me!* The vague memory of her body bouncing in his back seat as his vehicle careened along a rugged path tickled the edges of her mind.

She fixated on the garage doors, and her realization hit her with a forceful blow, expelling the air from her lungs. *This was where Poole and I sheltered our vehicles!* She hadn't paid much attention to the space when they'd parked her truck and his SUV to protect them from the hail of the impending storm but had noticed the interior in more detail as she said goodbye to him.

I'm at the estate! Oh God, the ones that had the drug runners!

She couldn't fathom how they knew she had been there the day they came. *Harry!* Gasping as she remembered telling her boss she'd been there on Sunday, the revelation that he must have been in contact with them nearly bowled her over. *This is why they sent him to come for me. What a goddamn fucker!*

Still sitting on her ass, with her legs bent and her arms draped over her knees, she swiped her hands over her face and focused on taking deep breaths to help clear the lingering fog of the drug-induced stupor that still plagued the outskirts of her memories. Her arm ached, and she looked to see the bruise extending from the bloody prick point.

She bent forward and pushed herself up to stand slowly, continuing to breathe deep to battle the wooziness. Turning, she startled at the sight of boxes stacked against the back wall. She staggered closer, seeing numerous manufacturer boxes in one area with pictures of drones on the outside. It reminded her of holiday time at superstores, where they piled up boxes of electronic devices to put on sale. Only, this was no superstore, and there was no sale. The conversation she'd overheard came back to her.

"Your idea of using drones as well as helicopters instead of just trucks interests me. You will not be able to carry as much per trip, and I have concerns about this."

"I understand, but, sir, transporting the product with trucks is becoming harder and harder. It's slower, more cumbersome, and has a much higher rate of being stopped by the authorities."

Looking at the other, non-labeled boxes, she had no idea what they contained but wasn't about to open one to see. *I have to find a way out of here!* She tried to hurry, but her weak legs made her movements slow as she passed the stack of boxes. A gasp forced air from her lungs as her gaze landed on another body lying near the garage's back door. Stumbling to a halt, she stared dumbfounded before recognizing the hideous brown suit Harry had been wearing when he came to her apartment.

Assuming they'd given him the same drug he'd given to her, she was tempted to keep walking. The last thing she wanted to do was waste any time saving his wretched ass, but she couldn't just leave him. Kneeling behind him, she called out, "Harry! Harry! Wake up!" He didn't move, and she grabbed his shoulder and strained to roll him onto his back.

The gruesome sight that met her eyes caused her entire body to shudder violently. His vacant eyes were open, staring straight ahead, slightly bulging as though he'd seen something frightening just before he was killed. A deep, jagged gash across his throat with congealed blood soaking the front of his clothes and the floor was the obvious cause.

Gagging, she struggled to turn away from the scene before her and began to retch. Little was expelled since her stomach was empty, but waves of nausea continued as her body attempted to purge whatever contents were possible.

She scrambled back and sucked in desperate deep breaths as fear jolted her synapses to fire, quickly shaking her out of the influence of whatever drug she'd been given.

The urge to escape surged within her, propelling her to stand, wishing she had a way to see outside the garage. Throwing open one of the large bay doors would certainly announce to anyone outside that she was awake and trying to escape. Casting a hesitant glance behind her, she realized she had no choice except to navigate around Harry's body to get to the back door. Trying not to look down, she inched her way toward the door.

Recalling the estate plan, she knew she wasn't far

from the back wall that led to the desert. Not exactly the most hospitable environment, but considering that her fate might be the same one dealt to Harry, she was keen to try anything.

With her trembling hand on the doorknob, her hopes were dashed when she discovered it was locked. She glanced around the empty garage to see if she could use anything to help her open it. Just as desperation was setting in, a noise shattered the silence, causing her to whirl around and watch in fear as the door opened.

A man stepped forward with calculated purpose before his gaze landed on her, and his eyes widened in surprise. "You're awake. How nice. Since you can walk, it saves me from having to drag you."

Her mouth opened, but words failed to materialize, lost in the grip of paralyzing fear as he lifted his hand, and her focus centered on the gun barrel pointing straight toward her.

———

Poole was wrapping up plans for his next mission when Rachel walked in and immediately said, "Poole? Tricia's father is on the line. He wants to talk to you."

His chin jerked back as his brows lowered. "Put him through."

Rachel pressed a button on her phone, then nodded toward Poole.

"Jack? This is Frederick."

"I'm so sorry to bother you at work, but I wondered if you'd heard from Tricia today."

Instantly on alert, he glanced at the other Keepers staring at him when he shook his head and said, "No, I haven't. I was going to talk to her when I got off work. What's wrong?"

"Her mom and I decided to make a surprise visit to see if we could do anything to help with her packing. Her front door was unlocked when we arrived, but she wasn't inside. Her purse and phone were on the kitchen counter, but her keys were missing. Since her truck is in her parking spot, we went out and spied her keys on the ground."

Jumping to his feet, he looked over at the other Keepers in the room. Rattling off her address, he barked, "Get the security feed up from Tricia's place!"

Natalie and Leo immediately turned to their computers and began typing.

Poole hit the speaker and said, "Jack, you're on speaker with the rest of my co-workers. Is there no sign of her around?"

Jack's voice cracked when he said, "No. None. But that's not all."

Poole's heart pounded as he growled, "What else?"

"A hypodermic needle was on the ground, partially under her truck. It had blood on it. I would assume maybe it was somebody's drug paraphernalia if she wasn't missing. But, Frederick, I think somebody took my daughter." Emotion shook his last words.

Poole's heart no longer pounded as he was certain it had stopped.

Natalie called out, "There's no security around her building, but I have a street camera with a line of sight aimed toward part of her parking lot. Let me rewind a few hours and see what I can find."

"That'll take too long!" Poole argued as he dialed Tricia's number, praying she would answer even though she hadn't for her parents.

"Divide it up!" Carson ordered.

With multiple Keepers going through the traffic video, it still took several minutes before Rick called out, "A Roche Electrical car pulled in. It was there for ten minutes and then pulled back out." He rattled off the license number. Leo responded after only a few seconds. "It belongs to Harry Roche."

Poole shook his head. "There's no reason for him to be there. She had already quit and gotten her last paycheck."

Adam growled, "If the cartel has him do their dirty work…"

He turned to Abbie and said, "Her necklace. She was still wearing her lighthouse necklace."

While Abbie focused on her screen, Poole looked around at the others, his gut clenching. "She told Harry that she was there that weekend. He grumbled and complained about not paying for extra time, but he wanted the job done. If he's in bed with the cartel, then they've discovered she was there through him."

"I've got her!" Abbie said, turning from her screen. "She's at the Munez estate."

Poole forced his body to move as the others rallied around. Carson barked orders, and Dolby and Adam on either side of Poole, forcing him to the equipment room, were all that kept him from running out heedlessly.

"Keep your head in the game, man," Dolby said.

Bennett moved up behind him, shoving body armor, firearms, and ammunition at him. "We go in, we go in ready." He grabbed Poole by the shoulders and held him tight, looking into his eyes. "And we'll be ready."

25

Tricia couldn't take her eyes off the gun barrel pointed at her, but she forced the air in and out of her lungs to keep from fainting. She didn't recognize the man holding the weapon... he could have been there the day she and Poole had watched from the safe room when they'd almost been caught in the house. *Oh God... he must know I was here.* The barrel jerked to the side, but she stared dumbly, not moving.

"Go. Someone wants to talk to you."

Her legs trembled with an overwhelming sense of terror, but the fear of being shot if she didn't move was greater. Without casting her gaze downward at Harry's lifeless body, she hesitantly put one foot in front of the other.

With the weapon pointed directly at her, she was uncertain if she was supposed to follow him or start walking ahead. He stepped to the side when she drew closer and signaled that she should proceed by the cold touch of the gun barrel pressing against her back.

Her tentative steps came to a halt once they reached the path outside the garage, having no clue which direction he wanted her to go. He tapped her right shoulder with the gun, and she turned obediently in that direction. She'd spent enough time at the estate that she easily recognized the path he indicated for her to take. It wound from behind the garage toward the main house, and as they got closer, he forced her to walk through the garden and past the swimming pool.

She anticipated seeing guards with their guns slung over their shoulders, but no one was around. *Are they hiding? Are they just waiting for me to try to run away, and they'll kill me like Harry?*

The water in the swimming pool was clear and fresh, and her gaze shifted to the steps leading from the shallow end. Memories flooded of her and Poole together. *Was that only two weeks ago?* Her life had changed drastically since she'd first encountered him, and now she was struck with the possibility that she would never again be in his arms. Her arms wrapped around her waist, wishing she were in his embrace.

She knew he would look for her once she was discovered missing. *But how long will that take?* The idea that he would stumble over her body like she had Harry's sent a shiver along her spine.

The sliding glass door leading into the kitchen opened, and she moved through. Now, even more, she was in familiar territory.

"Stop."

Her feet stuttered to a halt, but she remained facing away, not daring to move unless he gave the order.

Footsteps came from the hall, and she looked up to see a man in a dark suit enter the kitchen. She recognized him— the mustachioed man from the safe room security cameras. He didn't have a weapon she could discern, but considering the guard behind her had his, she remained perfectly still except for her racing heart that threatened to leap from her chest.

The man stared without speaking. His hard gaze started with her face, then slowly moved down her body to her feet and back again. There was no change of expression, but it didn't feel like a leer. It was as though he was intently assessing, but for what, she had no idea. If he wanted to determine how much her legs were shaking, it wouldn't take much for him to determine she was barely standing.

"You were here on Sunday," he stated, his accent pronounced.

She blinked at his words but didn't say anything since he hadn't asked a question. She focused on breathing to remain upright.

"I want to know what you saw."

She swallowed, her throat so dry she wasn't sure she could speak. "I... I came to work. Um... the electrical system... for... um... the security."

"I know that. Your worthless employer gave me that information."

Thinking of what had happened to Harry, she nodded slowly, saying nothing.

"Unless you want to end up with the same fate as he, tell me what I want to know. You were here when others arrived, weren't you?"

"I was here by myself—"

The crack of his hand against her face was so unexpected that even as her head jerked to the side, she didn't feel the pain for a few seconds. And then, her cheek felt like it exploded. Gasping, she cried out.

"Do not waste my time. You will answer me, answer me correctly, and answer me fully!"

Before she had a chance to speak, he continued. "Very soon, there will be other men who arrive here. Men who are not as refined as me. Your death will not be quick. I will let them have fun. They'll pass you around, and you will wish for death by the time they finish. So answer my questions. Where did you hide when the others arrived?"

She had no idea if she could lie to him and survive. She had hoped to put him off, but that wasn't working. With her hand pressed gently against her already swelling cheek, she dragged in a breath. "I got caught out here when the storm came up so quickly. I waited it out and fell asleep upstairs where there was carpet. A noise woke me, and I looked out and saw that someone was arriving. I thought it was the real estate agent and didn't want to get in trouble for being here."

A slow smile curved his lips, but nothing about it was handsome. "And where did you hide?"

"I knew there was a safe room that I could lock from the inside. So I did and waited."

"Ah, just as I suspected. And what did you see while you were in there?"

She shook her head, jerking slightly, praying her expression was appropriately blank. "I don't know what you mean. There are no windows in the room. Only a sofa and a table and a bed. There was a bathroom—"

"You didn't turn on any other computer equipment?"

She furrowed her brow as she shook her head, adopting the most incredulous expression she could muster. After all, Poole turned on the equipment, not her. "No. Why would I?"

His eyes narrowed as he stared unwaveringly at her. His expression held violence, and her insides quivered again. Finally, he asked, "Then what?"

"I waited for several hours and then stuck my head out the door, and it was quiet. I looked out the window in the front, and the vehicle was gone, so I left."

"Where was your vehicle?"

"When the storm came up, my phone app said that hail was expected. I pulled it into one of the far garages that was unlocked."

Again, he held her gaze, but she refused to look away. She wasn't sure, but she hoped that giving him mostly the truth would be the best way to keep herself alive. And even though she figured that his end goal was to kill her because she knew too much now, if she could stay alive and keep him distracted, she just might have a chance to escape.

"You expect me to believe that you were in a room with security cameras, and you didn't look?"

"I only handle the wiring. I didn't look at the computers... I didn't have a reason to," she whispered, then cleared her throat. "I assumed the real estate agent was coming because all the work had been completed on the house, but I was double-checking for my boss."

"He asked you to come out here?"

"He wanted everything done correctly and knew I had the skill to do it. But since I'd fallen asleep in one of the smaller bedrooms, I didn't want to have to try to explain that to Ms. Pence, the real estate agent. I've seen her a couple of times when I was out here working, and while she was nice, I didn't think she'd appreciate a worker spending the night in the house."

His dark eyes kept their intense focus on her, but he seemed to be carefully pondering the veracity of her words.

A noise was heard from outside, and he jerked, his head snapping around to look toward the front of the house. "Fuck!" Grabbing her arm, he shoved her toward the guard behind her.

"Take her upstairs. Put her in a closet in one of the upstairs bathrooms... one in the back... and lock her in. He held her gaze and leaned in until his face was directly in front of her. "Stay there, and stay quiet. Someone has come and brought the guards I was referring to, so if you think they will help you by screaming, I assure you, you would be praying for death."

The guard dragged her to the bottom of the staff's stairs, poked the gun barrel at her back, and said, "Go!"

Clueless as to what was happening, she heeded his warning, and with adrenaline racing through her blood, she sprinted to the second level with the guard on her heels. They hurried down the hall with the guest bedrooms. Terrified of being caught with the multitude of guards, she didn't argue as he opened a closet door in the bathroom. He pointed to where he wanted her to go with the gun.

Swallowing her fear, she complied and stepped inside. Turning, she was met with a lascivious grin spread across his face. His gaze descended slowly, tracing a path down her body while his tongue darted out to slide over his lips. The air rushed from her lungs as he slammed the door.

The carpeting silenced his footsteps, and she prayed he went downstairs to be with the mustachioed man. *Who came? Just guards?* The questions echoed through her mind as she wondered why he had her hidden. *Whoever came, he doesn't want them to know I'm here. Why?*

Nothing made sense, but she pushed those thoughts from her mind. She knew this would be her only opportunity to escape. *But how?* Even if she could flee the house, she had no vehicle and was stranded miles from civilization. Squeezing her eyes as she pressed her hands on the locked door, she knew she'd be safer in the desert alone than staying in a gorgeous estate that was now her prison.

She gazed upward, grateful for the light on the closet wall. There was no trapdoor leading to the attic, but being a linen closet, the shelves created a ladder. Just like before. *Oh my God! I did it once... I can do it again!*

Discarding any doubts before they had time to settle, she scaled up the shelves until her head was close to the ceiling.

With nothing but her fists at her disposal, she desperately hoped they would be strong enough. She clenched her hand and pounded against the ceiling, barely making a dent in the drywall. By the third hit, pain sliced through her hand, and she was sure that she'd broken a bone. Grimacing, she stifled her cry, swallowing the agony. Not able to afford the time to inspect her injured hand, she lifted her foot and slipped off her shoe and sock. Wrapping her fingers in the sock and then slipping her hand into the shoe, she hit upward with force, knocking a small hole in the ceiling drywall, ignoring the continued pain.

She had little room to maneuver but managed to get the shoe back onto her foot before using her sock-covered hand to pull down on the drywall ceiling, allowing chunks to fall to the floor. Having created a hole just big enough for her body to slip through, she felt a preemptive sense of elation. *Thank God I have my mother's narrow hips.*

She had no idea how long she had before the mustachioed man or guard came back, but with all the drywall remnants scattered in the linen closet floor, he'd instantly know she had left through the attic. She truly had no time to waste.

As soon as her body squeezed through the hole and she was in the attic, she looked around, taking a few seconds to orient herself to where she needed to go. She had a long way to traverse if she went all the way to the other wing of the house and climbed down the way she had the other day. *But that's familiar to me, I know I can do that.*

But there was a similar HVAC system in the wing she was in, and she knew the extra seconds it would take to get to the other side of the house would waste too much precious time.

With a large dose of faith and an intense determination to survive the day, she scrambled quickly over the maze of two-by-fours, intertwining pipes, intricate electrical wires, and the labyrinth of air ducts to come to the space leading down all the way to the crawlspace. This time, though, it was dark, and traversing the attic was vastly more difficult without her cell phone light to guide her or a Keeper to communicate with her. And she sure as hell didn't have Poole offering encouragement as she forged ahead.

Thoughts of him tugged at her heart, but if one thought urged her forward, it was that the mustachioed man seemed oblivious to the fact that she had not been alone. If it cost her her life, she'd ensure Poole was safe.

The attic had the barest hint of light seeping through the slats in the eaves. However, the darkness enveloped her as she approached the shaft leading downward. The apprehension of becoming stuck or trapped caused her to hesitate, and she sat at the top of the chute with her feet dangling down. The oppressive heat pressed on her, urging her to take action. Waiting wasn't an option. *Nobody knows I'm gone. Nobody's going to be looking for me.*

The idea that her parents would be left without a body to bury twisted her heart with pain. *It's now or never.*

Pressing her feet on either side of the shaft, she cautiously pushed aside the pliable air ducting and shimmied down. With no light available, she had to rely on touch as she maneuvered down. The skin on her right hand felt tight, and it wasn't hard to imagine the swelling. Still battling the pain, she continued down, gritting her teeth as her hands and arms snagged on nails not hammered in all the way. Her feet slipped more than once, and each sound seemed to echo. She prayed no one could hear her.

She strained to maintain her focus solely on her escape, but her thoughts continually rolled to what awaited her when she escaped from the crawlspace. *If I can make it that far.*

She couldn't imagine who had arrived at the estate that would cause the mustachioed man to want to hide her unless he was an underling and didn't want his boss to discover that anyone had been there and possibly seen them. *But then, they would've just killed me, and the threat would be over.*

Her attention was jolted back to the immediate urgency of maneuvering downward when another sharp piece of metal sliced her arm. Squinting in pain, she clamped her mouth shut to keep from crying out. When she'd performed the same task with Poole, it had seemed easier. But now, every movement caused her shaking limbs to almost lose their grip.

Navigating down the tight confines, she reached the first-floor level. With nothing but darkness engulfing her, she had to rely on tactile sensation beneath her feet to gauge when she would come to the bottom, preparing to drop into the crawlspace. After what felt like an eternity, her feet lost their hold on the last piece of wood, and she realized she made it. Or, at least, made it this far.

Once again, with no light, she was terrified to drop down. It was one thing to drop onto the dirt floor of the crawlspace when she could see that it was about four feet below and there was nothing to hurt herself on. In the pitch dark, it was as though she stood at the edge of an abyss, with nothing but endless space below her.

Her legs dangled below, and she tried to hold her weight as long as she could with her grip on the wood surrounding her, but her injured hand made that impossible. Then, finally, desperation overtook her fear, and she loosened her fingers while clamping her elbows tightly in, holding her hands over her face as she dropped straight down.

Her feet landed on the solid ground, and an abrupt jolt reverberated throughout her body. Her head collided with the side of the chute before she collapsed to her knees. Wounded and bruised, a flicker of elation ignited that she wasn't simply waiting for someone to come back and kill her. True escape was a long way off, but taking action offered a semblance of hope.

Now relegated to her hands and knees because she was unable to stand in the crawlspace, she was disoriented. Panic threatened to overwhelm her, and she struggled to breathe in the musty air.

Raising her hands above her, she felt the soft ductwork coming from the chute she'd just come down, noting it continued to the left. Reoriented, she turned straight ahead and began to crawl. Finally, the faintest hint of light showed along the edge, and she knew she'd made it to the outside entrance. As her hands touched the wooden slat door, she remembered the last time she was here two weeks ago. When the door opened, Poole's face was what she saw. She yearned for the same sight to greet her again. Knowing that was a futile wish, she grabbed the wood and slid it up until the bottom edge past the lip of the outer edge. Sliding it just an inch to the side, she was met with evening shadows and the sounds of boot steps in the distance.

Whoever came must've brought some of their gunmen with them. A heavy sigh escaped her lips. She'd come this far but had a long way to go to get to the outer wall of the estate grounds. It would take all her wits and a dose of a miracle.

26

The pair of helicopters carrying the Keepers touched down several miles from the secluded estate, concealed under cover of darkness. Poole wanted to be closer, but they couldn't afford the risk of audible or visual detection. Natalie kept a vigilant eye on the satellite feed, updating them on the evolving situation. During their flight to the estate, she had noted the arrival of multiple SUVs. According to Abbie, Tricia's sensor from her lighthouse necklace continued to emit a signal indicating she was still at the estate. But that didn't tell him if she was harmed or alive or if her necklace had become lost and she was no longer there. Blowing out a deep breath, he made a futile attempt to lock down the rage inside.

Landon, with a contingent of FBI and DEA agents, disembarked from one of the helicopters. Donned in tactical attire like the Keepers, theirs sported their identifying initials plastered on the front and back. Poole acknowledged Landon with a chin lift, glad to have their support but knowing their missions differed. The DEA wanted the drugs. The FBI wanted the cartel members. And all the Keepers wanted was the safe rescue of Tricia.

Poole turned toward Dolby, Adam, Jeb, Ian, and Bennett, gaining strength from their presence. He'd spearheaded a shit ton of missions, often with the objective of rescuing one of their women. Yet this was the first time the woman in peril already had a grip on his heart.

A convoy of DEA agents in Jeeps converged at the helicopter landing site. The FBI agents and Keepers clambered aboard and were driven closer to their objective, stopping at a nearby hill. With the practiced stealth of professionals, they fanned out and made their way to the estate's outer wall. With a keen awareness of the vulnerable spots, the DEA focused on the gates near the front, not wanting anyone to escape by vehicles. The Keepers focused on the wall nearest the house.

"Jam now," Dolby radioed to Leo, stationed at the LSIWC compound. They had maintained the ability to interfere with the security at the Munez estate, and their plan necessitated the deactivation of cameras and alarms.

"You're good to go," Leo radioed in return.

Scaling the wall, Poole and the others lay flat on top, silently observing through night vision goggles that guards walked around, their weapons casually slung over their shoulders. Surprised at the lax vigilance, he blew out a slow breath, knowing they could easily overtake those present.

Carefully descending the inner side of the wall, he came to the garage that had previously housed his and Tricia's vehicles during the storm. Suppressing the surge of memories that threatened to distract him, he summoned every ounce of concentration. Dolby swiftly circumvented the lock and pushed the door open. Poole stepped inside and spied the crates on the far side. Several rushed over and discerned what was stored in the garage. "Drones and drugs," he radioed, knowing DEA would take possession.

"Shit," Dolby said from behind him.

Poole pivoted swiftly, noting Dolby fixated on the floor near the far side. Hurriedly approaching, Poole spied the bloodied body of a man he recognized from their files. Harry Roche, with his throat slit from side to side. Poole's stomach dropped as he whirled around, searching for Tricia. Not seeing her, he bolted out the door. "Natalie. Abbie. Talk to me," he demanded.

Ian's hand landed on Poole's chest, halting him. "Steady, man. FBI just cleared two other buildings."

"Her location is at the main house. There's no way to tell where."

The tranquility of the night shattered with the sounds of shouts and gunfire, signaling the abrupt end of the DEA raid's element of surprise. Poole dropped low and sprinted toward the house, keeping his head down. Every fiber of his being clamored with the conviction that she had to be alive if she was still in the house. His heart raced with anxiety, but he felt certain no one would have killed her inside the dwelling. The agonizing uncertainty of what she was enduring inside the house had him rushing forward.

Poole relied on his faith that the other Keepers had his back, letting the FBI and DEA agents maintain the upper hand with the cartel guards. Still crouching low, he swiftly navigated past the foliage surrounding the swimming pool, then fired several shots toward the sliding locking mechanism on the glass door leading into the kitchen as he approached. The metal exploded, and he threw open the door unhindered. Despite the estate's dual role as a drug transport hub, the absence of furniture indicated the main house remained unchanged since he was there with Tricia. Tomas Munez hadn't relocated his family, making it easier to search without fear of a wife or child in the way.

The Keepers spread out, their footsteps echoing through the empty rooms as they raced through the lower level of the house. Closet doors swung open with force as each room was searched with determination. Rounding the bottom of the staircase, he started to ascend with the certain knowledge that she wasn't on the first floor.

The sound of gunfire met Tricia's ears, followed by shouting, and a gasp left her lips. She froze, and panic threatened to ensue. Her first fear was that her disappearance had been discovered, but then she quickly debunked that notion, knowing gunfire wouldn't accompany her absence. Whatever was happening, the urgent need to continue fueled her actions. Her chances of slipping away unnoticed increased if the guards were busy with another threat. Crawling through the opening, she was grateful for the concealment the bushes planted close to the house offered. Crouching behind the shrubs, she peered out to ascertain the best route to take.

The glow of light from the house cast illumination toward the swimming pool. While it was hard to turn away from the lighted area, her path to freedom necessitated the cover of shadows. She remembered trees on the far side of the garden that were not far from the back wall. At the time, she simply thought the landscaping added an element of beauty to the desert surrounding, and their shade was necessary. Now, those trees promised to become her way to scale the outer wall.

Staying behind the foliage near the house, she skirted around the corner to where long shadows were cast. Ignoring the gunfire, she kept low and darted away from the house toward the trees. Grateful that the lush grass camouflaged her fleeing footsteps, she ran until she reached the wall, her chest heaving from the exertion.

Wanting to be as far away from the ensuing commotion as possible, she hurried along the shadowed expense of the wall until she reached the closest tree. In the distance, she could hear boot steps running and more shots ringing out. Praying she could avoid detection, she used cacophony and confusion to mask her escape. Her gaze lifted at the decorative tree, its frail appearance not inspiring confidence. With no alternative, she began an awkward climb with her injured hand but quickly prayed the spindly trunk didn't break before she could grab the top of the wall.

Small branches and limbs scraped against her already wounded arms, but she buried the pain and continued to scramble up. The tree trunk began to bend with her weight, but she shifted so that it leaned toward the wall. With a desperate maneuver that lacked grace but somehow, by a miracle, managed to work, she was able to latch her upper body onto the top of the wall. Summoning strength she didn't know she had, she swung one leg to the top and then was able to shift her body so that the other leg followed.

Lying prone on the concrete wall, she refused to look back toward the house, terrified of catching somebody's attention. She had no doubt that the threat of what the guards would do to her was true. She would undoubtedly wish for death as swift as Harry's if they caught her. Shuddering at the remembrance of finding his body, she looked over the other side of the wall, but the darkness impeded her ability to see how far she had to drop to reach the ground.

Hearing shouts coming closer, she sent up another quick prayer. Then she swung her legs over the far edge of the wall and shimmied down until she was holding on by her hands for a few painful seconds before letting go and dropping into another abyss.

A jarring impact reverberated through her legs as her feet collided with the hard-packed ground. Her ankle twisted, and she sprawled face down. A shock wave of pain shot up her leg. "Dammit!" she cried softly, the torment of the past hours draining what little energy she had left. With tears falling unheeded, she looked around, once more determining the best direction to begin. She needed to escape while keeping the compound in sight. The last thing she wanted to do was die when wandering in the desert. Her only plan was to get close to the road leading back to civilization, and she would still need to avoid vehicles. *I'd rather walk for hours than be caught!*

27

Poole surged up the grand front staircase, his pounding footsteps echoing through the opulent foyer. The other Keepers trailed him closely. They swiftly split at the top of the stairs, half following Poole toward one wing while the others raced toward the guest bedroom wing.

Poole bolted through the owner's bedroom, then dashed into the walk-in closets before running into the bathroom. His gaze involuntarily lingered on the glass-walled shower, and the memory of the moment she gave herself to him hit him. Releasing a painful breath, he turned, checked the linen closet, then darted back through the room. Now, glancing toward the fireplace, he remembered their passionate night together.

Running out of the owner's suite, he met with Dolby coming out of the smaller bedroom on that hall. He started to look into the safe room when his name was shouted from the other side of the second floor. Sprinting down the hall and across the breezeway, he followed the voices into one of the guest bedrooms.

"Poole! In here!" Ian called. Arriving at the en suite bathroom, he spied Ian and Adam in the linen closet. Seeing shredded drywall on the floor, he looked up to see the hole in the ceiling.

"Holy shit, that was her!" He grabbed the shelves and climbed far enough to poke his head into the attic. "Tricia! Tricia! It's Poole!" The attic was silent, but he knew where she'd gone. Dropping back to the floor, he turned to his friends and gasped, "She escaped like before. Down the HVAC duct chutes to the crawlspace. She may still be there."

Gathering the other Keepers, they retraced their steps, flying down the stairs and through the kitchen, not stopping until they were on the patio.

Landon met them outside. "Compound secured. We've disarmed the guards around. We have Ricardo Cordova, but Tomas Munez wasn't here."

"Tricia escaped," Poole said, still running to the side of the house. "She went through the attic and down into the crawlspace like before."

Bennett radioed for the outside security lights to be turned on remotely by LSIWC, and a few seconds later, the area was filled with illumination.

Now able to see clearly, Poole spied the crawlspace door shifted to the side. Dropping to his hands and knees, he yelled through the opening for her but got no response.

"Poole," Natalie radioed. "She's on the move right now. Heading southwest. She's about a fourth of a mile in the desert, southwest of the front gate."

"How fast is she moving?"

"Not enough for a vehicle. Her tracer is barely moving. She has to be on foot."

Standing, he turned, dragging in a breath that made his chest ache. "She's escaped. That means she's in the desert, in the dark, on foot. We need a vehicle."

"Damn, she's resourceful!" Dolby said, admiration in his voice.

"She's smart," Natalie agreed through the radio.

Poole didn't give a fuck what words anyone else used to describe her. All he could think of was she was alive.

Landon came around the corner, tapping his earpiece, then looked at Poole and inclined his head to the side. "Two Jeeps, ready for us to use."

Two Jeeps came careening around the corner a few seconds later, kicking up dust as they skidded to a stop. The agents hopped out as Dolby got behind the wheel of one and Ian in the other. Ian was one of the new Keepers, having only joined them recently, but he'd jumped in as though he'd always been with them.

The remaining Keepers jumped on, and Poole was grateful for the headlights and spotlights. As they roared through the compound's gates, he shouted, "Be careful! She's going to be scared and not expecting us."

Knowing she couldn't have gotten far on foot, the Keepers slowed their speed once they were through the main gates. Here, with the lights of the compound behind them, the desert stretched out in complete darkness, broken only by their headlights.

Tricia was torn between wanting to keep trudging forward and turning back. The lights of the compound now glowed on the distant horizon behind her, serving as a reminder of how she'd narrowly escaped. Although relief washed over her that it seemed no one was following her, the desert night was so dark she was unable to see the road. With a sprained ankle, her movements were slow.

Limping while shuffling each step was the only way she could tell that her feet were still on the asphalt. She was oblivious as to when the road curved, only discovering it when her feet encountered dirt, sand, and gravel. Then she was forced to shift, dragging her canvas sneaker in front of her to find the road again. The laborious process kept her progress slow and painstaking. Her body ached, the cuts and scratches stung, and the shuffling movement was exhausting. *But I'm not being tortured or killed... at least not yet.*

She tried to recall the number of miles separating the compound from the gas station on the main highway. *A twenty-minute drive means I'd have to walk... oh God... too long.* Convinced that her survival would depend on staying awake at night and could fare better in the morning when she could see around her. Certain that she didn't want to encounter anyone visiting a drug cartel's residence, she planned on avoiding all travelers on the desolate road.

A sudden rumbling sounded behind her, and she whipped around to peer over her shoulder. Her heart leaped in her chest at the sight of tiny headlights emerging in the distance. Gasping, she staggered to the side, inadvertently veering off the road. Terrified of being discovered and equally terrified of losing her bearings when the vehicle passed, she crouched down, desperate to scuttle out of sight.

In her frantic attempt to hide, she tripped over a rock. She threw her hands out to break her fall and landed flat on the ground. Her body protested the abuse while exhaustion threatened to overwhelm her. But she refused to be captured again without a fight.

Flattening herself on the ground, she offered a silent prayer that no scorpions or rattlesnakes lurked in the dark. Glancing over her shoulder, she strained to discern the approaching headlights. Panic surged within her, realizing that if she could see them, there was the possibility that they could see her as well. She lay motionless, afraid to move again in case they noticed movement, and zeroed in on her.

"Do you see anything?"

"Where can she be?"

"Swing the light to the left."

"She's got to be here."

Tricia's senses heightened as the shouted words reached her, and she was struck with the realization that the guards must be hunting her in the vast desert.

"Tricia! Tricia!"

Her body jolted as the headlights neared, and she heard her name. Terrified to make any movement, her breath stuck in her lungs.

The first vehicle passed slowly, not seeming to

detect her, and she glanced back to see the second vehicle almost to her.

"Tricia! Tricia! Where are you? It's Poole! It's Poole, baby!"

Another gasp leaped from her lungs at his voice calling her name like a beacon through the darkness. Scrambling to her knees and attempting to stand, she was desperate that his vehicle didn't pass her by. "Poole! I'm here! Poole! I'm here!"

A chorus of men's voices erupted.

"Did you hear that?"

"Stop the Jeep!"

"Swing the spotlight over there!"

"Poole! I'm over here to the side!"

A powerful spotlight swung in her direction, blinding her momentarily. Fear gripped her heart that maybe his voice had been a mirage. She held her breath as the sound of boots thumped on the asphalt. The spotlight created a silhouette of a large figure approaching her from the darkness. And then he spoke.

"Babe. Oh God, Tricia."

Tears streamed down her face as a surge of relief washed over her. She stumbled toward him as she lifted her arms like a child. He rushed forward and enveloped her in his embrace. A sob escaped as his arms tightened around her.

"Are you hurt? Oh baby, are you hurt?"

Gasping between sobs, she couldn't contain her tears as she clung to him. He carried her to the Jeep with great care, and the others shifted in positions as he took a seat while cradling her tenderly.

"Get us back to the bird," someone said, their urgency palpable.

Holding him tightly, she felt the Jeep lurch as the driver executed a U-turn on the road and accelerated. They bounced over the terrain, but she felt deep within her soul that she was safe as long as he held her.

28

Poole lay in bed, his arms encircling Tricia as she slept peacefully. Sleep would elude him tonight as his restless mind replayed the day's harrowing events. Despite the knowledge that she was now safe, his heart continued to pound in his chest whenever the vivid images of her injuries surfaced in his thoughts.

Torn and dirt-streaked clothes, evidence of the struggle she had endured to escape. Bloody cuts and scratches that marred her skin. The prominent lump on her forehead was a painful reminder of her landing in the crawlspace. Her sprained ankle was swollen and discolored, as was her hand from a broken bone. A puffy, bruised cheek from when Ricardo hit her. The mere thought of that injury ignited a fury within Poole, fueling a desire to visit Ricardo in jail just to beat the shit out of him.

In the hospital's chaotic emergency room, Landon had managed to interview her between x-rays, the applications of splints, and stitching her lacerations.

Poole learned that DEA had confiscated the illicit drugs, drones, and the entire property. Ricardo Cordova was taken into custody, and they had a warrant for Tomas Munez. The DEA had wanted more but was satisfied with the halt in the new cocaine pipeline. Hearing the threats Ricardo had issued made him want to beat the shit out of the man even more.

Dolby finally pulled him to the side. "Let the FBI do their thing, and you focus on Tricia."

Poole stood with his fists on his hips, stared down at his boots, and nodded. Lifting his gaze, he agonized, "But what if I can't take this away for her?"

Dolby grabbed the back of Poole's neck and squeezed gently. "Man, you can. All you have to do is be there for her. That's it. Just be there for her."

"It's that easy?"

"Fuck no, man. Nothin' about this is easy. But it'll work. And the other Keepers would tell you the same thing."

Sucking in a deep breath, he nodded and headed back into the ER bay, determined to erase the worry in her eyes.

"Are you okay?" Her simple question was laced with hesitation.

He sat next to her and wrapped his arm around her shoulders. "I've got you in my arms, babe. Nothing is better." As her body relaxed into him, he knew Dolby's words had been true.

Following her discharge, Hop flew them back to the LSIWC compound, where Carson and the others waited. Abbie and Natalie hugged Tricia, promising that they would see her soon. Carson told him that Jeannie wanted to meet Tricia soon, and since she was a nurse, Poole decided he didn't want to wait long before she did.

During the entire rescue, hospital trip, interview, flight, and finally, the drive to his apartment, she remained quiet, although she'd made a brief phone call to her parents to reassure them of her safety. Once at his place, she'd barely looked around before saying, "I need a shower."

Without hesitation, Poole scooped her into his arms and carried her to the bathroom despite her protests that she could manage independently. He'd set her down gently on the closed toilet seat while he turned on the water, ensuring the temperature was right. Then, with the utmost tenderness, he'd unwrapped the bandages from her ankle and hand, gently pulled her shirt over her head, and slipped her pants down. Once she was stripped, he'd quickly discarded his clothes and stepped into the shower with her.

He'd washed her carefully, tending to every cut and scratch. His fingers had massaged her scalp as he shampooed her hair. When finished, he'd stepped out and quickly dried himself before assisting her out, taking care of her every need.

She'd claimed she wasn't hungry but finally agreed to nibble on crackers and drink a glass of milk before they crawled into bed. She'd curled tightly into him, and with the aid of the painkillers prescribed by the doctor, she'd fallen asleep.

Poole lay in bed and tried to settle the whirlwind of

emotions that consumed him. He'd been on dangerous missions all over the globe, both in the service and with the Keepers. He'd faced death and killed when needed. But nothing had ever prepared him for the overwhelming sense of loss, fear, desperation, and lack of focus gripping him when Tricia was taken.

His phone vibrated on the nightstand, and he glanced down at Tricia, who remained peacefully asleep. Checking the caller ID, he slipped from the bed and connected as soon as he walked out of his bedroom.

Bennett's voice came through the phone, concern evident in his tone. "Just wanted to see how you were doing?"

"She's asleep," Poole replied, his voice tinged with weariness.

"I figured she'd be fine 'cause she's got you. And she'll have the women swarming soon to make sure. What I wanted to know is, how are you holding up?"

Poole closed his eyes and dropped his chin to his chest, feeling the weight of his emotions bearing down on him. Blowing out a long breath, he squeezed the back of his neck. "I don't fuckin' know, Bennett. We're trained to anticipate all the possibilities. So how the fuck did I not think that they would find out she'd been there?"

Bennett's response was firm and reassuring. "None of us thought she was in danger, man. This isn't on you. But what you have to hold on to is that she'll be fine. She's hurt, but she'll heal. She's shocked, but she'll have lots of support. And she's got you."

"It's that easy?"

Bennett snorted. "Hell, no. I didn't say it'd be easy for either of you. But she'll realize she now has a whole team in her corner. And you'll realize that you'll be even stronger with her by your side."

Poole thought about how it felt to hold her in his arms while she slept. Her warm body curled up next to his. Her little puffs of breath skimming over his chest. Her silky hair caressing his arm. Her steady heartbeat as it pressed against his.

"You're right," he conceded, grateful that she was now safe and determined to make a life with her. "Thanks for calling, Bennett. Appreciate it."

"Take some time off. Hold your woman. Talk to her. Let her talk to you. Then, when you're ready, let us know. We'll throw a party to celebrate another Keeper finding happiness."

Chuckling softly, he agreed before ending the call. As he turned, he caught sight of a sleepy, tousled-haired Tricia standing in the hallway. She fidgeted with the hem of his T-shirt she'd worn to bed. He fuckin' loved seeing her in his shirt. "You should be asleep, babe. Did I wake you?"

"No. I just woke up and discovered I was alone."

"Bennett called to check on you. I was just coming back to bed."

She nodded, then sighed. "I was scared." Her voice was small, as though confessing the emotion made her less.

"We're going to get through this, Tricia. I promise I'm right here. I won't let anyone hurt you again. But, sweetheart, you are so courageous. It blows my mind when I think of what you went through to escape."

She looked up before leaning forward to rest her head on his chest. "Thinking of getting to you is what gave me the courage. I just wanted to get to you."

He lifted her chin with his knuckle and smiled at her confession. "I just wanted to get to you, too."

He waited, his heart warming as her lips curved ever so slightly. "Come on. Let's go back to bed." Scooping her up again, he walked into his bedroom and settled her under the covers with his body curved around hers. And despite his initial thoughts, he fell asleep soon after she did.

29

Poole and Tricia drove away from the mansion they had been working on, a feeling of accomplishment running through her. "All systems checked out," she said, talking on the phone. "Yeah, Jeb, once you finish testing the G27 system and everything on your end, we should be good to go. The owners will have the state-of-the-art security system they need, and we've got satisfied clients."

Disconnecting, she turned her attention to Poole and noted his lips quirking upward like he was holding on to a secret. "What are you smiling about? That smirk looks strangely suspicious."

His brows knit together, and his eyes widened as he swung his head around. "Suspicious?"

"Okay, how about devious?"

"That's even worse!" he exclaimed, feigning shock.

She huffed, crossing her arms in a playful manner. "Then what?"

"I was just listening to you talk to Jeb and loved it… uh… admired it would be a better way of putting it."

"You loved hearing me talk to another man?"

Now, it was his time to huff as he hurriedly corrected her. "No! I just mean that getting to work with someone I love is something I never thought would happen. And hearing you so competent and confident with our co-workers is more than I could ever hope for."

Her breath caught in her throat, emotion welling in her eyes as her top teeth bit into her bottom lip. Finally, after swallowing a few times to steady her voice, she said, "I love you, too, you know."

A deep, warm chuckle rumbled from his chest, resonating with her heart. "I hope so. 'Cause we've got an appointment after we check back in with headquarters."

Excitement flowed through her veins at the mention of the appointment. "I can't wait."

Soon, they pulled into the compound and parked. Walking in, she sucked in a deep breath with awe. She had only been working for LSIWC for two months, but goose bumps rose on her arms each time she entered the impressive compound. After all the education and training, she finally had a job she loved with people she enjoyed. And that didn't include the perk of working with the man she wanted to spend the rest of her life with.

With Poole by her side, life was filled with promises and dreams. Her parents were thrilled, and her dad finally cut back on the jobs he worked on so they could travel. With the money she made as a contract Keeper, she no longer had to worry about the business. She still had non-LSIWC jobs but could provide the installations they needed.

"Hi, Rachel," she greeted as they walked past her desk. Greeted warmly in return, she felt the goosebumps return as they went past security doors and into the main compound room. With a quick smile toward Poole, she made a beeline to Jeb. Checking the camera angles and audio on the job they had just completed, she was satisfied.

"Looks good, guys," Jeb said before winking at her.

"You didn't wink at me," Poole jokingly complained.

"Sorry, man. You just don't do it for me," Jeb shot back.

As she walked over to Abbie, she whispered to Poole, "I'll do more than wink later, big guy." Not giving him a chance to respond, she hurried to the bank of computers where Abbie and Natalie monitored a mission that Dolby and Leo were working.

Carson walked into the room, drawing her attention. "Adam," he called out. "The assignment postponed for the professor is back on the table. I'll send you the new information, and you leave in three days."

Adam nodded and turned back to his computer, and from what Tricia had learned, he would already be studying the new information. Adam was a good friend of Poole's and had always been sweet to her, but he displayed a seriousness and focus that never wavered.

Soon, it was time for the appointment she had been waiting for. One look at Poole's face, and she knew he was anxious, too. Leaving with the congratulations ringing out from everyone, they hurried out to the SUV.

"Ready for the next step?" Poole asked as he leaned over to kiss her lightly.

"A thousand times yes!" she murmured against his lips.

Poole and Tricia had left the title agent's office, having just purchased the house of their dreams. As they pulled onto their winding driveway framed by lush greenery, he glanced to the side. His heart was light as he gazed at Tricia, her face lit as she bounced in her seat. Reaching over the console, he tenderly grabbed her hand, and their fingers intertwined as naturally as their lives had come together.

"Excited, babe?"

Her hand jiggled his as her smile radiated elation. "Oh, you know the answer to that!"

They had given their real estate agent the challenging task of finding a four-bedroom house with proximity to the ocean so they could easily get to the shore and a view of the majestic mountains in the background. Much to their surprise, she lucked into a listing from an older couple, ready to pass on the dream they'd nurtured for years. Poole had wanted turn-key ready, and it was for all practical purposes, aside from a few small items they would update or improve.

Now, the house stood before them as they approached the drive's end.

"Oh God, Poole. It's really ours!" she exclaimed, a hint of disbelief mixing with her obvious delight.

He tugged on her hand, capturing her attention with his eyes. Still grinning, she leaned over at his unspoken request, and their lips met in a deep kiss. Finally, mumbling against her lips, he whispered, "Let's go in and see *our* house."

They walked together as they stepped through the door, hands still linked, hearts pounding in unison. Moving into the living room, she turned to him, bouncing on her toes.

"What do you see in here?" she asked with laughter in her voice.

They'd been planning each room since they'd first seen the house a month ago, imagining their lives unfolding within these walls. But standing in the living room, knowing it was now theirs, made it all seem more real. "I guess this will be the last time we play this game, considering the movers are bringing our things tomorrow."

"Come on, play along!" she cajoled, still bouncing.

"Okay," he said, eager to acquiesce. "I think the sofa should be on that wall, facing the fireplace, and the television can be in that corner. The comfy chair from your place will be perfect near the bay window."

"A new rug on the floor," she enthused, excitement building. "And we'll buy new lamps."

She loosened their hands to wrap her arms around his waist. He easily picked her up and twirled her around. "Babe, we can buy everything new if you want."

She leaned back while her feet still dangled in the air

as he held her securely. "Nope. Your stuff is fabulous, and my things have sentimental value!"

They wandered through each room, planning where to place the furniture and what upgrades they would tackle first.

"Why did we skip the owner's bedroom?" she asked as he'd pulled her to the other bedrooms first.

"Because I have a surprise for you."

Her wide eyes held his gaze, and he couldn't wait anymore to lead her into the bedroom that would be theirs. Throwing open the door, he waited so she could step in first. Her gasp, followed by a squeal, made him smile.

She raced to the new king-sized bed placed just where she'd planned, against the wall facing the windows that gave a view of the water and mountains. Hopping up on the new comforter-covered mattress, she spread her arms wide in silent invitation.

With no hesitation, he joined her there, eagerly deciding that spending their first night in the new house in bed with the woman he loved was the best place to be.

Don't miss the next Keeper release!
Adam

ALSO BY MARYANN JORDAN

Don't miss other Maryann Jordan books!

Baytown Boys (small town, military romantic suspense)

Coming Home

Just One More Chance

Clues of the Heart

Finding Peace

Picking Up the Pieces

Sunset Flames

Waiting for Sunrise

Hear My Heart

Guarding Your Heart

Sweet Rose

Our Time

Count On Me

Shielding You

To Love Someone

Sea Glass Hearts

Protecting Her Heart

Sunset Kiss

Baytown Heroes - A Baytown Boys subseries

A Hero's Chance

Finding a Hero

A Hero for Her

Needing A Hero

Hopeful Hero

For all of Miss Ethel's boys:

Heroes at Heart (Military Romance)

Zander

Rafe

Cael

Jaxon

Jayden

Asher

Zeke

Cas

Lighthouse Security Investigations

Mace

Rank

Walker

Drew

Blake

Tate

Levi

Clay

Cobb

Bray

Josh

Knox

Lighthouse Security Investigations West Coast

Carson

Leo

Rick

Hop

Dolby

Bennett

Poole

Adam

Hope City (romantic suspense series co-developed

with Kris Michaels

Brock book 1

Sean book 2

Carter book 3

Brody book 4

Kyle book 5

Ryker book 6

Rory book 7

Killian book 8

Torin book 9

Blayze book 10

Griffin book 11

Saints Protection & Investigations

(an elite group, assigned to the cases no one else wants…or can solve)

Serial Love

Healing Love

Revealing Love

Seeing Love

Honor Love

Sacrifice Love

Protecting Love

Remember Love

Discover Love

Surviving Love

Celebrating Love

Searching Love

Follow the exciting spin-off series:

Alvarez Security (military romantic suspense)

Gabe

Tony

Vinny

Jobe

SEALs

Thin Ice (Sleeper SEAL)

SEAL Together (Silver SEAL)

Undercover Groom (Hot SEAL)

Also for a Hope City Crossover Novel / Hot SEAL…

A Forever Dad

Long Road Home

Military Romantic Suspense

Home to Stay (a Lighthouse Security Investigation crossover novel)

Home Port (an LSI West Coast crossover novel)

Letters From Home (military romance)

Class of Love

Freedom of Love

Bond of Love

The Love's Series (detectives)

Love's Taming

Love's Tempting

Love's Trusting

The Fairfield Series (small town detectives)

Emma's Home

Laurie's Time

Carol's Image

Fireworks Over Fairfield

Please take the time to leave a review of this book. Feel free to contact me, especially if you enjoyed my book. I love to hear from readers!

Facebook

Email

Website

ABOUT THE AUTHOR

I am an avid reader of romance novels, often joking that I cut my teeth on the historical romances. I have been reading and reviewing for years. In 2013, I finally gave into the characters in my head, screaming for their story to be told. From these musings, my first novel, Emma's Home, The Fairfield Series was born.

I was a high school counselor having worked in education for thirty years. I live in Virginia, having also lived in four states and two foreign countries. I have been married to a wonderfully patient man for forty-one years. When writing, my dog or one of my four cats can generally be found in the same room if not on my lap.

Please take the time to leave a review of this book. Feel free to contact me, especially if you enjoyed my book. I love to hear from readers!

Facebook
Email
Website

Made in United States
North Haven, CT
28 February 2026

89300385R00189